SEA CHANGE

OCTOPIAN SHIFTERS BOOK 2

ANNA KENSING

Cover photo: Period Images

Cover design: Anna Kensing

Editing: Laura Blackwell

ISBN: 978-1-7342344-2-8 (ebook)

ISBN: 978-1-7342344-3-5 (paperback)

CHAPTER 1

*D*eclan Fitzgerald splashed through the cold surf on the shoreline and rolled the whiskey cask up the short rocky beach. He could barely see his fingertips when Joey Carrigan took the barrel from him and stacked it atop the others inside a shallow cave hollowed out in the bluff, but he imagined they were as blue as his lips felt. A small lantern lit Joey's face in a ghostly grimace.

"Colder than a monkey's brass balls," Declan commented. He helped Joey stack a dozen or so whiskey casks against the back of the cave. It had been a natural depression in the bluff before Declan's men had chipped away enough to make a decent hiding place.

"'Least you can look forward to your man warming you up tonight," Joey said with a sly smirk.

Declan cuffed the boy across the back of the head. "Less lip from you, lad, and more stacking. Thomas is right behind me with a half a dozen more of these to get in before the clouds clear."

Joey ducked his head and hoisted a third barrel atop one of the stacks. Not so much a boy anymore. He was still slight of frame, but the last few years of working as first mate aboard Declan's ship had built enough lean muscle to handle the heavy barrels of the liquor Declan smuggled into Washington on his frequent voyages between the States and British Columbia.

He was beardless and short enough to stand upright in the small cave, but his face was sunburned and weathered, making him look older than his eighteen years, and he'd lost the gangling adolescent awkwardness he'd had when Declan first found him stowed away aboard his ship. Joey carried himself with the confidence of a man living life on his own terms now.

Once they finished unloading the liquor, they'd round the peninsula at Point Wilson, sail into Port Townsend Bay, and declare the goods they'd brought that didn't have exorbitant excise fees. This section of the beach was inaccessible during high tide, so they'd return during tomorrow afternoon's low tide in a wagon to collect the liquor.

In town, they'd tap the casks into plain brown jugs, dilute about half of them with water, and pack the jugs into the wagon for distribution to the restaurants and saloons in Port Townsend, Port Ludlow, and a handful of other towns in Jefferson County.

Then he'd pack the *Black Dove* with goods to take to back to the various towns in British Columbia he traded with, maybe sail to San Francisco for anything he couldn't get here, and head back to start the circuit again.

After a few weeks of shore leave in Port Townsend. Declan stepped out from under the cave's opening and stretched to his full height. He twisted left, then right, cracking the kinks from stooping under the cave's ceiling out of his back, then wrapped his arms around himself and chafed his cold hands up and down to warm up. He might be getting a little old for this life. At least he could look forward to a fire and a hot dinner at the Bishop house, followed by some even hotter activities with Elliot later in the evening. A hot meal, a stiff drink, and a good fuck, and he'd be back in form in no time.

"Speaking of your man." Joey's voice sounded behind him.

"Let's not," Declan replied. Joey went on as if he hadn't heard him.

"Tomorrow's full moon is a supermoon, ain't it?"

Declan glanced at the dark sky above. As if he needed reminding about the supermoon. Thick clouds rolled in front of the nearly full moon, obscuring most of its light, but a faint corona gleamed behind the drifting clouds. The new moon was better for avoiding the revenue cutters, but they'd been delayed by fog at the entrance to the Strait of Juan de Fuca a week longer than Declan had planned.

As proud as Declan was of his first mate, he could do without this newfound habit of sassing his captain. He'd undoubtedly learned it from Thomas Cuevas, the *Black Dove*'s cook, who was now rowing the small gig toward them with the last of the barrels. On the other hand, Joey could just as likely have inherited his mother's absolute disregard for authority along with her small chin and delicate features.

At least the dim light made loading and unloading a little easier. The north beach of the peninsula was only a couple of miles as the crow flies from downtown, but most townsfolk rarely ventured this far. The handful of S'Klallam who remained on the peninsula still portaged their canoes from this beach, over a series of marshy ponds, to the lagoon, then down to the bay, avoiding the riptides around Point Wilson. But more often, the beach was a convenient place to offload wool, liquor, opium, or other items under the noses of the excisemen. Some crews had smuggled Chinese folk from British Columbia since the Chinese Exclusion Act had outlawed immigration, though Declan generally kept to transporting goods rather than people.

"Not that it's any of your business," Declan growled. His crew paid as much attention to the position of the moon and stars as any sailor did, but Joey, Thomas, a handful of others, knew something of the significance the supermoon had to Declan and Elliot.

"We're just glad you'll be reunited with him soon. Maybe a walk on the beach, full moon overheard? Kinda romantic, ain't it?" Joey's tone was jovial, but the faint starlight reflected the glint in his eyes as he nattered on.

"Jesus, Joey, fucking drop it, would you?"

"See?" Joey sidestepped out of Declan's reach quickly, but didn't quit. "You've been madder than a spitting cat for weeks. If you don't get some soon, Thomas and I was going to drag you from the ship to the nearest brothel and leave you there until your mood improved."

Joey splashed into the surf's edge and grabbed the bow of the gig, holding it steady while Thomas disembarked, then helped Thomas drag the craft a few feet up the beach. "Ain't that what we said, Thomas?"

Thomas cast Joey a dour look, and Declan winced internally. It'd been more than a year since Declan had been with Thomas, and they'd never been permanent. Still, he tried not to rub his relationship with Elliot in Thomas's face.

"Drop it, Joey. Drop it right the fuck now."

"Sounds like you're the one in need of a good fuck, Jo-Jo," Thomas said. He lifted a barrel over the gig's side with a grunt. He rolled it up the beach toward the cave, tossing over his shoulder, "About time we take him to the Cliff House, don't you think, Captain?"

The Cliff House, less than a mile as the crow flies, was nestled at the base of a high cliff between Point Wilson and Point Hudson. Declan chafed his hands against each other, trying to rub some feeling back into his fingers. It would be warm there, the whiskey and beer would flow like water, and the sounds of music and revelry that roared within would drown out the pounding of the surf against the sands. The *Black Dove*'s crew would smoke, drink, gamble, and dance the night away with the rest of the Port Townsend residents who enjoyed the kinds of entertainment the Cliff House specialized in.

But these enticements paled in comparison to what Declan really wanted. The thought of Elliot's tentacles wrapped around his waist and Elliot's thick tentacle cock pushing into him stiffened his own cock. He'd fucked and been fucked by Elliot in his fully human form countless times, and that was always good, but he couldn't deny a shiver of anticipation at the idea of putting his hands all over the velvet softness of Elliot's half-devilfish skin, and of the extra limbs that held him tight.

"Keep a barrel to take to the Cliff House and give Oregon Jack my compliments," Declan said to Thomas. "I'm heading home for the evening." The crew would have more fun without him, and Declan couldn't wait any longer to be with Elliot. Even if he didn't shift until tomorrow's supermoon, they'd have all night to make up for his months away.

Thomas nodded, and Joey opened his mouth, no doubt for more teasing. Thomas shouldered him roughly and jerked his chin at the last barrel waiting to be stacked in the cave. "Basta, cabrón," he said, and for once, Joey listened to his elder. Joey finished rolling the barrel up the beach and disappeared into the cave.

Thomas offered Declan a drag from one of the vile cigarillos he had a habit of smoking, but Declan shook his head. "Give my regards to your stepbrother," Thomas said on an indrawn breath, then bent over and hacked out a rusty cough. Declan pounded him on the back until he spit a gob of something on the beach and straightened up. "Tell him he owes me the end of that story he was reading to us last year."

Declan chuckled. "Will do." They waited in companionable silence until Joey returned. Still another couple hours until they rounded Point Wilson, guided around its rocky shoals by the lighthouse there, and docked at Union Wharf. But then he'd be home. Where Elliot was waiting for him.

CHAPTER 2

*E*lliot Bishop should have known better than to host a supper party on the night before the supermoon. It had been almost a year since a full moon reached perigee, the closest point to Earth in its orbit. And just as the supermoon caused higher than normal high tides and lower than normal low tides, its gravitational pull tugged at the blood in his fingertips and wrists, pooling in his groin. The same blood he'd learned last year made him different from the other men seated around his dining table tonight.

Different enough that he should have chosen another night for this supper for the trustees of the Port Townsend Southern Railroad and their wives to celebrate the beginning of the railroad's construction. The whole town had turned out for the groundbreaking three weeks ago, bringing picnic baskets out to the portion of the farm Albert Briggs had deeded to the railroad. Judge Briggs himself had turned the first spadeful of dirt. Elliot had been attending similar celebrations since, but he'd somehow forgotten how hard it was to concentrate on company when he knew what was coming.

And Declan was late. Elliot had been expecting him for days, to give them time to reconnect after his months away at sea. Before Elliot changed, before he needed Declan's help to change back.

Elliot turned his face toward Mrs. Lawrence Hastings, seated a few seats down, who was complimenting him on the new electric lights he'd installed. It cost a pretty penny for the new service —forty-five dollars a month for four thirty-two candlepower lamps and another eight sixteen candlepower lamps—but it was worth it. He responded with some pleasantry he hoped would suffice. The incandescent lights in the chandelier over the table made the jeweled combs in her hair sparkle, much like the way the moon's light glittered on the tips of waves in the small cove he'd be swimming in tomorrow night, assuming Declan arrived in time.

If he didn't, well, Elliot wouldn't think about that now. He crossed one leg over the other, the fall of the tablecloth hiding his half-hard erection, and pushed the remains of his food around his plate. The gold-rimmed Limoges china service had been a wedding gift Declan's father had brought from France for Elliot's mother. His mother was able to shift back and forth at will, but Elliot changed only at low tide during the supermoon, when staying out of the water was impossible and he gave in because he had no other choice.

He caught sight of Mrs. Terrell Jackman halfway down the table's left side, twitching uncomfortably in her chair, too. Her cheeks were flushed pink, and her eyes met his, something knowing in her gaze that Elliot turned away from. Just over her shoulder, his housekeeper, Sally Jenkins, motioned to him from the kitchen doorway.

"Excuse me a moment," he murmured to Judge Swan, who had been trying to draw Elliot into his conversation with Mr. Eisenbeis about land values increasing when the railroad made it all the way to Portland.

"Someone waiting for you in your study," Sally told him.

There was a note of suppressed glee in her voice, and her eyes were bright with a happiness he rarely saw on her brown face.

Hope and relief surged in him. "Declan?" It couldn't be anyone else. Everyone he'd invited tonight was here, and supper was more than half over.

Sally gave him a little push toward the door. "Go on, then. See for yourself."

Elliot rushed through the kitchen and across the hall. The door to his study was open a crack, and when he pushed through it, Declan was standing in the middle of the room, his cheeks above a full, bushy beard flushed pink from the spring evening's chill and his chestnut hair mussed from the wind.

"Ellie, my boy!" Declan said, a broad smile crossing his full lips and crinkling the corners of his eyes.

Elliot barely had time to close the study door behind him and open his arms before Declan barreled into them. Declan's arms wrapped around him, and Elliot tucked his face into Declan's neck. He breathed in the scent of pipe smoke, sea salt, and something else that was uniquely Declan. Declan's arms squeezed him closer, and Elliot hugged him back just as hard.

"You're home," he breathed, his lips against Declan's warm skin. He inhaled another whiff, Declan's beard tickling his nose, then pulled back. Declan held him at arm's length and glanced up and down his body.

"'Course I'm home," Declan said, a twinkling glint in his green eyes. His fingers plucked at the leaves and vines embroidered in blue thread on the charcoal-gray vest under Elliot's black jacket. The vest had been a gift from Nance Carrigan and matched a version with silver thread that Declan owned. "Bit overdressed for me, aren't you?"

Declan had clearly come straight from his ship to the house. He was wearing plain black wool trousers, vest, and jacket, all of which were a little the worse for wearing several days in a row. His neckcloth was untied, his collar open, and Elliot wanted nothing more than to put his mouth at the hollow of his throat and taste the brine of sea and sweat there. Declan would probably want a bath and a shave as soon as could be arranged, but Elliot wondered if he could talk him into keeping the beard for a little longer.

"I'm having a supper party tonight," he answered. "Judge Swan, Lawrence Hastings, Henry Landes, the rest of the trustees, a few others, their wives. We're celebrating the progress in finally starting the railroad construction."

Declan raised an eyebrow. "Celebrating, eh?" He curled his fingers around Elliot's jacket lapel and tugged him forward just a touch. "Don't we have other things to celebrate?"

Elliot's abnormality wasn't something he ever wanted to celebrate, but his desire for Declan long predated his discovery of what he really was. He cupped Declan's face in his hands and took his lips in a hard, bruising kiss. He'd meant to start soft, and take his time with it but Declan thrust his tongue into Elliot's mouth in matching desperation. He pressed his hips against Declan's, the answering hardness between the layers of cloth separating them, tearing a low groan from the back of his throat.

Declan snaked his arms under Elliot's jacket, then slid his hands down the small of his back and under the waistband of his trousers. He gripped Elliot's ass cheeks in both hands and squeezed hard. Elliot slipped one hand around Declan's neck and into his hair, tugging on the silky strands curling over his collar. He tugged a little harder and nipped at Declan's earlobe, and Declan inhaled sharply.

Elliot pulled back to catch his breath, and Declan followed him, still seeking his lips. Elliot put his other hand against Declan's chest. "We can't right now. Half the town is in the dining room, and I can't keep them waiting. But join us after you've washed up."

He slid the hand down Declan's chest, the rough wool of his jacket prickling against Elliot's palm, and cupped the bulge in

Declan's trousers. Declan groaned and dropped his head against the door behind him. "Later," Elliot promised.

"What if I can't wait that long?" Declan said. "Come on, Ellie, you know it won't take long." He palmed Elliot's own erection, then fumbled the buttons of Elliot's trousers open with one hand. Elliot opened his mouth to protest, but Declan dropped to his knees, and that was it. His guests would just have to entertain themselves for another few minutes.

Declan's mouth engulfed him, and Elliot bit his lip to stifle a sound that might travel to the dining room, where the faint clink of silverware on china echoed across the hall. No, it wasn't going to take long at all.

The soft heat of Declan's mouth sent Elliot over the edge in a throbbing rush, and his knees nearly buckled. Declan swallowed and kept sucking gently until Elliot stilled him with a hand on his head.

Declan looked up at him, knees spread wide on the carpet, his ass resting on his heels, his lips shiny and wet. Elliot ran his fingers through Declan's hair, then cupped his cheek, and Declan tipped his head into Elliot's hand. Then, Declan pushed to his feet with an audible crack in his knee and wiped the back of his hand across his mouth.

"Getting a little old for that," he grumbled, but his eyes held the lazy happiness that Elliot loved to see in him. He pulled Declan closer and kissed him, curling his tongue around Declan's, tasting himself.

The aching need that swelled within Elliot with the upcoming supermoon eased a little, but Declan's hard length still pressed against his leg. He fumbled the buttons of Declan's trousers open without ending the kiss and slipped his hand inside. He gripped and squeezed, driving a low grunt from Declan, and passed his hand over Declan's cock head, slicking his palm with the wetness at its tip.

He wanted to suck Declan in return, close his lips over that silken thickness and feel Declan thrust into his throat, but he'd stroked Declan no more than three or four times when Declan groaned into his mouth, stiffened against him, and spilled into his hand.

He rested his forehead against Declan's until their heartbeats returned to normal. Finally, Declan pushed him a little and stepped back into the middle of the room. He tucked himself back into his trousers and handed Elliot his handkerchief, slightly grubby from being in Declan's pocket on the ship. Elliot took it and cleaned his hand off. If he used his own, he'd have to go upstairs for a clean one or go back into the dining room smelling like what had just happened. Declan winked as he took the handkerchief back.

"Join us after you clean up," Elliot offered again. "You must be hungry, surely?"

Declan grinned and looked Elliot up and down lewdly. "I'm always hungry. But I suppose I could have some supper after that first course, before dessert."

Elliot pushed him toward the door. "That's not what I meant, and you know it. Sally can fix you a plate. Judge Swan was just asking after you, so try not to scandalize the neighbors, hm?"

Declan gave him an angelic smile. "I'm always on my best behavior, little brother."

Elliot shivered at the tiny illicit thrill Declan's reference to their relationship always sparked in him. They weren't related by blood, but Declan's father had married his mother when he was an infant, and they'd been raised together. Elliot had looked up to his older stepbrother as a boy, until that hero worship turned into a different sort of worship.

He watched Declan disappear through the study door and listened to him climb the stairs, his boots thumping softly on the carpeted steps. The jaunty tune he was whistling faded when he reached the second floor, and Elliot smiled to himself. Thank God Declan was home again.

He checked his reflection in the hall mirror on the way back to the dining room. His cheeks were nearly as pink as Declan's had been, and his eyes were perhaps a little bright, but he otherwise looked normal.

Lawrence Hastings glanced at him as he resumed his seat, though. A thrum of something passed between them, an extra awareness that wasn't the covert glance of a man seeking the attention of another man, but there was a knowing quality to Lawrence's gaze, like he knew what Elliot had just been up to. He raised his wine glass in a silent toast to Elliot. Elliot felt himself blush and looked away.

Mrs. Jackman was also staring at Elliot again. The weight of her gaze dragged at the edges of his mind. Like she had the same capacity for sensing him the devilfish women he'd met last year did. But that was silly. This wasn't his mother's island in the middle of the Pacific Ocean, where a few hundred half-human, half-devilfish women operated independently, but all for the benefit of the group. He was in his own dining room, safe in Port Townsend, with friends and neighbors he'd known since he was a boy.

He looked away, and Mrs. Jackman finally turned her attention back to Mrs. Eisenbeis, seated next to her. She looked like what she was—a respectable uptown matron, chatting pleasantly about a husband's successes, children's antics, and the upcoming social to be held at the Key City Club next week. But Elliot could still feel her mind pushing at the edges of his, questing for a connection he didn't want to have with anyone, much less the wife of a business acquaintance.

Declan appeared at the dining room's door, hair damp and in fresh clothes, his beard combed and trimmed but still present. The ensuing commotion of greetings and handshakes distracted everyone, including Mrs. Jackman, thankfully. She left Elliot alone for the rest of the evening, and he resolutely put out of his mind anything more unusual than business talk and dessert.

CHAPTER 3

$\mathcal{B}$y the time the last guest left Elliot's interminable supper party in the wee hours, Declan was too tired and not sober enough to do anything more than leave his clothes draped over a chair and climb into Elliot's four-poster bed. Elliot said he'd be in after locking up, but Declan had fallen into a deep sleep before Elliot came to bed. Now he was awake, his head still swimming with all the whiskey he'd drunk and his mouth drier than a hardtack biscuit. Elliot wasn't next to him, and the small lamp Declan had left burning on the bureau was sputtering with the last of its oil.

Declan glanced around the room. His clothes were still draped over the chair. Elliot's wardrobe was closed, and the bureau's surface clear of his collar, cufflinks, or other accessories he'd have left there if he had undressed for bed.

Declan slid from under the warm covers and shivered in the room's chill air. He pulled his shirt and trousers on and rinsed his mouth with water from the pitcher on the washstand. He padded barefoot from the room and peered down the stairs. A light spilled from the open door of Elliot's study, and Declan headed there, figuring Elliot must still be wired from supper and didn't want to disturb Declan's sleep. Now that he'd had a couple hours of sleep, he'd see what he could do to get Elliot to relax.

But Elliot wasn't in the study. Nor was he in the parlor or dining room or any of the other rooms on the first floor. The house was quiet, Sally and her girls long since retired to their own rooms. The fire in the study's fireplace was banked for the night. After a second round through the empty first-floor rooms, Declan realized where Elliot must be.

When they'd returned to Port Townsend from the octopians' den, Elliot had found a secluded spot in the Kah Tai lagoon where he could shift without anyone seeing him. It was early for the shift to come on him, but the day or two before the super-moon made Elliot restless.

Declan returned to his room to finish dressing. His kit was half-open at the top of his sea chest, and a small, cork-stoppered bottle was under the jumble of other items in it. His stepmother had given him the bottle last year, and he held it up to the kerosene lamplight and flicked a fingernail against it. A small piece of seaweed lay in the bottom, which had kept Marie's blood from clotting, but there was no blood left now. She'd warned him that it might not be enough to keep the consequences of being with Elliot at bay, but he'd followed her suggestion and taken her blood at the new moon before each supermoon.

Until the most recent new moon. He shook the little bottle again, but no liquid sloshed in it, and the blood-soaked seaweed clung limply to the bottle's base. He tossed the bottle back into his kit and left the room. Whatever would happen would happen. He wasn't going to stop fucking Elliot, no matter the consequences. He'd figure it out later.

He grabbed his greatcoat on the way out the front door and hustled west through the quiet uptown neighborhoods to where the street ended at a tidal marsh. The plan was to build a bridge across the lagoon for the railroad, according to the trustees at Elliot's supper tonight. He'd joined the men tonight in toasting the railroad's groundbreaking and listened to Lawrence Hastings and Terrell Jackman argue with Judge Swan about how much property values in town would increase when the railroad was complete.

He doubted the railroad would ever come to fruition, though. Swan had been an early booster for the Northern Pacific Railroad building an extension to Port Townsend from the Columbia River, but the terminus went to Tacoma more than a decade ago, and no other railroad lines had come knocking since. Declan agreed with his father, God rest the old man's soul. Port Townsend would be better served by focusing on what it already had going for it—its deepwater bay and unparalleled access to Oriental and Alaskan trade—and relinquishing the pipe dream of an intercontinental railroad connection.

Elliot was a dark shadow, standing at the end of a short dock that stretched out over the lagoon. When the tide was high, the dock floated just about at the waterline, but it was ebbing now, nearly all the way out, and the waters were barely deep enough for Elliot to swim in. A good thing from Declan's point of view, since he didn't have Elliot's talent for swimming, and the dock's pilings gave him something to hold on to.

The thick clouds from earlier in the evening had mostly cleared, and stars winked in and out from the wispy remains over the bay. At least the lagoon's waters were warmer than the ocean at Admiralty Inlet.

A small kerosene lantern cast flickering shadows at Elliot's feet. Declan's steps thumped against the dock, but Elliot didn't react to his approach until Declan fetched up next to him. The tension in Elliot's body radiated from him in waves, like the waves lapping gently at the dock's pilings. He kept his face forward and his jaw clenched, though his voice was soft when he said, "I didn't want to disturb you. You looked like you needed your sleep."

As if Declan would ever stop looking out for Elliot. He put a hand on Elliot's back, which was rigid with strain, and stroked down from Elliot's shoulder to his waist. When Elliot relaxed slightly under his hand, he leaned in and pressed a soft kiss to the side of Elliot's jaw. Then he stripped off his clothes and folded them into a little pile in the center of the dock. He dropped into a crouch at the end of the dock, then eased down until his ass was perched on the end, legs dangling over the side. He shivered, anticipating the cold water, took a deep breath, then pushed off the dock and into the water. At least it was warmer here than other spots near town they'd tried. He grabbed onto a cross brace between the pilings to keep from going under completely and looked up at the dock. "Come on, Elliot. What are you waiting for?"

A heavy, deep sigh came from above, but Elliot stripped off his clothes and joined him. He submerged and swam a little way out and Declan waited for him to get his sea legs, so to speak. The moon shone on the little ripples that trailed in Elliot's wake, and then the ripples stilled, and Declan turned his face up to the sky.

He wondered idly whether he could talk Elliot into relocating to someplace tropical. Hawai'i was warm this time of year. Hell, the waters off the coast of Mexico were warmer this time of year too, and closer than Hawai'i.

Elliot returned, surfacing just before Declan, and slicked back his wet hair with one hand. He crowded close to Declan and wrapped an arm around his waist. A glancing touch of smooth, strong muscle brushed against Declan's leg, and he chased after it, wriggling closer to press his chest against Elliot's.

He shivered again, and Elliot kissed his cheek, his lips warm and wet. "We don't have to," he said against Declan's ear. Of course they had to. Once Elliot shifted under the supermoon, there was one way they knew to change him back to fully human. And it wasn't as if it were a hardship for Declan.

"Shut up and fuck me, Elliot," he said. He'd warm up when they got going; he always did.

He let go of the cross brace, and Elliot's other arm wrapped around his waist, keeping him afloat. Two of Elliot's tentacles immediately twined around his legs, the suckers on the undersides flexing and squeezing against him. Elliot's eyelids fluttered, like he was concentrating on the sensations from his tentacles caressing Declan's skin. The shorter tentacle between their bodies lengthened and thickened, and Declan spread his legs to give Elliot's cock room to slide under his balls. The slick muscle fondled his sac, driving a sigh of pleasure from Declan, then slipped past it and circled his hole.

Declan breathed out shakily as Elliot's tip breached the first ring of muscle. God, he'd missed this. Elliot's arms tightened around him, and he pressed slowly farther and farther in, spreading Declan open and filling him up. He was holding back, Declan could tell, being careful not to hurt him. Declan wrapped his legs around Elliot's waist and used them to pull himself down on Elliot's tentacle cock, matching Elliot's low groan with one of his own.

"Take it, Ellie," he whispered against the shell of Elliot's ear. He caught Elliot's earlobe between his teeth and bit down. "Fuck me hard, like I know you want to. You know I want it, too."

Elliot's cock expanded inside him and undulated against that spot inside that sparked sharp waves of pleasure building and cresting from the base of his spine to the tips of his fingers and toes. His own cock rubbed against the wet velvet of Elliot's web just below his navel. Declan pulled his knees up, opening himself more, and let Elliot fill him until he couldn't feel the cold water anymore, just Elliot's hot cock inside him and the tentacles wrapped around him, squeezing and stroking him until he shuddered his release with Elliot's arms holding him against his chest.

Elliot followed a few moments later, groaning into Declan's ear as he pulsed within him. Declan tucked his face into Elliot's neck briefly, breathing in the sea salt and sweat, then disentangled himself from Elliot's tentacles and grabbed the cross brace again.

"Don't say it," Elliot said, with a hint of laughter in his voice. The water rippled gently as Elliot's tentacles shifted back into his two human legs. "You want a fire and a warm bed. You didn't have to leave those things for me tonight, you know."

As if Declan wanted to be anywhere else tonight. "Come home with me and prove it, then," he said, matching Elliot's light tone. He hauled himself up to the dock platform and rested a minute before pulling his clothes on over his wet skin, wincing a little as he tucked his shirt into his trousers. He wasn't usually so sore afterwards, but he supposed it had been a while.

Elliot was putting on his own clothes, and Declan waited until he was dressed and let him lead the way to the Bishop house. He stamped his right foot a few times as they climbed the hill at the end of Taylor Street, trying to shake out a tingling numbness running from his hip down his leg, then ignored the sensation. He was probably just tired, or his leg had fallen asleep while fucking Elliot. Nothing a warm bed and a few more hours of sleep couldn't fix.

"Come out to Point Wilson tomorrow." They trudged up the Bishop house stairs, Elliot stumbling sleepily against him. "There's something I want to show you."

Declan murmured agreement, then pulled Elliot's clothes from his unresisting body and tucked him under the covers. He shucked his own wet duds and, with Elliot's warm arms around him, he fell asleep again only minutes after they crawled into bed.

CHAPTER 4

*E*lliot woke with a start, his heart pounding, Declan staring down at him. Declan's hand was gripping his shoulder, like he'd been shaking it, and his eyebrows were drawn together, that familiar look of concern on his face.

Elliot blinked at him a few times, trying to get his bearings. He was in bed, in his own room. The bed-curtains were tied back at the bedposts. The sheets were twisted in his hands at his waist, damp and clammy. Declan was propped on his elbow, his warm body pressed along Elliot's damp, bare skin.

Right, Declan had come home last night. Elliot turned his head on the pillow. He couldn't see the bedside table clock with Declan in the way, but a thin shaft of bright light jabbing through the crack in the drapes suggested it was well after sunrise.

"You're back," Elliot said, his voice coming out rougher than he expected. He swallowed a few times, moistening his dry mouth, soothing the harsh tickle at the back of his throat. Declan's green eyes narrowed at him.

"Of course I'm back. Got back last night. You don't remember? How much did you drink last night?"

Elliot now noticed the dull throbbing over his left eye. He'd definitely drunk too much last night. "Of course I remember," he said. "Just…" He trailed off, still not quite in the here and now.

"Nightmare?" Declan asked softly. He slid the hand on Elliot's shoulder up the side of his neck to cup his jaw and Elliot shivered, the sweat coating his body cooling now in the room's chilled air. He turned his face against Declan's bare chest, and Declan hugged him closer, stroking his warm hand down Elliot's back.

"Yeah," he said. His lips grazed Declan's nipple, which tightened into a peak, but Declan didn't do anything else to encourage him, just stroked Elliot's back the way he always had when Elliot had nightmares.

"Same one?" Declan's voice was still soft and even. "Thought those ended last year. After—"

After Elliot learned what really happened to his mother, who had disappeared when he was a boy. After Elliot's fiancée disappeared the same way, the night before they were to be married. After he and Declan had spent weeks searching for Celeste and found her and his mother, and they learned what Elliot really was.

"No," he said. "I mean, yes, I haven't had one of those since we came back. This was different." He squirmed a little closer to Declan. Sleeping with Declan was like curling up around the belly of a fully stoked stove, and he pressed against as much of Declan as he could, chasing away the cold dread the nightmare left in his mind.

"Different how?" Declan tightened his arm around Elliot, his voice rumbling low in Elliot's ear. Elliot draped an arm around him, running his palm firmly up and down Declan's back, ignoring the puckered and raised scars that covered him from shoulders to hips. Declan's other nipple was at the end of his nose, and he licked it, then breathed softly over it. It tightened into a peak, and Declan hummed appreciatively, but still didn't take the hint.

"It doesn't matter," Elliot said. "It's over now." Or he could put it out of his mind, with Declan's help. He scooted his hips closer and slid his hand down to the curve of Declan's ass, pressing Declan's morning wood against his lower belly. His own cock nestled between Declan's thighs, the tip nudging the rough hairs on Declan's balls.

A clang of metal against wood sounded outside his bedroom door and a perfunctory knock. "Morning, Mr. Elliot."

"Good morning, Eugenia," Elliot called back, after clearing his throat and lifting his head so his voice wasn't muffled in Declan's shoulder. Declan pinched a bit of flesh at Elliot's hip.

"Clarice," he hissed. "You still can't tell those poor girls apart?"

"Not unless I'm looking at them, and half the time, not even then. I swear they do it on purpose to confuse me." He pulled Declan's hips closer and nudged his cock against Declan's balls again. He didn't want to talk about how to tell his twin house-maids apart. He wanted to roll Declan over and fuck him. In a bed, like a normal man, even if normal men didn't fuck other men. But the kind of abnormal man who fucked other men was better than his other abnormality.

He slid the hand at Declan's hip over the curve of his ass and gently probed a finger along the crack. Declan reached back and moved his hand away. "Little too sore for that today, Ellie."

He said it easily enough, but Elliot went cold all over, like he'd plunged into the icy waters of the bay. "Christ, Declan, I'm so sorry." He rolled onto his back, a flash of his nightmare returning.

Declan beneath him, still and cold, while Elliot pounded into him over and over, tentacles wrapped around him, keeping him still, spreading him wide to take more and more of Elliot. The image did nothing to diminish his erection, but his mind rebelled at the thought of hurting Declan like that.

He covered his face with one hand. Christ, what was wrong with him? "You said it was alright last night, but I shouldn't have. I'm so sorry," he repeated.

Declan scooted toward him and stroked a warm hand down Elliot's chest. "I did say and there's no need to be sorry. I'll be fine by tomorrow. You can pound my arse as hard as you want then."

Elliot shook his head, still not looking at Declan. He'd have to be more careful. Last night was only a preview of what he'd feel when the moon was full and the tide was ebbing. It was a mating imperative, his mother had told him, never mind that Elliot wouldn't be fathering any children on any of the octopian women in his mother's island home, much less on Declan.

But being with Declan was the only thing that kept him sane, especially once he'd learned about his true nature; it kept him from becoming the monster in his childhood nightmares. And he'd be damned if he'd give into that impulse to fuck Declan as hard as the blood rushing through him demanded.

"Hey," Declan said, tugging Elliot's hand from his face and turning his chin to look at him. "I'm not damaged, Ellie, just a little tender. You know I like it rough sometimes." He dipped his head and kissed the corner of Elliot's mouth, then his jaw, then just under his earlobe. "Like to feel where you've been the whole next day, reminding me every time I sit down what we did together."

Elliot shuddered, his cock hardening even more. Would he ever stop wanting Declan so much it hurt to breathe? Not likely, since he'd felt this way his entire life. Even when he was a boy, before he'd known anything about sex, he'd wanted to crawl inside Declan's chest and huddle there, wrapped up safe within. He knew it was selfish beyond words, to constantly take and take from Declan, and yet, Declan always seemed to have more to give.

"In the meantime," Declan whispered, kissing the other corner of his lips and nudging his head aside with his nose to kiss along his jaw to his other ear. "There's plenty of other things we can do."

Elliot squeezed Declan's hand and kissed him back. "I should get up. The water Clarice left is probably getting cold, and I've plenty of work to do today."

Declan pulled back, propping himself up on an elbow and gesturing lewdly to the erect cock jutting from his reddish bush, a gleam of fluid winking at the tip in the dim morning light. "You've got a job you could do here first," he said.

"You're incorrigible." Elliot smiled. The nightmare was receding in the face of the brightening morning light and Declan's cheerfulness.

"Big words from that pretty mouth." Declan smiled back. He tapped Elliot's hip and twirled his finger in a circle. "Come on. Swivel around and we can suck each other at the same time."

He lay back against the pillows and spread his thighs open. Elliot's mouth watered. He disentangled his legs from the bedclothes and swung one leg over Declan's chest. There was a bit of awkward fumbling, Elliot navigating where to plant his knees astride Declan's broad shoulders, and then he was ass up over Declan's face, with Declan's cock in front of his lips.

He glanced back at Declan, feeling his face redden at how much he was exposed. "Nice view, Ellie lad," Declan winked at him, then grasped his hips with firm hands and pulled him down into his mouth.

Christ, that was good. Declan's mouth was soft and wet, his tongue pressing against the sensitive underside of Elliot's cock. He turned back to Declan's and licked the beads of fluid from the tip, swallowing the salty bitterness before sliding his mouth down Declan's length until he couldn't take any more.

It wasn't the best French job he'd ever done, he knew that. Declan's steady sucking was distracting, and Elliot kept losing his rhythm. Declan didn't seem to mind too much. He made encouraging noises around Elliot's cock, and Elliot pushed Declan's thighs wider so he could get his hand in between, cupping Declan's balls and tugging gently, bobbing his head up and down.

Waves of pleasure built in his groin, Declan's cock battering his throat and washing the last vestiges of his nightmare away. Declan tipped his own chin up, and Elliot's cock slipped into his throat, and that was it. He pulsed down Declan's throat, his own mouth going slack around Declan's cock, and Declan stroked the backs of his thighs until his whole body quivered with the aftershocks.

He was too wrung out to stay up on his knees now, and flopped onto his side, planting one foot behind the other knee and tugging Declan's hips with him to keep his cock in his mouth. Declan's head was resting on his leg, his beard softly tickling Elliot's inner thigh. His breath blew hot on Elliot's damp, softening cock. The angle changed, and Elliot took more of Declan's cock in his mouth.

He couldn't move his own head much, but he had a good grip on Declan's hip and pulled him closer, then let him slip back a little. Declan didn't take over, just let Elliot fuck his own mouth, but the low moans and clutch of his arm around Elliot's lower back and Elliot knew he was close.

He squeezed a handful of Declan's ass and relaxed his jaw, keeping his tongue firmly pressing up. Declan groaned and stiffened against him. The hot salt of his spend burst on Elliot's tongue, and he swallowed until Declan twitched in his mouth and tapped his fingers on Elliot's side.

He let Declan's cock slip free, and Declan rolled onto his back, breathing heavily. He brushed the back of his hand against Elliot's belly. "That's a job well done, El." His voice was huskier than usual, but lazy with satisfaction. "Whatever else you do today, you can take pride in this bit of work."

Elliot swatted him, then swung his legs around and got up from the bed. "And what are you working at today, hmm?" He glanced at Declan, still sprawled across the mattress, bedclothes rumpled around him, hair tangled across the pillows, his soft cock still exposed between his spread-open legs. "Or are you planning to stay in bed all day?"

Declan flapped a hand at him. "I'll get up in a minute. Try not to use all the hot water, eh?"

Elliot snorted and reached for his silk dressing gown. He wrapped it around himself and went to the door to fetch the coal and water. "I'm quite sure it's cold now, thanks to you." He used the water closet in the upstairs hall, washed and dressed, then returned to the bed, where Declan had at least propped himself up against the headboard and pulled the sheet up to his waist.

He perched on the side of the bed and kissed Declan lingeringly, tasting himself on Declan's tongue, then pulled away. "I'll see you at Point Wilson around two, yes?"

Declan nodded. "Tell Sally I'll be down in a bit for breakfast."

It wasn't like Declan to linger abed in the morning, but they had had a late night. Maybe Declan was relaxing some of the austere habits he'd learned from the Captain. The skin around his eyes was papery and thin, but still crinkled at the corners the same way it always did when he smiled at Elliot.

"Get on with you. Let a man dress in peace, eh?"

Elliot stroked his hand over Declan's beard, then pushed off the bed and went downstairs to start his day, resisting the impulse to fuss over Declan. Elliot had plenty of work to get done before tomorrow's supermoon. If Declan said he was fine, Elliot would have to take his word for it.

CHAPTER 5

Declan waited until Elliot's footsteps receded downstairs before swinging his legs from under the covers to the side of the bed. The tingling in his right leg that started last night after fucking Elliot was worse now. It reached all the way to mid-thigh, like being jabbed with thousands of tiny pins and needles. He planted his feet on the floor and couldn't feel the pile of the wool rug under the sole of his right foot.

He could stand, though, and did. And he could walk, even if he stumbled the first few steps. He put Elliot's dressing gown on, the thick brocade silk still holding a hint of Elliot's body heat.

Of course, the water was cold by now. Declan shoveled some extra coal in the stove and set the ewer on top to warm up. He borrowed Elliot's slippers, too, and padded to the water closet, shuffling along like an old man and bracing a hand against the wall. Whatever the hell was wrong with his right leg had better clear up soon. He had a full day ahead of him, same as Elliot. He'd wasted enough of the morning already.

Not that being with Elliot was a waste. It was a luxury he didn't get enough of, to fall asleep next to Elliot and wake up together. He'd never turn down an opportunity to enjoy their

limited private time together, even if he couldn't do everything
that Elliot wanted this morning.

He shuffled back to Elliot's bedroom, washed, and dressed. He
trimmed the beard, but kept it, since Elliot liked it so much. He'd
be fine by tomorrow. And he'd prove to Elliot, again, that neither
of them needed to be ashamed of who they were or what they did
together.

When he reached the north beach, Joey and Thomas
looked surprisingly well-rested for a pair of sailors who'd
spent an evening of debauchery at the Cliff House. Joey was
gazing down the beach toward Point Wilson. He had a
dreamy, abstracted look on his face. It was Thomas who
threw a sharp glance at Declan's limping progress across the
beach.

He could have done without Thomas staring at him navigating the debris thrown up by the sea. The sand nearest the bluff
was hard enough to walk across, his boots crunching and sliding
side to side, but the rocks were worse, turning under his feet and
throwing him off balance. He had to wind his way around dozens
of driftwood logs, some as long and thick as a barkentine's main
mast, and those he couldn't lift his right foot high enough to step
over.

Thomas's arms were crossed over his chest by the time
Declan reached them, though all he said when Declan puffed to a
halt at the mouth of the small cave was, "And how was your
evening, Captain?"

"Fine," Declan said shortly. He gave Thomas his most forbid-
ding obey-your-captain look. Thomas's lips thinned, but at least
he didn't fuss.

"Let's get this hooch to town," Declan said. It would be a job to
get all the barrels up over the bluff to where he had a wagon
waiting and one of Elliot's more placid horses tied loosely to a
tree branch, lipping at the tall grasses within his reach.

Joey shook himself out of his reverie and trotted across the beach toward the small cavern, whistling a tuneless snatch of a popular song the crew had a habit of singing in the mess.

"You're chipper this morning," Declan commented. He ducked his head under the cavern's overhang and had to lift his right leg by gripping a handful of trouser to get it over the threshold. Thomas crowded behind him, just outside the cave's entrance, and Declan started passing barrels to him.

"Jo-Jo here had an evening with Janie June," Thomas told him.

The barrel Declan was handing over nearly slipped from his numb hands. Thomas narrowed his eyes at Declan, and he put an exaggerated look of surprise on his face to cover his fumble. "Did he, now?"

Joey turned his back on them and reached for another barrel, without confirming or denying.

"Spent the whole night with her, far as I could tell," Thomas said.

Janie June claimed to be from Paris, though she'd once confided to Declan that she'd been born back East and had come to Washington Territory with a logging crew. A few years younger than Declan himself, she'd been a fixture at the Cliff House since before he started sailing with his father. She spoke French she'd picked up from sailors, rouged her cheeks and painted her lips, and sang an impressive array of bawdy songs in a high, quavering soprano.

The postcards advertising her services—in the wallets of half the sailors he knew and a good number of Port Townsend businessmen—used a painted backdrop with the Eiffel Tower, Janie dressed as a can-can girl, a distinct bulge under her ruffled drawers. She had a smallish cock—and a pair of tits big enough to pass as a natural woman when she was fully dressed, which wasn't often.

Declan had had her a time or two, and he knew Thomas had, too. And there was that one night when the three of them, rip-roaring drunk on the worst rotgut hooch Declan'd ever had, got up to shenanigans he had only jumbled recollections of. Thomas grinned at him, also apparently remembering something about that night. She was an experience, all right. It was only a matter of time before Joey experienced her.

He was a little surprised, though. He hadn't thought Joey was interested in anyone like that. He'd taken a fair bit of ribbing from the crew for being a virgin, which Declan kept an eye on. He was fairly certain he was the only one who knew Joey's secret, but he wouldn't stand for anyone giving the lad grief for the way God had made him.

When another barrel slipped from Declan's grasp, this one landing on Thomas's foot, Thomas let loose a string of curses in Spanish. "For fuck's sake, Captain, let us handle the rest of it."

Declan lifted the barrel off Thomas's foot. "I'm fine," he said, but Thomas took the barrel from him and jerked his chin at the cavern's entrance. "You ain't, and I ain't in the mood for your shamming otherwise." He hefted the barrel over a shoulder and motioned for Declan to switch places. "Ain't room in this cave for the three of us anyway."

Declan sighed and got out of the way. He settled on a large driftwood log and dug his fingers into the meat of his right thigh, trying to massage some feeling back. Only while Joey and Thomas weren't looking in his direction, though. He didn't like sitting here, twiddling his thumbs, while his men did all the work. Other ships' masters did that, but Declan had been a sailor far longer than he'd been a captain and sitting still too long chafed at him.

He stretched his leg out and shifted his arse on the log, seeking a more comfortable position. Nothing was comfortable with his leg the way it was, damn it. His toes were numb in his boots, though that could just be from the wind. It gusted around him, blowing sand into his face and numbing his fingers as much as his toes. He buttoned his wool greatcoat and turned the collar up at his neck. It was a mild mid-April day, and Thomas and Joey were both in shirt-sleeves, but the bit of sweat he'd worked up while moving the barrels was drying cool on his back. Just sitting here wasn't making him any warmer.

Joey and Thomas finished piling up the barrels at the base of the bluff, and Thomas trotted down the beach to where it widened and sloped inland, to get into position for hauling the barrels up. Joey dropped into a cross-legged position on the sand next to the log Declan was sitting on. He draped a fatherly hand on Joey's shoulder.

"Janie treat you right?" He wasn't quite sure how to ask, or even if he knew what he should be asking. If Joey were his son, he'd give him the same speech his own father had given him years ago about the etiquette of engaging whores. Pay her up-front, ask for what you want, treat her with respect before and after. Joey's fair, smooth cheeks blushed pink and he ducked his head.

"She was nice. We didn't…like that. I mean, we did some things, but mostly we just talked. She was nice," he said again, and Declan snorted. Janie was a lot of things—vain as a peacock, tart like a lemon, entertaining as all get-out—but "nice" wasn't one of the words he'd use to describe her. He squeezed Joey's shoulder, then let him go.

They sat quietly for a bit, Declan watching the ripple of the waves washing gently on the shore. Joey cleared his throat awkwardly and said, not looking at him, "She said Mrs. Viola might have a girl or two who wouldn't mind me being the way I am."

Declan remembered a night at the Green Light a few years ago when Mrs. Viola had arranged a show where one of her girls used a carved ivory dildo to split the quim of another girl. The show had been popular among the other Green Light patrons, but he'd been with Thomas then, and it hadn't been the main event of his evening. He smiled fondly at Joey, even though the lad was gazing at the Cliff House and wouldn't see. "So, it's girls you like, then?"

No reason he should be surprised by this. Just because most of the *Black Dove*'s crew fucked men didn't mean Joey wanted to. Hell, Declan himself liked both men and women. Thomas, too. Seamus and Luca were either fucking each other or celibate and nasty about being so, and Reginald…well, who the hell knew what Reginald liked. He'd never said.

The tips of Joey's ears blushed even redder, and he nodded. "Like to get married some day. Own my own ship, like you do. Find a nice girl, build her a big house, settle down someday in one place for a while." He shrugged. "Not likely to happen, I know. But still."

Declan stifled the urge to wrap Joey in a firm embrace. "It'll happen," he said, injecting a note of confidence in his voice. "Stranger things have happened in this world." Five years ago, he wouldn't have predicted that he'd be fairly settled down with Elliot, spending more time in Port Townsend than on the water. In a big house, no less.

"Ain't that the truth," Joey said, and made an obscene gesture that looked like tentacles swimming through the air. Declan swatted at the back of his head, but Joey leaned out of reach and snickered.

"Ahoy!" Thomas shouted from the top of the bluff. "Quit jawing with the captain, Joey, and help me get this shit up."

Joey popped up and disentangled a rope from where it was hidden in the foliage growing up the bluff's side. The other end of the rope went up and over a sturdy tree branch and was tied at the top of the bluff, where Thomas was waiting with the wagon. Joey opened the sling at the end of the rope and rolled the first barrel into it, then wrapped the sling around it, cinched it tight, and gave a sharp tug on the rope. Thomas hauled it up, hand over hand, to the top of the bluff, then tossed the empty sling back down for the next barrel.

It didn't take long for Thomas and Joey to finish the job. Declan checked his pocket watch and gazed out along the shoreline to Point Wilson, shielding his eyes from a shaft of sunlight with a hand over his brow. His leg was worse now. Sitting on his ass in the stiff breeze had turned the tingling into cold numbness. It ached, too, right down to the bone. He tried wiggling his toes inside his boot, but couldn't tell whether they were actually moving.

"Got an appointment, Captain?" Joey said behind him.

"Promised to meet Elliot at the lighthouse," Declan replied. "But he can wait a bit while we take the hooch back to the warehouse."

Joey shook his head. "Thomas and me got it," he said. "Ain't like we never done it before." He trotted a few feet down the beach, then scampered up the bluff the way only a young man had the energy for, using tree roots as hand holds. He rolled over the lip of the bluff, brushed the dirt from his clothes, and waved down at Declan.

Declan waved back. He didn't relish the jolting wagon ride back downtown, nor the work hefting the barrels into the back of one of Elliot's warehouses. Nor the long walk back uptown if he didn't take the wagon with Thomas and Joey, to be honest, but he'd promised to meet Elliot and see what he had to show him.

"All right," he called up to them. "I'll catch up with you downtown later." Thomas gave him a lazy salute and swung up to the wagon. He clucked to the horse and Declan listened to the wagon lumber off, then turned toward the lighthouse and Elliot.

CHAPTER 6

*E*lliot never tired of the view from the spit of land leading out to the Point Wilson lighthouse. From here, he could see Admiralty Head across the inlet and from the hill atop the bluff, on a clear day, one could glimpse Vancouver Island. At two o'clock on the dot, he heard a sharp, long whistle behind him. He turned and felt a smile spreading across his face. Declan was trudging up the beach, strands of his chestnut hair blowing in the stiff breeze.

Except that he seemed to be limping. Elliot's smile faded. He was covering it admirably—he grinned back at Elliot and waved an arm over his head—but Elliot knew him better than nearly anyone else and he caught not only the hitch in Declan's gait but also the way his right hand was clenched into a fist and pressed against his hip.

"What's wrong?" Elliot demanded, as soon as Declan was within earshot.

"Nothing's wrong." His instant denial was as good as an admission that something was wrong.

"You're limping," Elliot retorted. "And in pain. You think I can't tell?"

"Just getting too old to be flinging whiskey barrels around, not to mention riding a poorly sprung wagon from your house over a rutted muddy track with a driver who don't know his gee from his haw."

Declan reached him and clasped his hands behind his back, the way he stood aboard his ship, as if he never stopped feeling the rocking of waves under his feet. A characteristic posture, but it also hid his hands from Elliot's sight.

"I've a mind to turn this part of the business over to Joey permanently," Declan said. "He's still young enough to see it as an adventure, instead of the damned inconvenience it is."

Elliot looked him up and down, trying to decide whether that was all, but decided to let it go. For now. Declan otherwise looked like he always did—a little pale, maybe, squinting against the sun's light, but handsome as ever—and he was in good spirits. No doubt because the smuggled whiskey and other spirits were on their way to the warehouse for watering down and sale to the saloons in Port Townsend and other nearby towns. Elliot could hardly fault him for bringing in a sizable portion of the money he'd been using to finance his other recent projects.

Speaking of other projects. "What did you want to show me?" Declan asked, after they'd stood there several minutes, watching a flock of gulls squabbling over something at the water's edge a few yards away. The wind gusted against their faces, and Declan sniffled next to him. If he couldn't fuss over Declan, the least he could do was get him under shelter and out of the wind.

Elliot turned and gestured Declan to follow him. "Come on, I'll show you."

He led Declan to a chiseled-out, arched entrance in the bluff, their steps crunching along the beach. It had taken his workers weeks to excavate the cave in the bluff and shape it to his specifications. Thanks to Declan's offhand comment about the small cavern he'd chipped out for hiding smuggled goods, he'd hit upon this idea of doing the same here, albeit at a much larger scale, and for different purposes. This cavern needed to be more accessible than Declan's, while still private when he needed it to be.

"I'll build better steps to get down here, of course," Elliot said, tracing a finger in the air along a set of rickety wooden steps from the top of the bluff. "Something that ladies find easy to navigate with their skirts."

"The hell are you building here that uptown ladies would want to visit?" Declan asked. "Or are you talking about down-town ladies?" He nudged an elbow into Elliot's side. "Investing in a brothel sounds more like something I'd do than you."

Elliot declined to take the bait. "You'll see." He went through the entrance first, then turned around so he could see Declan's reaction.

Declan's eyes widened, and Elliot held his breath while he took in the space. It had started as a shallow cave, probably similar to the one on the north shore Declan used for smuggling, but Elliot had had the bluff excavated to give a ceiling of twenty feet or so overhead and a central depression about five feet deep. Then his men had created a series of small alcoves surrounding the central well, smoothed and shaped from a mixture of silt and loess excavated from the cavern, and flooded the pools with salt water.

"It's like the caves under the island where your mother lives," Declan said, turning slowly around in a circle.

"Exactly," Elliot smiled. Declan was the only other man he knew who'd seen the octopians' dens and lived to tell about it. Their island was built atop a hydrothermal vent, which naturally heated the water surrounding it. From a ship, it looked like an uninhabited rock in the middle of the Pacific, but underneath a tall plateau covered in foliage and nesting sea birds, the interior of the island was a series of sandstone caves and canals that provided living spaces for the octopians both in and out of the water.

He'd rejected his mother's plans for him to live with the other octopians, but that meant he needed a more permanent solution to living with his abnormality. With the railroad construction, the town would inevitably expand west, and there was already talk about building bridges across the lagoon. Soon, there would be too much activity around the lagoon to risk shifting there. So, he'd spent the winter consulting with civil engineers and explosives experts and cobbled together a plan to replicate some aspects of the octopians' den here.

Elliot gestured to the entrance. "There's a pipeline buried under the beach to circulate the water and a steam engine to heat it. It'll be a little like the hot spring at Nance's."

Declan raised an eyebrow. "Yeah? What for?"

Elliot felt himself blushing a little. "Well, you're always begging me for fire and a bed. I know this isn't quite the same, but it will be warmer than in the lagoon."

"I don't beg," Declan protested. When Elliot just looked at him, he winked and grinned. "Well, all right, except when I do beg." He wandered around the cavern, poking his head into a couple of the alcoves. Elliot noticed how Declan was slightly dragging his right leg behind him, but he didn't say anything about it.

Declan leaned against a short wall that divided one of the alcoves from the central pool. "You built this for me?" His eyebrow was raised again, but his hands weren't clenched into fists anymore. Still, he couldn't look more suspicious if he tried. Elliot blushed again.

"Well, not entirely for you." If he was going to go through the expense of excavating the cavern and building the pool, he might as well turn a profit from it. "Eventually, I'll open it to the public as a spa, like Saratoga Springs. Folks can come here to relax and enjoy themselves, take the waters."

"It'll take a lot of coal to heat these waters," Declan commented, that eyebrow still raised.

Elliot shrugged. What else was coal for? "When the railroad connection is finished, more people will come to Port Townsend, which will bring more opportunities for development. Key City will become as much a destination as London or Paris."

Declan clasped his hands behind his back and gazed around the cavern. "I assume you're not funding it entirely yourself?"

Elliot shook his head. "Eisenbeis and Jackman have already invested in it. Modeling it after Saratoga Springs was Mrs. Jackman's idea. And Judge Swan has agreed to lend his name as a regular customer in advertisements for it."

He crossed the cavern to Declan and put his arms around him. "Do you like it?" he said softly. "I really was thinking of you when I planned it."

Declan's eyes twinkled in the shaft of sunlight streaming into the cavern. He clasped his hands at the small of Elliot's back and pulled his hips forward against his own. Elliot hardened instantly, and Declan's cock rose to meet his. "A heated pool for fucking during the supermoon? Of course I like it."

He ground his hips against Elliot's, and Elliot tightened his own arms around Declan. "Could have used this last night." Declan grumbled, though Elliot could tell he didn't mean it. "It'll be nice to be warm for a change."

"It wasn't ready last night. And besides, you're the one who insisted last night. I was planning to wait." He'd been too restless to go to bed after the dinner party, even with Declan waiting in it for him, and he'd hoped that a walk would settle him enough to sleep. But then he'd found himself at the lagoon, the nearly full moon tugging at his blood, and Declan had joined him and despite his better nature, he'd been unable to resist.

Tonight would be worse. He couldn't deny that fucking Declan in his other form was the most pleasure he'd ever experienced, and it had been months since the last supermoon. Declan had always seemed game enough for it, but the least Elliot could do was make a place they could be together that wasn't a frigid marshy swamp with reeds and grasses that tangled in his tentacles and muddy silt that coated both their skin.

Declan kissed him and Elliot squeezed a handful of his ass hard enough to make Declan grunt, then let go. "The water pipes into the cavern are laid. I just need to light the boiler to heat the water and turn on the gas line to light the fixtures."

He gestured at the sconces installed at intervals along the cavern walls. They were strategically placed to provide enough light so that the spa could be used at night, but far enough apart that the interior of each alcove would be dim. Bathers in the alcoves could enjoy the hot water without worrying about other patrons being able to see inside.

Privacy and discretion—these were the keys to making the spa a profitable venture. And to using it with Declan when he shifted. Whatever happened between people in the alcoves would stay private.

Elliot bent his head to lick along the column of Declan's neck. He tasted a bit of salt from the sea air and Declan's sweat, which just increased the need building under his skin. He took Declan's earlobe between his teeth and bit gently, tugging on it. Declan's shaky breath puffed against Elliot's own ear, and his hips thrust against Elliot's.

If he could, he'd take Declan right now, spend the rest of the afternoon touching him, exploring all the secret places that pleasured Declan, until the moon rose and the tide changed, and he could get this rut out of his system. But they couldn't count on privacy much longer. The workers would be back from their midday break shortly. "Tonight," Elliot whispered in Declan's ear. He pulled back and let go of Declan, but didn't step away from him.

Declan smacked Elliot's ass as Elliot pulled away, which did nothing to make his erection go down. "Can't wait, Ellie, lad."

He should have waited last night, but Declan's hands were

relaxed at his sides now, and his limp seemed better as he pulled away from Elliot and wandered toward the back of the cavern. The warm water would surely be more comfortable for both of them. He'd let himself get carried away last night, but he'd be more gentle tonight. He hoped.

CHAPTER 7

*E*lliot shoved another shovelful of coal in the firebox and adjusted the regulator. He'd asked the foreman to leave the boiler ready to turn on when the workers left for the day. They'd run it all day, and it shouldn't take long to heat the water back to a comfortable temperature.

Declan hovered a short distance away on the beach, a pair of towels slung over his shoulder. "Is that thing even safe?" he called. "Steam boilers explode all the damn time, don't they?"

"It's perfectly safe," Elliot tossed over his shoulder. He made another adjustment, and the pumps started churning the water through the boiler tubes. Declan should really consider installing a steam boiler on the *Black Dove*. He'd have his engineer draw up some plans for Declan's approval. Tomorrow, or the next day.

He turned back to Declan, standing on the beach, the light of the full moon shining on his hair, picking out a few stands in silver. "It's ready," he said softly. The tide was ebbing, and Elliot's skin was tight and hot, his clothes chafing him. He ached to be in the warm water, holding Declan, feeling Declan's even warmer skin sliding against his.

Declan's boots crunched against the sand as he came toward

him. A boardwalk would be good here—a walkway from the cavern to the water's edge, so bathers could alternate between the hot spa water and the cold ocean. He tucked that thought away for later, too. Tonight was for them.

Declan followed him into the cavern and audibly sighed when he stepped inside its steamy warmth. He loosened his tie and unbuttoned his collar. "Nice, Elliot."

Elliot smiled back at him. "The walls retain the heat really well, don't they?" He watched as Declan moved around the cavern, exploring the alcoves, running his fingers along the stone dividing walls.

Declan stopped by the one in the center, slightly larger than the rest, and opposite the newly widened arch of the cavern's entrance. "This one, I think, yeah?" Without waiting for Elliot's answer, he stripped his clothes off with efficiency and sat on the pool's edge, putting his legs in the water with a sigh that bordered on a groan. "Oh, yeah," he said. "This is much better."

The muscles in his back and arms flexed as he lowered himself into the pool, and Elliot let the anticipation build under his skin, watching Declan's obvious pleasure in soaking in the pool. Declan submerged to his chin and spread his arms wide, then lay back until he was mostly floating, gazing up at the cavern's ceiling with his eyes half-closed. "First time I've been truly warm all day."

Elliot got out of his own clothes and joined Declan in the pool. He couldn't hold back the shift any longer. Each leg split into two thick muscled tentacles, and a fifth one grew from the base of his spine. He didn't reach for Declan right away, though. He wanted to, so badly, but Declan's forehead still had a slight crease to it and even in the dim lighting, he could see the dark shadows under Declan's eyes. Taking him tonight at the height of the supermoon would surely be rougher than last night.

"We don't have to, you know," he said.

Declan chuckled, a sound that always caused a tingle in his

stomach. "That's what you said last night, but it's a little late for that, don't you think?" He gestured at Elliot's tentacles, swirling in the water below his waist. They were stretching towards Declan like they had a mind of their own. Elliot moved a little farther away from Declan, despite his every instinct begging him to grab Declan and split him open. He clenched his hands at his sides to keep from reaching for Declan.

"No, really," Elliot said. "Maybe we shouldn't this time. Until you're feeling better."

Declan straightened and looked directly at Elliot. "What are you talking about? I'm fine. It's not like you dragged me here against my will, Elliot."

When Elliot didn't move any closer to him, Declan sighed and leaned back against the side of the pool. "So, what, you're just going to suffer through it on your own? How do you think that will work out?"

Elliot hadn't had to suffer through it on his own so far, because Declan had been with him for each supermoon since he discovered what he was. The first time he'd shifted, he'd been caught unprepared for the rush of lust that demanded he take everything Declan had to give.

"I'm not an animal, Declan. I can control myself, and I'll be fine once the tide turns." He spread his tentacles and stretched his web wide enough to feel the heated salt water swirl against his hole. He let one of his own tentacles circle around it and wrapped another around his cock. It wasn't the same as touching and being touched by Declan, but it felt good. He'd never touched himself like this before, but maybe it would be enough and he could resist taking Declan.

Declan must have noticed what he was doing, because his lips curled up in a sly smile, and he wrapped his own hand around his cock and stroked it slowly from root to tip. "If you're going to take care of yourself, then the least you can do is let me watch." He motioned to Elliot with his free hand, and Elliot couldn't stop himself from floating closer. Could this work? Could he jack himself off next to Declan and avoid fucking him until he changed back to human?

Declan was so near, his eyes shining in the lantern light, his full lower lip caught between his teeth, his face and chest flushed with his own desire. Elliot watched Declan's cock slip through the circle of his fist under the water. He wanted that cock inside him, and he wanted his cock inside Declan even more. He closed his eyes and continued stroking his own cock, the tentacle slowly pushing its way inside him.

Declan's breath sped up beside him, and Elliot increased the pumping of his own cock within the tentacle coils. One hand clenched around the pool's stone lip until he felt Declan's hand wrap around his and squeeze. He squeezed back and plumped the tentacle in his ass. It wasn't the same, fucking himself instead of encouraging Declan to fuck him, but it was still good, and he groaned as the tentacle expanded even more, filling him until he wasn't sure he could take anymore.

Declan rolled on top of him, straddling Elliot's waist, his knees pressed against Elliot's lower ribs. "Come on, Ellie," he breathed into Elliot's ear. "Don't keep me waiting now."

He squirmed against Elliot, his cock rubbing against the tentacle wrapped around Elliot's. He released Elliot's hand and gently unwrapped the tentacle surrounding Elliot's cock. Then he lifted himself on his knees and guided Elliot's cock to his opening. He sank down, and Elliot pushed inside. Declan's tight heat bloomed open slowly, and Elliot groaned, giving in to what they both wanted.

He flipped them over, cushioning Declan's back from the stone seat with his arms wrapped around him. He looked down into Declan's eyes and saw only bright encouragement. He moved inside Declan slowly, and Declan responded by wrapping his legs around Elliot's waist and pulling him closer.

He bent his head and kissed Declan, and Declan kissed back

enthusiastically. Declan's hands cupped Elliot's face when they broke apart. He stroked one hand from Elliot's jaw to temple, then smoothed Elliot's hair from his forehead. "Don't you under-stand, Elliot? I need you too. Nothing else matters."

Elliot pushed into Declan's body until he couldn't get any closer to him. His nipples tingled as they brushed against the hard nubs of Declan's, and so did his lips as he trailed them along the side of Declan's neck. He was overwhelmed with the sensa-tions of each tentacle wrapped around Declan, each sucker tasting Declan's skin, drinking in the feel of him. Elliot pressed Declan's thighs down, spreading them more open for Elliot to move against him.

Declan's head dropped back against the stone ledge, and his arms splayed out to the sides. His eyes were closed, his mouth open, and he was making little hitching, moaning sounds, his whole body shuddering in Elliot's embrace. He spent his release between them, and the slick wetness sliding against Elliot's web added to the lubrication Elliot was already making. Elliot ground against him, shamelessly rubbing his slippery web against Declan's softening cock, rolling over and around the tender skin of Declan's sac, slipping against all secret places between his legs.

He thrust his own cock again and again into Declan, swelling inside and pulsing against that special spot, milking more and more pleasure from Declan until he tensed in Elliot's arms and came again, spurting weakly against Elliot's belly. Elliot finally let himself go then, everything that had been building up at the base of his spine, unloaded into Declan in pulsing wave after wave he felt would go on forever. Declan's body jolted with each thrust, quiet now, his eyes rolling back into his head, arms and legs loose in Elliot's grip.

Declan stayed that way even when Elliot finished and with-drew. Elliot untangled his tentacles from Declan's limbs and flopped next to him, breathing hard. He could hear Declan panting next to him, hitching a little every few breaths. Elliot rolled onto his elbow and looked at him. Declan's head lolled in his direction, but his eyes didn't focus on Elliot, and his face was pale. Elliot stroked the side of his face and whispered his name.

Declan's eyes blinked, and he slowly seemed to come back to himself. He smiled at Elliot and breathed out a soft "Hiya, Ellie."

"Hey," Elliot whispered, tracing a thumb softly over Declan's cheekbone. The skin under his eyes was papery and gray. He seemed shrunken and brittle, like his skin was drying up before Elliot's eyes, even as he lay half-submerged in the pool. Declan lifted his right hand weakly and shook it, closing his fist and opening it again.

"What's wrong?" Elliot asked. This was more than just basking in the afterglow. Declan rolled his head against the stone bench as if he didn't have enough energy to shake it.

"Nothing's wrong," he said, but Elliot knew he was lying. "Give a man a minute to get himself together after that." He shook his right hand again and Elliot caught it between his own. His hand was cold, and Elliot chafed it between his palms. He squeezed Declan's fingers, but Declan didn't squeeze back. "Can you feel this?" he asked. Declan smiled at him, an attempt at his trademark grin that didn't quite reach its full strength.

"I'm going to feel you for days after that," he joked feebly and tugged against Elliot's hand to free his. Elliot didn't let him and instead turned Declan's hand palm up in his own.

"Make a fist," he told Declan.

"Later," Declan said, winking at him. "If you think you can handle that."

"I'm serious, Declan," Elliot said. "Show me that you can make a fist and I'll leave you alone."

Declan sighed and curled his fingers into his palm. They stopped about halfway, and his face paled even more as his eyebrows drew together with the effort. Elliot folded Declan's fingers into his palm and covered it with his other hand. "What else is wrong?" Declan opened his mouth, and Elliot narrowed his eyes at him. "The truth, goddammit, this time."

Declan rolled his eyes. "I can't feel my legs," he finally confessed. "And my hand is completely numb. So's my arm, up past my elbow." He pushed himself upright with his left hand, and Elliot helped him sit up against the ledge. "Stop looking at me like that," he groused. "I'll be fine. Just need to—" His face turned a ghostly white, and his body slumped against Elliot, who caught him just before he tumbled under the water's surface. He held Declan tight against his chest. Fine shivers ran through Declan's body, and his eyes were half-closed, a glimmer of the whites showing through his wet lashes.

CHAPTER 8

*D*eclan woke in slow fits and starts, first noticing the softness of the mattress beneath him, then the faint scratch of the linen pillowcase under his face. He was in bed at the Bishop house, then. Not on his ship. It always took a few days of sleeping in port before he woke without missing the familiar rocking motion of the *Black Dove*, the creak of her timbers, and the splash of water against her hull.

He was warm, and glad to be so, though fuzzy on why that seemed so surprising. The room's fireplace must be stuffed full of coal, and he was sweating slightly under the weight of the bedclothes pressing down on him. He turned his head on the pillow and felt a flurry of movement at the bedside.

"Declan?" The concern in Elliot's voice woke him the rest of the way up. He opened his eyes and promptly squeezed them shut against the light stabbing into them.

"Sorry," Elliot murmured, and the light source behind his closed eyelids moved away. Declan tried again, slitting his eyes at first, then opening them more. Elliot's bedroom, the drapes closed tight, but with what must be every electric lamp in the house brought in to clutter every surface.

Elliot himself was hovering over Declan, brows drawn together with concern. His hazel eyes were bloodshot and red-rimmed, and he had a couple days of stubble shadowing his cheeks.

Declan moistened his dry mouth and tried to give him a reassuring smile. "Morning, Elliot." His voice was thick, and he cleared his throat with a rasping cough.

Elliot moved back and sat down at a chair pulled close to the bed. "It's afternoon, you damned fool, and you scared the hell out of me last night." He scrubbed both hands over his face and dragged his fingers through his hair. "Christ almighty, Declan, why didn't you stop me?"

Declan hadn't wanted to stop him. He smiled at Elliot and squirmed under the bedclothes, stretching his limbs and feeling the pleasant aching soreness that followed a good fuck. Last night had been the first time Elliot had really let go and fucked him the way Declan knew he wanted to.

He'd wanted it too, wanted to be held tightly within Elliot's tentacles, filled beyond capacity by Elliot's cock, fucked hard and long until he couldn't take it anymore. He'd tried to convey this to Elliot before. Last night, it seemed he'd finally gotten the message.

Elliot didn't smile back, though. He looked terrible, his face drawn and hair mussed from all the times he must have run his fingers through it. He was still wearing last night's clothes, which he must have pulled haphazardly on, because his vest was buttoned the wrong way and his shirt was untucked.

Declan's heart ached at the desolate look on Elliot's face. He disentangled a hand from the bedclothes twisted around him and groped for one of Elliot's. Elliot let him have it and squeezed. Declan squeezed back, pulling all his strength in it to show Elliot that he was fine.

"Sorry, Ellie," he said, managing to sound almost normal, his voice maybe a little husky, but it usually was in the morning. "Guess we went a little overboard last night, eh?"

Elliot tugged his hand, but Declan didn't let go. "Christ, Declan, this isn't a joke! You passed out in my arms last night, and I couldn't wake you." He tugged again and this time, Declan let him free. Elliot planted his elbows on the bed and covered his face with both hands.

"You said you wanted it," he whispered, his voice broken and filled with shame.

Declan lifted his hand, which took nearly all the energy he had at the moment, and dropped it on Elliot's head. He ran his fingers through the soft strands. "Of course I wanted it," he said softly. "Elliot, how many times do I have to tell you? I'm not ashamed of wanting you. There's nothing about you that I don't want."

"But being with me is hurting you." Elliot lifted his face and looked directly into Declan's eyes. "I can't be with you if it hurts you like that. I won't."

Declan sighed. "It's not your fault, Elliot." When Elliot just glared at him, he tugged gently on a strand of Elliot's hair, then let his hand fall to the bed. "It was bound to happen eventually. But you can't help the way you are any more than it's my fault that I'm the way I am."

"What the hell do you mean, it was bound to happen eventually?"

Declan tried to push up to his elbows, which shook with fatigue almost immediately. Elliot got an arm around his back and helped him shimmy up to lean against the headboard, then tucked a couple of pillows behind him to prop him up.

"You remember Nance Carrigan telling us about that ship that docked at her compound years ago? The one with the naturalist on board, studying marine creatures?"

Elliot's hands, still fussing with the blankets covering Declan, stilled. "I remember she told us that half the crew died after they found my mother's island." He smoothed a lump from the blanket over Declan's leg, and Declan ignored the fact that he didn't feel anything in that leg—not the bedclothes against his skin, not the weight of Elliot's hand, nothing. Surely the feeling would come back soon, though he'd take this lack of sensation over the painful pins and needles from the other night.

Elliot resumed his seat by the bed. "I always assumed one of the women there killed them. Maybe Mother did." He turned his head away from Declan and swallowed. "Like she killed the Captain." He glanced back at Declan, his eyes sad. "I never said...I mean, we were trying to get away, and then I had to shift back, and we never talked about it."

Declan patted his knee, pressed against the side of the bed. "It's all right, Elliot. I know." Elliot's relationship with Declan's father had been contentious for a long time, but Father had treated Elliot like his own son, despite the town's rumors of his conception, and Declan knew the man had loved Elliot in his way. "Father knew the risk he was taking."

Lunging after the huge octopus that had taken his wife and stabbing it with a copper harpoon was his form of revenge, but he'd paid for it with his life, after he was poisoned by the beast's ink, and Elliot's mother had killed him before he died in agony from it.

Elliot blinked his eyes a few times quickly, then got up from his chair and went to the bureau. He came back with a glass of water for Declan. Declan took the water with a grateful smile and drank the entire glass in one long gulp. It went a long way toward moistening the dryness in his mouth.

"Anyway, some of the sailors in the ship Nance told us about may have been killed outright, but I think a number of them weren't. There are only women living at your mother's island, right? I think some of them couldn't resist what must have seemed a golden opportunity to them."

Elliot stared at him until comprehension dawned on his face.

"You think some of them forced the women?"

Declan snorted. "I doubt that. All the women I saw could take care of themselves, and any man foolish enough to try to force her. But women have needs too, despite what some folk say about the purity of womanhood."

Elliot looked slightly uncomfortable. Declan couldn't tell whether it was because they were talking about sex with women in general, or the idea of his mother having sex. "What does this have to do with what's happening to you?" he asked.

Declan sighed. "Your mother told me that men tend to get sick after having relations with her women. Something to do with the differences between human blood and octopian blood." He shrugged. "She didn't go into very great detail, and I didn't ask."

Elliot pushed from his chair and paced across the room. He stopped at one of the tall casement windows and jerked the drapes open, letting in a shaft of bright sunlight that hurt Declan's eyes. He shielded them with his hand while Elliot gazed out the window, his hand clenching around the sill.

"So, it is my fault."

"No, Elliot. I told you—"

Elliot whirled around and glared at Declan. "If being with me—"

Declan summoned all his energy and spoke over Elliot. "The same thing happened to Father."

Elliot stopped, some of the fight draining out of him. "What?"

"Father," Declan repeated patiently. "When he was with your mother. He loved your mother so much he'd have done anything for her. Is she to blame for hurting him, when she can't help who she is, either?"

"She's to blame for a lot of things," Elliot muttered under his breath, but Declan chose not to respond to that. He hadn't exactly forgiven her for killing Father, himself. The point here was to make Elliot see that this wasn't his fault, that he wasn't to blame for what was happening with him.

"I never saw anything wrong with the Captain," Elliot argued. "The man always seemed invincible."

"Well, you were eight years old when your mother left," Declan retorted. Elliot winced a little, that childhood wound still tender. Declan imagined he'd never really get over it. "Father wasn't going to tell a child about the challenges of loving a woman with a few key differences from him. It's not like he told me anything, either."

"Then how do you know?"

Declan gestured at the glass on the bedside table, and Elliot took it and refilled it from the pitcher on the bureau. Declan drank the whole glass thirstily again, and Elliot wordlessly refilled it a third time for him.

Declan had to rest the bottom of the glass in his lap because his hand was starting to tremble from the weight of it. He glanced up at Elliot, still standing beside the bed, his arms crossed over his chest. "Quit hovering, man," he said. Elliot huffed an annoyed breath, but sat back down in the chair.

"Marie told me," he said. "That's how I know about Father. She said that the longer a man is with a woman like her, the harder it is to resist her, but that they all sicken. She wasn't specific about the symptoms, but I guess we know those now." He shrugged when Elliot gave him a pointed look and offered, "She said that Father lasted longer than most, so that's a good sign, don't you think? Maybe I will, too."

"How?" Elliot asked.

Declan glanced down at the water glass in his lap. The surface was rippling a bit from the tremor in his hand. He explained how Marie had cut herself while she stood over his father's body and given him a small bottle with the blood that ran from the cut. He explained her instructions to mix it with his blood at the new moon before a supermoon. He left out that she warned him she didn't know whether, or how long, it would work for him.

"How did you take it?" Elliot said. He was up from the chair again, rummaging in his shaving kit on the washstand.

"Put it in a shot of whiskey and drank it before the last two supermoons." When Elliot turned around to stare at him, he shrugged. "Didn't quite know how else to do it."

Elliot had found what he was looking for in his kit and tapped the side of his straight razor against his lips. "She probably meant for you to mix it with your own blood, to find a way to inject it into your own veins."

"Maybe," Declan conceded. "But it's not like she gave me a whole lot of instructions about it. And there was a lot going on at the time."

Elliot nodded absently, fiddling with the razor in his hands. "Why didn't you tell me about this?"

Declan shrugged again, trying not to think about what Elliot intended to do with that razor. "It's a little bizarre and disturbing, isn't it? Drinking my stepmother's blood?"

Elliot barked out a harsh laugh. "That's where you draw the line? That's the part of all of this that you find bizarre and disturbing?"

CHAPTER 9

A knock at the door startled both of them, and Sally's voice rang through the paneled wood. "I ain't leaving this tray outside the door, so open up, boys, 'fore the coffee gets cold."

Declan frowned at Elliot. "Why the hell did you tell her?"

Elliot sighed and got up to fetch a shirt from the wardrobe. "You were barely conscious when I got you home, and I needed help to get you upstairs. You know Sally sleeps lightly anyway. It's not like I could keep it from her."

Sally'd known about them for years, probably since shortly after they'd started, when Elliot was seventeen and before Declan's father had taken him away. They'd never talked about it, but she was no fool and she knew everything that went on in the Bishop house. Hell, she probably knew everything that had gone on between his father and Elliot's mother, too. She was an understanding sort, in her tight-lipped, gruff way. Still, knowing she'd seen him naked and at his weakest gnawed at Declan, and he felt a brief flare of irritation at Elliot for putting him in that position.

Elliot tossed Declan the shirt, which fluttered softly into his lap, and Declan plucked awkwardly at the tails with stiff hands, then pulled it over his head. His fingers were too numb to manage the buttons, so he just tucked the button placket under the buttonholes and hoped it wouldn't be too obvious.

Elliot swung the door open wide, like there was no need to hide who was in his bed at this hour. Sally stood at the threshold, a tray between her hands and a bland expression on her face. The smell of coffee wafted toward Declan even across the room. Elliot took the tray from her and set it on the edge of the bed. Sally eyed Declan, but aimed her words at Elliot.

"Mrs. Jackman's in the parlor to see you."

Elliot was fussing around the tray, hopefully pouring Declan some of that coffee, and said over his shoulder. "Not now, please, Sally. Tell her I'll call on her later."

Sally shook her head. "Already tried that. She's insisting it's important. Won't leave until she speaks to you directly."

Elliot straightened up from the tray with a cup cradled in one hand. He sighed and set it on the tray. "Fine. Keep an eye on him, please?"

"Of course," Sally said, as if Declan wasn't even in the damned room, right in front of them. She advanced into the room with a pointed glance at Elliot's disarranged clothing. Elliot tucked his shirt in and buttoned his vest properly, then ran a brush quickly through his disheveled hair. He patted Sally absently on the shoulder and left the room.

Declan reached for the coffee, but Sally grabbed it before he could get at it. She looked into the cup and tipped it a bit toward him so he could see Elliot had lightened it with cream. Probably had far too much sugar in it too, the way Elliot liked it. Declan leaned his head against the headboard with a sigh and caught Sally's smirk out of the corner of his eye. For all his attention to detail in business, Elliot could never seem to remember how Declan preferred his coffee.

She poured him a fresh cup, black, and he took it carefully in both hands. A headache was gnawing just above his left eyebrow, and he took a much-needed sip, the hot liquid warming his throat. He sighed and closed his eyes to savor it.

When he opened them, Sally was still there, standing at the end of the bed, staring down at him, arms crossed over her ample bosom. He stared back at her, willing himself not to blush at the knowing look on her face. Jesus, the last thing he needed was Elliot's housekeeper, the woman who practically raised both of them, imagining the things he got up to with Elliot last night.

"What?" he finally demanded. If Sally had something to say to him, she could just come right out and say it, damn it. Or leave him in peace. He shifted his ass on the bed, seeking a more comfortable position, and tugged the covers higher up his waist. Bare-assed and sore in Elliot's bed was not the way he'd ever intended to discuss with Sally the true nature of his relationship with Elliot.

Sally opened her mouth, then closed it. "Got some nice porridge here for you," she offered. "Added a little maple syrup to it, like when you were sick as a boy."

Declan took another sip of coffee. "Thanks, Sal. But you know what would really hit the spot? Some of that hash you make with a couple eggs."

Sally raised an eyebrow at him. "Come on," he wheedled. "I'm not an invalid here. Don't need a nursemaid, either."

She snorted. "Same thing your father'd say when he had spells like this. You're as stubborn as he was."

Declan didn't want to know what she meant by that, but if his father experienced the same effects when he was with Marie, then maybe Sally would have some suggestions. How the devil to ask her, though, was the question.

"Hash and eggs fixed him right up, though, didn't it?" He put on his best smile, half hoping she'd take the hint and give up, half that she'd have some sort of solution for him.

She shook her head. "All I know is they quit happening after

Mrs. Bishop went away. It's a wonder he survived as long as he did with her."

Which was an answer of sorts, but Declan wasn't in a mood for cryptic complaints from Sally, as fond as he was of her. "If you've got something to say, Sal, spit it out."

"Just saying that sometimes the one you want ain't the right one for you. After Mrs. Bishop left, the Captain didn't have no more spells like this."

"And you knew this how?" he snapped, his patience shredding.

Sally lifted her chin. "I knew," she said, and it suddenly dawned on him.

Everyone in town called her Mrs. Jenkins, but as far as he knew, no one had ever met a Mr. Jenkins. Declan had asked her once when he was a boy, and she'd told some vague story about him being a logger up north somewhere who'd died in an accident, but that was before the twins were born.

"The girls are Father's?" he asked. Sally's cheeks pinked, but she looked steadily at him. "You loved him," he said softly, and she gave a small nod. Sally had been employed in the Bishop house since before his father married Marie, and he'd always assumed her loyalty was to the Bishop family. But Father had been essentially a widower for longer than he'd been married, and he could hardly fault the man for finding comfort where he could.

"Never mind, it's none of my business." Declan swallowed the rest of his coffee and turned the cup over in his hands. They weren't shaking anymore, which had to be a good sign. "That ship's sailed for me, Sal. There's no one else. So if you got any suggestions, I'm all ears."

Sally sighed. "Figured that was the case. I never knew what he did after he was with her. Never wanted to ask, I guess. Far as I could tell, it was time that did the trick. He'd usually be back to normal within a few days."

Declan nodded. He didn't say anything for a few minutes, and neither did Sally. She just watched him, though her arms relaxed some and her expression was softer. "Time and hash and eggs?" he finally said, with a small smile.

Sally snorted. "Mr. Elliot's gonna sack me for this," she grumbled, but she was already turning toward the door, bless her.

"You know he won't," Declan called after her as she left the room.

"Someday he might" floated back, Sally's routine response in their habitual exchange.

Alone in the room at last, Declan set the coffee cup on the bedside table. He pushed the covers down and swung his legs off the bed, planting his feet on the Oriental rug that covered most of Elliot's bedroom floor. Without the headboard to lean against, his sense of vertigo increased, and he wondered whether this was what seasickness felt like.

He tried wiggling his toes, and was reassured when it worked, his toes curling and digging into the wool fibers. His ass hurt—more than yesterday morning—and he pushed his hands into the mattress, lifting his backside to take the pressure off. He took a deep breath, steadying himself, and slowly pushed to his feet.

And promptly fell down, his knees buckling, and landing ass over teakettle in an ungainly sprawl on the rug.

"Fuck," he muttered under his breath, glancing at the door Sally had left open, hoping not to see Elliot or Sally rushing to his aid. The hall was silent, though, Elliot still presumably entertaining Mrs. Jackman and Sally probably in the kitchen, too far away to hear him upstairs.

He eyed his sea chest next to the wardrobe, only a few feet away. Clothes would make him feel better than any porridge or coddling. He'd figure out what to do next after he got his trousers on.

Ignoring the open door and trying not to think of how long Mrs. Jackman would be able to keep Elliot's attention, he crawled on hands and knees to the trunk, fumbled the latch open, and lifted the lid. There was a pair of trousers folded neatly on top, and he drew them out. He stuffed one leg into them, then the other, and managed to shimmy them up over his ass by leaning against the trunk and wiggling the fabric over his hips.

He didn't bother tucking his shirt in, but determinedly struggled with the buttons, his right hand stiff and numb, uncooperative. He got them done, though. The buttons on the fly of his trousers were a similar struggle, and by the time he was finished, his hands were shaking again. He tugged a vest from the chest and pulled it on, but left the buttons undone. He wasn't dressed for polite company, but at least he was decently covered and felt a little more like himself.

He closed the chest's lid, then propped a forearm on it and used his other hand to drag his leg forward so that his knee was positioned under his hip. He pushed himself up so that he was kneeling on that knee, then switched the arm he had braced on the chest and dragged his other leg into place. He straightened up so that his weight was on both knees and pushed both hands against the chest until his shoulders were over his hips and he was kneeling upright. The vertigo increased, and he swayed a bit on his knees, but then stabilized.

He let go of first one hand than the other and managed to stay upright. So far, so good. He braced one hand on the chest again, and grabbed his right ankle and positioned it where his knee had been. Pressing down into that right foot and against the chest with his hands, he managed to leverage himself to standing. He had to slap one hand against the wardrobe for support, but he had it now. He was standing on his own damned feet, without anyone's help. Just in time for Elliot to appear in the doorway.

CHAPTER 10

*E*lliot's relief at seeing Declan standing on his own two feet lasted only as long as it took for Declan to spread his arms and give him a smile. "See? I'm fine."

His knees started to shake, and Elliot knew that he wouldn't make it across the room before Declan fell. Declan managed to swing his left leg around by swiveling his hips, then collapsed on his ass on the chest. Elliot started towards him and ignored Declan's attempt to wave him off. He grasped Declan's upper arm and hauled him up, then manhandled him toward the bed.

"Goddammit, Elliot, let go," Declan panted, but he didn't have the strength to both protest and resist Elliot, so Elliot won the brief struggle. He shoved Declan onto the bed, where he landed in an ungainly sprawl. Elliot backed away from the bed before he did something else in his frustration and fear, like hit Declan to make him stay down.

Declan looked like he might hit Elliot, his chest heaving, two spots of color on cheeks that were otherwise still pale.

"Stay there," he ordered Declan.

"Fuck off," Declan retorted. "I don't take orders from anyone; I give them."

"This is my house, not your damned ship, and you'll do as I say while you're here." The look of shocked betrayal that flitted across Declan's face made Elliot briefly regret suggesting that this wasn't Declan's home, too, but then his stubborn stepbrother lurched ungracefully to his feet again.

"Well, I'll remove myself from your house, then," Declan said, in a cold, low voice, the voice that meant he was absolutely furious.

Some of Elliot's anger drained away, but the fear about what was happening to Declan and his guilt over being the cause settled deeper in the pit of his stomach, its weight hard and cold, like the *Black Dove*'s anchor dragging through icy water.

When Declan straightened up to his full height, he came forward and offered a hand to support him, but Declan slapped it away.

"I don't need you," he said, and the steel in his voice and the hard look in his flashing eyes crushed something small and child-like in Elliot. That's what he'd been afraid of his whole life, wasn't it? That Declan didn't need him, that no one did. Except his mother, but only for something he couldn't— wouldn't—bring himself to do.

He wiped a hand over his face and rubbed at his burning eyes. The grandfather clock in the parlor had chimed eleven while he was speaking with Mrs. Jackman, and his sleepless night of worrying over Declan was catching up to him.

"I'm sorry," he said. "I didn't mean that this isn't your house, too." He stepped back so he wasn't crowding Declan and let him take a few steps from the bed. He did look a little better. His face still pale, and his right hand still clenched in a fist at his side, but he took four shuffling steps on his own and paused at the chair Elliot had been sitting in, his other hand braced on the ladder back.

Declan sighed, and his shoulders relaxed a bit. "I know," he said.

"Would you like to sit down?" Elliot gestured at the chair and made it a request instead of a demand, the same polite tone he'd just used with Mrs. Jackman. "Sally will be up in a bit with some breakfast for both of us."

Declan gave him a suspicious look, but Elliot smiled as pleasantly as he could, and Declan swiveled the chair so its back was to the bed. "Don't mind if I do," he said, also making an effort at politeness. He sat, planting his feet under his knees, his hands resting on his thighs. The fingers of his right hand twitched against the black wool of his trousers and squeezed once, as if massaging the feeling back into his leg, and Elliot turned toward the fireplace so Declan didn't feel like he was being monitored.

He busied himself with stoking the fire, even though the sun streaming through the open drapes was already warming the room to a temperature comfortable for him. Declan's feet were still bare and his vest unbuttoned, and Elliot figured he'd appreciate the additional warmth. When he finished, he sat on Declan's sea chest, and clasped his hands between his knees.

"What did Mrs. Jackman want?" Declan asked, after a period when the only sounds were the hissing of the stove and the faint calls of a raven somewhere outside. His voice was mild, no trace of anger now. Elliot wondered how he could always do that—be the bigger man, smooth over a conflict, make the first move toward reconciliation. Did he never hold a grudge? He'd certainly had enough reasons to do so, against his father, against Elliot. He never seemed to, though.

Elliot stretched his legs out across the rug and leaned back against the wall behind the chest. He motioned toward a small bottle he'd put on the bureau when he came back to the room. "She brought something she said might help you recover."

"For fuck's sake, Elliot, did you tell the whole town about us?" Declan inhaled a deep breath through his nose, clearly trying to not to escalate their fight. Elliot hastened to reassure him.

"I didn't. She doesn't know exactly what happened, I swear. It's only…" he stopped, not sure how to explain.

Declan raised an eyebrow. "Only what?"

"We have a sort of connection," Elliot started, then blushed when Declan's other eyebrow went up. "I don't mean anything improper by that." Declan snorted.

"You mean something like what you have with the octopian women? You can hear their thoughts, can't you?"

"Not exactly," Elliot said, then cocked his head at Declan. "How did you know?"

Declan shrugged. "It was obvious you could hear something I couldn't while we were there. And the women who took me to your mother's island never spoke words to each other, but communicated well enough to sail the ship, so I figured there must be some kind of telepathy going on."

He gave a small chuckle, a faraway look on his face. "You won't remember this, but this medium passed through Port Townsend when I was about ten or eleven. She conducted a séance at the house one evening. Father didn't approve, I think, but your mother could talk him into almost anything. I was sent to bed early with you, but wanted to see it, so I crept halfway down the stairs and found a spot where I could see a little into the parlor. I don't remember everyone that attended, but I do recall Judge Swan and his wife were there. She said she could read people's minds, and whatever she read in Judge Swan's mind caused quite a stir. Mrs. Swan left in tears, and Father tossed the medium out on her ear."

His smile was delighted, like a boy watching a theatrical spectacle, though he wiped most of it off his face when he continued, "Judge Swan left for a couple months later to live among the Makah Indians for a while."

Judge Swan's abandoning his wife and children was a scandal Elliot had been too young to notice when it happened, but he'd heard whispers about off and on as an adult. He wondered whether the medium's mind reading had caused the breach, or if it would have happened anyway.

"You going out on the mind-reading circuit, Elliot?" Declan asked, an undercurrent of amusement in his voice.

Elliot shook his head. "It's not a parlor trick. It's not even that I can hear distinct thoughts. Just that I can sense things and sometimes feel what she's feeling or doing." He shrugged. "It's fainter with Mrs. Jackman than with Mama or Celeste. More like hearing an echo of her feelings and a general awareness of where she is and what she's doing, and only when I pay close attention to her."

"Huh. And can she sense your feelings and where you are, too?" Declan's forehead creased, and he frowned. "Because that would be...disconcerting."

Elliot's face heated, and he couldn't look Declan in the eye. "You're telling me. I don't think she can see things—Christ, I hope not—but you know she's from Port Angeles, right? Didn't the *Poulpes* appear there at least once?"

Declan nodded. "You think she's an octopian, too?"

Elliot shook his head. "I don't...think so?" He said slowly, considering how the connection with her differed from that with his mother and Celeste. "The connection's not as strong. But maybe she's related somehow to one of them?"

Declan tapped a finger against his lips. "Your mother said something about being selective in who they take. Maybe this connection is how they find the right ones." He stretched his right leg out in front of him and dug his thumb into the crease at his hip. Elliot was suddenly reminded of why they were talking about Mrs. Jackman in the first place. He got up and fetched the bottle she'd given him, snagged a spoon from the tray Sally had left and brought both to Declan.

"Take it," he said. "Two spoonfuls a day, she said, until you feel better."

"What's in it?" Declan hesitated before taking the bottle.

Elliot shrugged. "She didn't say. Just that it would help. But her intentions were good, Declan, I could tell. She genuinely wants to help."

Declan pulled the stopper from the bottle and sniffed the contents. Then he capped it firmly and handed it back to Elliot. "No, thanks."

"What? Why not?"

"Whatever else it's got in it, it's laudanum-based."

Elliot uncapped the bottle and sniffed at it. A sweetish aroma flooded his nose, followed by an astringent scent of something he recognized, but couldn't place. He poured a bit into the spoon. The liquid was a dark amber color and thick as molasses. He filled the spoon and held it out to Declan. "So?"

Declan crossed his arms over his chest. "So, I don't take laudanum."

"Oh come on, Declan. I know you mix a bit of hashish into your pipe tobacco."

"That's different," Declan retorted. "I don't take straight opium. I've seen well enough what too much of that shit can do to you. And laudanum is just as bad."

The heaviness in Elliot's stomach rose to tighten his throat. It was his fault Declan was in this condition, but for once, couldn't Declan cooperate? Did he have to be so bloody self-reliant all the time? "Please, Declan, just do it for me. I can't lose you again."

Declan glared at him for an interminable moment, then sighed. He uncrossed his arms and took the spoon from Elliot. "Fine." He swallowed the spoonful, made a face, and took the second spoonful with unconcealed irritation. "Satisfied?" he demanded, when Elliot capped the bottle and set it on the bedside table.

"Almost," Elliot said. "Sally's gone to the apothecary for a syringe. We're going to see whether injecting my blood helps, too."

"Oh, for fuck's sake," Declan said, casting a long-suffering glance at the ceiling. "I told you your mother said to do that at the new moon."

"Fine," Elliot said. "But at least we'll be ready to do it when the time comes." He returned to Declan's chair and hovered near him, putting his hand on Declan's shoulder, then cupping his jaw, tangling his fingers in the hair at the back of Declan's neck. Declan rolled his eyes, but let Elliot run his fingers through his hair. He closed his eyes, and Elliot bent to press a soft kiss against his lips.

"She said it might make you sleepy. I guess that's because of the laudanum. Maybe you should get back in bed?" He tried to make it a suggestion, rather than an order.

Declan tipped his head into Elliot's hand and hooked a finger in his waistband, tugging him closer. "Only if you get in with me. You need sleep even more than I do."

The exhaustion Elliot had been fighting all morning crashed over him, leaving his limbs heavy and his head woozy. "All right."

It was too much work to remove his clothes, other than his shoes, before slipping under the covers. Declan shrugged out of his vest and draped it over the back of the chair, then got in next to him. He pulled Declan's body against his, his chest pressed close against Declan's back, and draped an arm over Declan's waist.

Despite how tired he was, he didn't let himself sleep until he felt Declan drift off, pulled under by the laudanum's influence. When Declan's breathing settled into a deep, steady, rhythm, Elliot finally let sleep take him, too.

CHAPTER 11

*T*wo weeks of convalescence, as Elliot insisted on calling it, and Declan was going out of his goddamn mind. Sitting on his arse and wasting time was more like it. He'd absolutely refused to stay in bed the way Elliot wanted, but there wasn't much for him to do at the Mercantile. Elliot had taken over Father's office downtown and had the books for the import/export business well in hand. He'd invited Declan to a few meetings of the railroad trustees, which Declan had attended out of sheer boredom, but those entailed a lot of speeches about Port Townsend's need for a railroad and not much progress in luring one to put money into constructing it.

Evenings with Elliot were pleasant, at least. Sally's excellent cooking filled his belly, and sipping a good whiskey or port after dinner was better than watching Thomas curse a blue streak while struggling with the *Black Dove*'s temperamental stove or trying to sleep during a storm.

But he wasn't used to being idle for so long, and Elliot's constant watchfulness was chafing at him. Tonight was the new moon, and Elliot insisted they try injecting his blood into Declan's veins. Not that Declan needed it. He'd recovered within a day or two of the supermoon and hadn't experienced any further effects. But Elliot refused to touch him until after the injection, so Declan agreed to it, if only to prove to Elliot that they could get back to normal.

Elliot had dragged him into his study after breakfast this morning and pushed him into a wingback chair next to his big desk. There was a tray strewn with items Declan was trying not to look at on the desk, and Elliot was fiddling with the tray's contents. His eyebrows drew together in concentration.

"You even know what you're doing here, Elliot?" Declan asked.

Elliot nodded, picking up a small vial filled with dark red liquid and dislodging a cloth covering a syringe on the tray. "I talked to Dr. Calhoun. He showed me this diagram of where all your veins are and how to get the needle in the vein."

Declan's stomach plummeted alarmingly at the sight of the long needle on the tray, its sharp tip glinting in the sunlight streaming in from the bay windows behind Elliot's desk. He closed his eyes, which didn't make him feel any better. He could still see it behind his lids.

"What'd you tell him to explain why you were asking?" Maybe talking would distract him. Elliot didn't answer for a moment. Shit, maybe talking would distract Elliot. He sure as hell didn't want that. But then Elliot glanced up with a tiny smirk.

"I told him one of your crew has syphilis and I'd heard about the mercury treatment. I asked if he could show me how to do it so I could show you. He conducts the monthly examinations for most of the known prostitutes in town and treats half the sailors. So he says. He gave me a lecture on the evils of the flesh that I'll spare you, and said he was glad someone else in town was concerned about the health of our sailors."

Declan snorted despite himself, careful not to move his arm. "That's slander, is what that is," he protested mildly. "My men don't have syphilis. And I don't appreciate you casting indirect aspersions on Mrs. Viola or the ladies of the Green Light saloon, either."

"Or the androgyne at the Cliff House?" Elliot said, with an arch tone in his voice.

"How do you know about Janie June?" Declan asked. Declan had seen plenty of uptown bankers and merchants at the Cliff House, but Elliot didn't frequent the saloons or female boarding houses and wasn't on a first name basis with any whores that Declan knew of.

Elliot shrugged and picked up the syringe, suddenly reminding Declan what was about to happen. "I heard Mr. Hill tell Judge Kuhn about her." He stuck the syringe's tip into the vial containing his blood and drew up far more than Declan thought was really necessary. "It sounded like Kuhn was familiar with her." He grinned at Declan, who tried gamely to grin back.

"Sly dog," he managed, and his voice didn't even shake. His head was swimming, though, and black spots appeared before his eyes, the syringe in Elliot's hand wavering in his vision.

"Hey." Elliot's voice seemed to come from far away, until he grasped Declan's chin with his other hand and turned his face away from the syringe. "Are you all right?" His eyes flicked over Declan's face, and then the worry in them changed to something else. "Are you afraid of needles?"

"'Course not," Declan protested. Elliot's smile just got wider and smugger. He didn't say anything more, just looked like he was seconds away from laughing in Declan's face.

"Well, why do you think I mixed it with whiskey instead of sticking myself with it, Elliot?"

Elliot's lips twitched, but thankfully, he held himself in check. Declan glanced back at the syringe in his hand and hastily looked away again. Elliot patted the side of his face, though he wasn't especially gentle about it.

"Look out the window while I do it," he suggested. "That should help." He went down on one knee next to the arm of

Declan's chair and grasped Declan's forearm with one hand, pinning it to the chair arm and aiming the needle toward it.

Declan resolutely stared out the window over Elliot's shoulder. From this angle there wasn't much to see but the trees across the street and a solid bank of clouds threatening rain. He watched a few wisps drift across the main bank and felt a sharp pinch in his forearm. He held his breath and focused on the warm strength in Elliot's hand holding his arm steady until Elliot withdrew the needle and pressed a bit of cotton wool over the injection site.

"Done," Elliot said. "Now, that wasn't so bad, was it?" He had that singsong tone to his voice that mothers use when bandaging skinned knees on crying children. Declan shoved against Elliot's shoulder.

"Leave off me, you sadist."

Elliot rocked back on his heels, overbalanced, and sprawled on the rug, his dimples flashing as he grinned at Declan. It was the first real smile Declan had seen on his face in days.

Declan rolled his eyes at him and stood up. He peeked under the cotton wool, which had a spot of blood on it that he looked away from, but his arm was fine. Just a tiny red dot, no blood trickling from it, and he tossed the bit of bandage on the tray with Elliot's other accoutrements.

He reached a hand down to Elliot and hauled him to his feet. Elliot's grin faded, and he searched Declan's face. "How do you feel?"

Declan spread his arms wide. "Fine. Right as rain." He didn't point out what Elliot already knew, which was that Declan had improved within a matter of days after the supermoon and hadn't experienced any symptoms since the quarter-moon.

"Feel any different?" Elliot said hesitantly, his hands hovering in the air, like he wanted to touch Declan but didn't think he was allowed. He hadn't touched Declan other than in passing or that hand up just now since the morning after the supermoon. "I mean, can you tell if it's working?"

Declan stepped closer to him and snagged Elliot by the waistband before he could move away. "Don't know. Want to test it and see?" They hadn't done anything in days. Elliot slept beside him in his big bed, or at least pretended to sleep, since every time Declan woke, he could feel Elliot watching over him. Purple shadows bloomed under Elliot's eyes from the lack of sleep, and he'd been snappish and ill-tempered more often than not lately. Well, that was something Declan could fix, at least temporarily. If Elliot would let him.

Elliot's hands settled on Declan's shoulders, and he tipped to rest his forehead against Declan's. Declan slipped his arms around Elliot's waist and clasped his hands behind the small of Elliot's back. He stood firm, legs braced with no tingling or trembling, to prove that Elliot could lean on him. Elliot's breath ghosted over his lips.

"We can't," Elliot said. "Not until we know it's working." His voice was small and hopeless. Declan tightened his arms, pulling Elliot's hips against his hardness.

"Wasn't that the whole point of jabbing me with that damned thing?" He ground his erection against Elliot's, also hard, despite his words. "How will we know it's working until we test it?"

Declan had been through longer periods of enforced celibacy, but right now, Elliot was here in his arms, and he was damned tired of waiting for what they both wanted.

"And if the treatment takes time to work? I can't do that to you again," Elliot said. He tucked his face against Declan's neck, and Declan could feel his deep sigh.

"Your mother's blood worked while I took it," Declan argued. "And you're normal now, so there shouldn't be a problem."

Elliot's body stiffened and pulled back. Damn it. He knew Elliot thought of his other form as unnatural, and he wanted to snatch back his thoughtless words. He tightened his arms to keep

Elliot from pulling away again. "That's not what I meant," he said softly.

He stroked one hand up Elliot's back and cupped the back of his neck, tangling his fingers in Elliot's soft hair. "Come on, Ellie, don't make me beg."

Elliot kissed his neck, and Declan tilted his head to encourage Elliot to keep going. His lips brushed against the spot under Declan's ear that always made him shiver. But then Elliot said in a muffled voice, "You should go."

"Go? Go where?" The only place Declan wanted to go was upstairs so they didn't scandalize Sally or her girls.

Elliot pulled away and turned his back to Declan. His shoulders were slumped and his exhaustion was evident even facing away from Declan. "You had a voyage planned, didn't you? You should get back on your schedule."

A schedule that was planned around the four supermoons between April and June. But if he left now, he couldn't be sure about making it back before the May supermoon in two weeks. As if reading his thoughts, Elliot said, "I'll get though the next one on my own."

Declan swung around to face Elliot, who refused to look him in the eyes. The argument he was about to make died on his lips. Instead, he touched two fingers to Elliot's chin and gently lifted it so he could see Elliot's face. "Is that what you want?"

Elliot snorted mirthlessly. That bulge in his trousers didn't lie about what he wanted, but his eyes were red-rimmed with exhaustion and heavy with sadness. "Of course it's not what I want. I just can't keep waking up every morning with this false hope that we can be together."

"We can," Declan insisted. "We can figure this out, Elliot. Somehow." He pulled Elliot's head down to his shoulder again and kissed the side of his head.

A part of him wanted to drag Elliot upstairs and show him how he was recovered enough to do everything they'd been missing out on these last two weeks. But it wasn't fair to force Elliot, even though Declan knew he could. Elliot couldn't control the shifting at the supermoon, so the least Declan could do was let him control what else he did with his body.

In the meantime, Declan would do whatever it took to find more answers. He kissed the side of Elliot's head again. "All right. I'll leave for Nance's in the morning. She helped us last year. Maybe she can help us again."

Elliot nodded, his hair softly brushing Declan's neck. "Maybe." He didn't sound hopeful. Declan tightened his arms around him. He would just have to have enough hope for both of them.

CHAPTER 12

"*A*hoy!" Elliot called, clambering over the rail from the gangplank. Joey's head popped from behind the *Black Dove*'s wheel. Elliot waved at him, steadying himself against the gentle roll of the deck with his other hand on the rail. It had taken him a few days to get his sea legs last year. He was a little sorry he wouldn't be aboard long enough this time.

"Mr. Elliot," Joey called, waving back at him. He turned to speak to someone behind him, then hopped down the few steps from the quarterdeck to the main deck and brushed his fair hair off his forehead and out of his eyes.

Elliot shook his hand. He'd tried telling Joey that he could call Elliot by his Christian name, but Joey simply refused. At least he'd relented enough to stop calling him Mr. Bishop. Elliot understood that this was a big step for Joey, who still called Declan "Captain" every time.

Joey threaded his way toward him while Elliot surveyed the small ship. Reginald was forward of the foremast with Luca, gesturing at something in the rigging, and complaining loudly about something, as usual. Seamus was dashing back and forth along the starboard side, tying various lines and tugging on others, readying the ship for departure.

"Where's Declan?" Elliot asked, when Joey reached him.

Joey jerked a thumb at the hatch that led to the captain's cabin. "Below. Been expecting you."

Elliot nodded at him and headed belowdecks. He tucked the box he'd brought with him under his arm and rapped his knuckles once on Declan's half-open cabin door.

Declan was bent over the desk, hands braced atop it. Elliot had a brief urge to approach him from behind, slip his trousers down to his knees, and take him just like that. He stamped that thought out as soon as he had it. Could he not control himself, especially now that he knew what it was costing Declan? As much as he loved being with Declan that way, he never wanted to see him so still and helpless again.

At least, he told himself he never wanted that again. And ignored the small, utterly wrong, image that stole into his mind of Declan conscious but immobilized, willingly held still so that Elliot could do whatever he wanted to him.

Christ, what was wrong with him?

Declan glanced up at him. He looked healthy, no sign of the sickly pallor in his face, and his green eyes crinkled at the corners the way they always had when he smiled. Elliot eyed him carefully, trying to tell whether he was leaning against the desk for support, but then he lifted his right hand and made a small pencil mark on the chart spread across the desk. Elliot took a few steps closer.

"Is that the North Pacific chart? The Imray & Son one?"

"Mmph," Declan grunted affirmatively. He walked a pair of dividers across the chart, moving west from Cape Flattery to a small drawn-on circle in the middle of the ocean. He made another notation on the chart, then wrote something in the logbook open next to the chart. Elliot knew what he was measuring, but couldn't believe it.

"You're not going there," he stated flatly.

"Not at first," Declan said. "I'm hoping not at all. Just considering it as an option, if there's nothing Nance can suggest to help."

Elliot sucked a deep breath in through his nose, breathing in the air of sea salt, pipe smoke, and whiskey that filled Declan's cabin, trying to keep calm. He trusted none of the devilfish women living under that remote Pacific island, not even Celeste. And especially not his mother. Not with Declan's safety, anyway, or with that of the *Black Dove*'s crew. Elliot wouldn't put it past his mother to use Declan as a bargaining chip to get Elliot's further cooperation. She'd done that last year.

Declan swiveled around and leaned against on the edge of the desk. He tucked the pencil behind his ear and spread his legs apart, making room for Elliot. Against his better judgment, Elliot rounded the desk and stepped in between them. Declan clasped the lapels of his jacket and tugged him closer.

"What's this?" he asked, his hand brushing against the box still under Elliot's arm. Elliot opened the lid and tilted it to show Declan the contents. The blood in the glass vial gleamed a dark burgundy, the color of the wine he'd served at the trustees' dinner party, the night Declan had returned.

He'd drawn as much from his own arm as he'd dared, until he was too woozy to hold the syringe. He just hoped it would be enough.

Declan made a face, but obligingly rolled his sleeve up. Elliot set the box on the desk next to his hip and filled the syringe with the blood. He set the needle's tip against the pale inside of Declan's elbow and glanced up. Declan was staring fixedly at the stern windows. He finished the injection as efficiently as he could, stroking Declan's arm with the thumb of the hand holding him, steadily pushing the plunger until the syringe was empty.

He withdrew the needle and cleaned it, then tucked it back into the box with the vial of blood. "You'll have to inject the rest yourself," he said. "Can you handle that? I could show Joey how, if you'd rather."

"Absolutely not," Declan said. "I'll handle it, Elliot. It's just a needle."

Elliot searched his face, but Declan's grin held an easy confidence that looked genuine. He wasn't entirely sure the blood made a difference, though it was undeniable that Declan's condition had markedly improved. If Declan couldn't manage the injections on his own during the voyage, at least Elliot wouldn't be along to hurt him anymore.

Declan tilted his face up and kissed the point of Elliot's chin, then his lips. A soft, quick kiss, just barely pressing his lips against Elliot's before he let go.

"I still don't want you going there," Elliot said, returning to the other sore subject.

Declan sighed. "They're your people, Elliot. You don't think they might have some answers for us?"

"And how does that conversation go?" Elliot retorted. "Telling my mother what I've done to you, asking her how I can keep doing it without killing you?" Elliot's entire body filled with hot shame and his mind recoiled at the thought.

Declan shrugged. "Believe me, I don't relish that conversation. But she was with my father for years before she left, and he was fine. She knows about us anyway, and she did try to help last year. She might again. There's no harm in asking." As if discussing their illicit relationship with his mother was no more embarrassing than consulting a physician about a stomach complaint.

Elliot tried a different tack. "You know what she wanted me to do."

Move to her remote island and breed a new generation of devilfish sons like himself. Abandon his life in Port Townsend and everything normal that he'd built for himself. Elliot shuddered at the idea. He'd been willing to marry Celeste when he thought they could build a comfortable life based on friendship. But that was before he found out about their shared abnormality. And before Declan came back into his life.

"I don't ever want to go back there."

Declan smoothed a hand down his shirtfront. "I'm not asking you to, Elliot. But you're the one who wanted me to get back on the water. As long as I'm out there, might as well see what I can find out."

"You know what her women have done to sailors." Elliot took a breath, then played the last card he had. "Would you put your crew in danger like that again?"

Declan frowned at him, but Elliot held his gaze. If there was one constant in the world, it was Declan's unwavering dedication to the welfare of his crew.

"All right," Declan sighed. "I still think it's foolish to ignore the best source of information we have. But I won't go, if you insist."

He kissed Elliot again, softly, then deepened the kiss, slipping a hand into Elliot's hair and tugging gently. Elliot leaned into the kiss, letting Declan's hot tongue fill his mouth.

Without breaking the kiss, Declan unbuttoned the buttons of Elliot's trousers and dipped his fingers inside Elliot's drawers. Elliot closed his eyes, and Declan's rough hand wrapped around his shaft, filling Declan's hand and earning a low chuckle in his ear.

"Declan," he protested on a low groan, even though he didn't really want him to stop. He hadn't come here for this. But Declan's hand was warm, and Elliot was already dreading the weeks he'd be away.

"Gonna miss your birthday tomorrow," Declan murmured against Elliot's lips. "Consider this an early present." He stroked Elliot from root to tip, swirling his hand around the head and using Elliot's own fluid to slick his palm. He kept the strokes slow, so slow Elliot just got harder and harder. He rocked into Declan's hand to increase the friction.

Declan looped his other arm around Elliot's neck and pulled his head down to tuck Elliot's face into his shoulder. "Shhh," he whispered in Elliot's ear, "I got you, Ellie, just let me, just like this."

Elliot gave up trying to reach his climax and relaxed against the solid bulwark of Declan's chest. He let Declan stroke him as slow as he wanted. The hard calluses of Declan's fingers rasped against the sensitive underside of his cock, and a low moan escaped his throat. Declan's firm grip was perfect around him, and the slow speed amplified the pleasure building up in his balls. He kept stroking, twisting a little just under the head, still slow and tight, beyond the point Elliot was sure he couldn't take anymore. Elliot melted even more against him. He heard himself at a distance, keening a little against Declan's neck, his mouth open, tasting Declan's skin, salty and warm.

When the pleasure finally crested, it washed through his whole body, a warm tidal rush that sparked against every inch of his skin. Declan stroked him through it, holding him steady, his arm tight around Elliot's shoulders. "That's it, Ellie," he whispered. "Give it all up to me." His words caused another shudder through Elliot and another rush of pleasure.

Declan's hand finally stilled, loosely holding Elliot's softening cock. His breath was soft and steady in Elliot's ear. Elliot lifted leaden arms and draped them over Declan's shoulders. His skin was still tingling, and he pressed a kiss to the curve where Declan's neck met his shoulder. He stayed like that for another moment, then lifted his head and kissed Declan's lips. They curved into a sweet smile when he pulled back. Declan's eyes were shining and bright green.

Elliot grasped Declan's wrist and gently tugged his hand from Elliot's trousers. He sank to his knees before Declan and brought his hand to his mouth. He licked his own spend from Declan's hand, cleaning him thoroughly, twining his tongue around and between Declan's fingers.

"That's my boy," Declan said, his voice low and approving. Elliot shivered, his spent cock twitching where it was hanging limp from his still-open trousers. Elliot sucked each finger into his mouth, and Declan's breath caught. He reached for Declan's waistband and fumbled the buttons open.

The salty, acrid taste of his own spend was replaced by the sweet bitterness leaking from Declan's cock, and Elliot flattened his tongue, letting the head bump against the back of his throat. He grabbed Declan's hands and put them around his own head and Declan got the hint, tightening his fingers in Elliot's hair and pulling his mouth down on his cock.

He held Elliot there, his hard length filling Elliot's mouth. His nose filled with Declan's musk, crisp hairs tickling his cheeks. Then Declan pulled Elliot back with a firm grip on his hair and Elliot sucked a deep breath in through his nose. Declan pulled him down on his cock with a sharp jerk, and Elliot let his neck muscles relax into Declan's hold.

His hands cradled Elliot's face and he fucked into his mouth, his hips thrusting the last inch into Elliot's throat over and over, and that was when Elliot's mind finally quieted, the worries about where Declan was going and how Elliot would survive without him overwhelmed by the feel of Declan's hard length on his tongue, battering his throat. Spit dripped down his chin and tears leaked from the corners of his eyes, but none of that mattered because this was Declan finally taking something from him, instead of Elliot always taking from Declan.

Declan gave a low grunt and stilled, his fingers clenching hard in Elliot's hair. Elliot welcomed the pain, relaxed the back of his jaw, and swallowed the flood that filled his mouth. When Declan's hands relaxed, Elliot kept a steady gentle sucking, swallowing every drop, until Declan traced a thumb around where his lips were stretched around him and broke the seal.

Elliot let Declan's softening cock slip from his mouth and sat back on his heels. He rested there for a moment, sucking in air through his battered mouth, letting his breathing return to normal, until Declan dangled a handkerchief in front of his face. He cleaned the tears and spit from his face, then swiped over his cock and dabbed at a wet spot on the front of his trousers. He balled the handkerchief into one hand and let Declan pull him to his feet with the other.

"Tide's about to turn, and we need to get underway," Declan said softly. Elliot nodded, still not happy about Declan's plans. But he was the one who'd insisted Declan go. And Declan was perfectly capable of taking care of himself and his crew. He'd been doing it almost as long as he'd been taking care of Elliot.

He turned toward the cabin door, then swung back and grabbed Declan in a crushing embrace. Declan hugged him back just as hard.

"I'll be back," Declan said. "We'll figure it out, Ellie, I promise."

Elliot left the cabin and tried not to feel like this was some sort of permanent goodbye.

CHAPTER 13

eclan lifted his face to the stiff breeze belling the sails and inhaled the damp, salty air. It was good to be back aboard the *Black Dove*, where he was in control again. He didn't mind being in port, and never felt like he got enough of being with Elliot, but the last two weeks of idleness while Elliot hovered around him like a nursemaid had about driven him mad.

He ran one hand around the smooth wood and brass fittings of the ship's wheel, keeping it steady against the water's rocking pull with his other hand. He still doubted whether he'd done the right thing in leaving Elliot to deal with the next supermoon on his own. But Elliot had been adamant that he could handle it, and Declan understood why, even if he didn't like it.

If their positions were reversed, he'd have already thrown himself into the deep if that were the only way to keep from harming Elliot. He'd stayed away from Elliot for five years, to keep Elliot safe, to let him have a normal life. But he returned, and they'd learned what Elliot was and what he needed from Declan, and now, Declan was all in. He'd no intention of abandoning Elliot now.

His heart, not to mention his oblivious cock, was willing to be with Elliot until his very last breath, but his head was a bit more practical. It was impossible to deny that the consequences his stepmother had warned him about were something he'd have to deal with. He could only hope that Nance would have some answers. If she didn't, he'd sail to the devilfish den, his promise to Elliot be damned.

He stuck his hand in his greatcoat pocket and drew out the copper compass Nance had given them last year. He'd snuck it from Elliot's bureau drawer the night before he left, ignoring the stab of guilt he felt in not telling him he was borrowing it. He flipped the lid open, and compared it to the ship's compass on the binnacle. The ship's compass was reliable as ever, needle pointing north, indicating their course in a generally north-northwest direction.

The copper compass's needle, in contrast, was swinging around, as if searching for its true meridian. It paused frequently pointing west, in the direction of the devilfish den, but Declan had seen it pointing at Elliot regardless of Elliot's position in relation to the cardinal directions. If he had to, he'd use the copper compass to find the devilfish den and get his answers from Marie.

His thoughts were interrupted by Joey mounting the steps to the quarterdeck, clutching a lidded pewter mug in one hand. Declan dropped the compass back into his greatcoat pocket. If Nance had the information he needed, there'd be no need to use the compass and no need to worry the crew about a destination they might not need to sail to.

Joey passed the pewter mug to Declan with a shy smile. "Thanks, Jo-Jo," he said. Joey ducked his head and gave him a sidelong look.

"You know I hate that. It's Joey." He added, "Captain." Declan took a hasty sip to hide his smile. The coffee warmed his throat and down into his chest, and he savored another sip, then set the mug down on the shelf next to the binnacle in front of the wheel.

Joey stayed for a bit, standing next to Declan at the wheel, facing forward, eyes scanning the horizon, glancing occasionally at the compass on the binnacle, monitoring the sails, and periodically checking on the deck crew.

He was a natural sailor and had earned the respect of the crew, despite his youth. Declan had no trouble imagining him as master of his own ship someday. Hell, he'd sell the *Black Dove* to the lad if he ever got to the point of retiring.

That day was far off, though. For now, Declan was where he was happiest, minus the hole that being away from Elliot left in him. Goddamn, he really hoped Nance would have some ideas. He let go of the wheel for a moment to touch the copper compass again.

"Looking forward to seeing your mam?" Declan asked Joey, mostly for a distraction from his thoughts.

Joey made a face, but it turned sheepish when Declan glanced at him. "Suppose so," he said, his shoulders shrugging. They looked scrawny under a peacoat two sizes too big for him, but Declan knew the strength they carried, not just for hauling lines and shifting cargo, but for carrying the strain of his everyday life.

Despite the hardships the lad had been through, he had a sunny disposition that was infectious.

"Things were better during our last visit, weren't they?" Declan asked. He'd seen the effort Nance made to repair her relationship with her only child, and while he could understand Joey's suspicion, the lad could try meeting her halfway.

"Suppose so," Joey said again. He fidgeted with something in his pocket, then brushed a few wayward strands of hair out of his eyes. He had his mother's bone structure, but must have gotten those blue eyes and blond hair from his father. He'd been a Hudson Bay Company trader, already married with a handful of other children back East. Gone back to his wife before Declan met him, but he and Father had been thick as thieves, and Father had told Declan a few stories about their misadventures. Declan wondered idly what he would have made of the man Joey turned out to be.

"Just kind of waiting for the other shoe to drop, I guess."

"Give her some credit," Declan said mildly. "You never thought she'd come 'round this far, did you? She calls you by the right name now, don't she?"

"Not like some people," Joey retorted, and Declan chuckled.

"Everyone needs a nickname," he said, "and you don't get to pick it yourself."

Joey snorted. After a moment, he conceded, "She's trying. I see that. Mostly 'cause of you. I never thanked you for that, Captain." Something in Declan's chest clenched at the grateful look on Joey's face.

"No need," he said, taking another sip of coffee to melt the lump in his throat. "You know she loves you. She just wants to keep her baby safe."

Joey made a face. "Not a baby," he groused, the way only a young man would.

Declan stifled a smile. "She'd have come around eventually with or without me."

Joey shrugged. "Maybe. She didn't have no trouble accepting Mr. Elliot. But that was more about Aunt Charlotte, I think."

Declan glanced at Joey, still gazing forward. His head cocked to the side, and Declan followed his gaze to Reginald, who was pointing at the foremast topsail. Joey glanced back at Declan, a question in his eyes, and Declan nodded. Joey called out an order to adjust the yard. Reg repeated the order, and Luca hauled on the line to comply. The ship carried forward, wind blowing Joey's hair back from his face.

"Aunt Charlotte?" he asked. Far as he knew, Nance didn't have any family left. Her parents were long dead back East, and she'd never mentioned any siblings.

"She died before I was born," Joey said. "But I used to hear sailors gossiping in the bunk house before I left. There was something strange about her, they said. I never heard just what, but lately I been thinking she was maybe like Mr. Elliot."

"Why would you think that?" Declan hardly wanted to discuss Elliot's devilfish form with Joey. But if Nance knew a woman who could shift like him and hadn't told him before, then he'd take whatever information he could get before confronting her about it.

Joey blushed a bright pink. "Well, you know how sailors talk. Wasn't kind, anyway. Or the kind of shit Mam would have wanted anyone to be saying about her sister."

Declan snorted. He knew how sailors talked indeed. And how people in general often weren't kind about anyone different from what they considered normal.

"Mr. Elliot all right?" Joey asked. "No way we'll be back for the next supermoon. How's he gonna get through it without you?"

Declan choked on the sip of hot coffee he'd just taken. Joey helpfully pounded on his back until he waved him away.

"For fuck's sake, Joey, that's none of your goddamn business." His crew knowing that Elliot shifted was bad enough. He didn't care that they knew he was fucking Elliot, since half of them were that way, too, but he didn't think anyone knew precisely how Elliot shifted back during the supermoon.

"Sorry, Captain," Joey said, not sounding nearly as sorry as he should be. "I just," he glanced quickly at Declan, then away, his cheeks tinged pink again. "Just, you're always taking care of everyone. Like me, or Mr. Elliot, with whatever we got wrong with us, or when we're hurting some way. And I heard you were sick for a few days after the last supermoon. I just think someone oughta take care of you sometimes, when you hurt." He ducked his head and picked at something on the tail of his coat.

Declan put a hand on the back of Joey's neck and squeezed gently. "That's kind of you, lad, but I'm fine. Mr. Elliot and I will figure it out. Nothing for you to worry about."

Joey nodded. "You gonna talk to Mam about it?"

Declan sighed. Joey was like a puppy pushing its head into a hand for petting, heedless of whatever else a man might be doing at the time. "Guess so," he said, with a note of finality that he hoped would end this awkward conversation. Joey didn't take the hint, though.

"Or are we going back to that island with the devilfish women? Reginald and me caught a few glimpses of them swimming around the ship while Mr. Elliot and your father was inside that cave. They didn't bother us none, but some of them were real pretty." He sounded a little regretful, like he'd have liked to see more of them. Declan shuddered at the thought of Joey going through what he'd been through after being with one of those women.

"Not if I can get some answers from your mam," Declan replied, but then he cleared his throat and went for the direct approach. "I'm done talking about this with you, though. I appreciate that you care about me, but it's my business, aye?"

"Aye, Captain," Joey said cheerfully. He glanced over Declan's shoulder and his eyes widened. "Fog rolling in from the southeast, Captain. Think we can outrun it?"

Declan followed his gaze. Dense white clouds were clinging to the southeastern horizon, obscuring the sliver of Vancouver Island that had been visible and billowing toward them. He turned forward again and eyed the wind filling the sheets. The wind was picking up, too, and he'd rather turn into Nance's protected inlet before the fog caught up with them. "Better try," he said, and gave the order to increase speed.

CHAPTER 14

*E*lliot paused outside the door to the Green Light and glanced down Madison toward Water Street. The street was empty, construction nearly finished on the fire department and city hall at the end of the block, and the site quiet and dark. There had been some protest from uptown residents about locating the city hall next to the Green Light. The sign overhead read "saloon," but everyone knew that it primarily functioned as a brothel. The saloon part was just the first way of parting sailors from their hard-earned cash.

Elliot could have chosen one of the dozens of other establishments downtown, but he knew Declan was friendly with Mrs. Viola Garnett, the Green Light's proprietress. Of course, he risked word getting back to Declan about exactly what he was doing here, but he was going to have to tell Declan eventually anyway. And he doubted that Declan would be exchanging telegraphs with a notorious madam while at sea, even if they were friends. It was for Declan's sake he was doing this in the first place.

He steeled his resolve with a deep breath, the cool evening

breeze tinged with salt from the nearby waterfront, and pushed the door open. Inside, the saloon was stuffy and warm, and the close fug of tobacco smoke, whiskey, and male sweat almost knocked him back.

The main room was full enough that hardly anyone noticed him at first. The stools along the bar were all occupied, and most of the tables dotting the room were filled with groups of men playing cards, drinking, and smoking a noxious variety of cheap cigarettes, hand-rolled cigars, and pipes. A blue cloud of smoke filled the room. Elliot almost changed his mind.

He was a little surprised to see nearly as many women in the saloon as men. A few were clearly barmaids, scurrying back and forth between tables and the bar at the back of the room with tankards of ale and shots of whiskey, avoiding the customers pinching at their bottoms with giggles and squeals, tucking banknotes and coins into apron pockets tied over their low-cut dresses.

But most of the women were coiffed and dressed as if they were presiding over a dinner party uptown. Their necklines were maybe a bit lower than he was used to seeing, and most weren't wearing evening gloves, but otherwise, Elliot wouldn't have guessed they were prostitutes. Mrs. Viola clearly ran a higher-class establishment than he realized.

The men weren't all sailors and longshoremen, either. Elliot recognized a handful of them from the Key City Club. Another table of card players were business associates. Elliot found a seat at a small table in the corner, avoiding the eye of anyone he knew, while surveying the room, wondering how he would be able to pick Mrs. Viola out of the crowd.

Then the swinging door at the other end of the long bar opened, and a woman bustled through, paused, and seemed to zero in on him.

He caught her eye, and she gazed at him for a moment, head

cocked to the side. Then someone behind the bar flagged her attention and she moved in and out of view behind the crowd. She seemed to be gradually making her way to Elliot's corner, so he held onto his patience, despite the voice in his head telling him this was a terrible idea.

When she finally reached his table, she had a glass of amber liquid in her hand and set it down in front of him. He half rose from his seat, but she waved him down and pulled out the chair opposite him herself before he could reach it, perching on the edge of the seat to accommodate her skirt's bustle.

She was short and curvy, and Elliot could see that she'd be popular among most of the men he knew. She was pretty, with pink cheeks and bright eyes crinkling just a little at the corners. She'd be in her late thirties, Elliot guessed, though she hardly looked older than him. Her hair was dressed elaborately in what he remembered one of his associates' wives explaining was the latest fashion. She folded her small hands together and rested her plump elbows on the table's surface.

"What can I do for you this evening, Mr. Bishop?"

He was a little surprised she recognized him, but he was fairly well known in town. Or Declan may have talked to her about him. Christ, he hoped not in too much detail. Although the more she knew about him, the less he would have to explain what he was here for. He felt his cheeks flush with embarrassment already.

"I'm seeking—" Elliot started, then trailed off. He cleared his throat and tried again. "I would like to inquire about—" Christ, this was awkward. How on Earth did Declan do it? He knew Declan had visited the Green Light dozens of times, not always for sex, but often enough. Did he just come right out and ask how much for a particular girl? Elliot wasn't even sure he could pick one, much less how to know whether any of Mrs. Viola's girls were willing to accommodate his particular needs. How was he going to explain himself?

Mrs. Viola waited, no sign of impatience on her face but no help there, either. "You gotta ask for what you want, Mr. Bishop," she said, when his silence became unbearable, despite Elliot's opening and closing his mouth. "Ain't nothing that can't be had for the right price, but you gotta say the words."

Elliot nodded. He took a deep breath, then said, all in a rush, just to get it out, "I have certain needs and am looking for some female companionship to accommodate them." He winced at how formal and awkward he sounded.

Mrs. Viola's lips twitched, like she was about to smile, but her eyes were kind. "First time's always the hardest, hon," she said. "It gets easier." She gave him a saucy wink, and Elliot answered with a smile he didn't really feel. He highly doubted it would get easier for him. And he still had to explain exactly what his needs were.

Mrs. Viola rubbed her hands briskly together. "Now, what's your pleasure tonight? You like your girls skinny or plump? Hair color or eye color preference?" She twisted a little and looked over her shoulder at the rest of the room. "Mariela, over there, now." She gestured at a tall, willowy woman with milk-white skin and dark eyes. "She's one of my best girls. Tall enough to be a good match for you," she said, eying Elliot's legs stretched out in the space between the table and the wall, since there wasn't quite enough room under the small table for their length.

Mariela turned her head to speak to another girl, and something about her profile reminded him of Celeste. He shook his head. Not her. This was going to be hard enough as it was.

Mrs. Viola seemed to understand. "Bettina, then, maybe?" She indicated the girl next to Mariela. Bettina was blonde and even plumper than Mrs. Viola, though not as short. "She's good with first-timers," Mrs. Viola continued. "Accommodating, too," she said with a wink. "That what you said you wanted, right?"

Elliot tried to imagine Bettina undressed and underneath him, his tentacles wrapped around her round limbs, squeezing that firm flesh and leaving marks on her skin. He shuddered a little, but not from arousal. He closed his eyes and rubbed his thumb across his forehead, trying to clear the mental image of Bettina lying as slack and helpless as Declan under him.

No. He couldn't do this. Not even to a whore.

Before he could tell Mrs. Viola he'd changed his mind, a loud tinkling crash cut through the chatter in the saloon, followed by a roar of masculine amusement. Elliot glanced up, and Mrs. Viola swiveled her head around. A barmaid had dropped a tray of glasses and was shouting good-naturedly back at the catcalls and whistles from nearby men watching her bend over to pick up the pieces.

Mrs. Viola huffed a frustrated noise. "Such a butterfingers, that one," she muttered. "Might have to start docking her pay if she can't learn to carry a tray properly." The affection in her voice belied her caustic words, though. She patted Elliot's hand, then pushed herself to her feet.

"You think on what you want, Mr. Bishop, while I clean up another of that girl's messes." She jabbed a finger at his untouched glass. "Drink up. Might take the edge off and help loosen your tongue. I'm sure we'll find the right gal for you."

She turned away with a rustle of skirts and pushed through the crowd toward the barmaid, calling for a rag and a bucket, and genially shoving patrons out of her way.

Elliot eyed the glass she'd left him. Whiskey, by the smell of it, and probably some of her best. He took a small sip and let the liquid coat his tongue before swallowing. It was the same whiskey Declan brought in from Canada and kept for his own enjoyment, only slightly watered down.

He took a larger sip, then another one. Maybe it would help, like she said. He closed his eyes to savor the feel of the whiskey warming him from the inside out, wishing he were tasting it on Declan's tongue instead of his own.

A chair scraped roughly across the floor, followed by a heavy thump, and Elliot opened his eyes.

"The fuck are you doing here, pendejo?" Thomas Cuevas demanded.

CHAPTER 15

*E*lliot blinked at the man glowering across the table. The *Black Dove*'s cook was the last person he'd expected to see tonight, here or anywhere else. "What are you doing here?" he asked. A sudden stab of hope, followed by a brief burst of shame, speared through him. He looked around the saloon, hoping and yet not hoping to see Declan chatting with the rest of his crew in another darkened corner. They couldn't be home so soon. Unless they'd turned back for some reason.

Thomas could tell what Elliot was doing. He shook his head impatiently. "He ain't here. I stayed behind for this one. I'll catch 'em up on the return."

Elliot stared at him. "You stayed behind? Why?" Declan never would have dismissed Thomas. He ran a tight ship, but every man who worked for him counted himself lucky to do so. He kept as minimal a crew as possible, partly for economy, but also because he tended to adopt folks he worked closely with, the way Henrietta Maynard adopted stray animals. Once a sailor joined the *Black Dove*'s crew, he became part of Declan's family. And Declan always put family first.

Thomas shifted awkwardly in the chair. "Busted my damn

leg," he admitted. "My fault. I was loading the food stores and hadn't secured the flour sacks the way I oughta have. Ship rolled unexpected-like and I didn't get outta the way of the sliding sacks quick enough. I told Captain Fitz gimme a splint and a crutch and I'll be fine, but he ordered me to stay off it 'til it's fixed."

Thomas spat a wad of tobacco on the floor next to his splinted leg and made a face indicating his opinion of Declan's orders. He'd followed them, though. Elliot resisted pointing that out.

"Anyways, don't matter what I'm doing here. The question is, why the devil are you here?" Thomas continued. "I saw you talking with Mrs. Viola. The only business she conducts at this hour is for her girls."

"What of it?" Elliot said sharply. "It's none of your concern what business I engage in, or with whom."

Thomas narrowed his eyes and glared at Elliot until Elliot looked away. "You do this to Captain Fitz, and you ain't half the man I thought you was. He would never do it to you, and you know it."

Elliot snorted. "Please. Declan's probably on a first-name basis with at least half the girls here, not to mention Mrs. Viola herself." He returned Thomas's glare. "And not just girls, either."

The old jealousy that had tortured him during the five years Declan had stayed away from Elliot before his return reared up again.

"Sure," Thomas said, a hard glint in his eyes. "We used to share a girl in every port, you know that? Paid her extra to take us one after the other. Me, I always liked to go last, so I could feel how sloppy and wet she was from him. Later, he'd fuck me into that soft mattress in his cabin. You must know the one, because I bet you let him do the same."

He'd lowered his voice to an angry growl, since what he was talking about carried a sentence of ten years of hard labor, even if rarely prosecuted.

He cocked his head at Elliot, who was shocked into speech-lessness at Thomas's bald admissions. "But maybe it's the other way 'round with you. He never let me do that to him, you know, but he'd do anything for your precious arse. Bet when you begged real pretty, with those puppy-dog eyes of yours, Fitz'd roll right over and let you stick your—"

"Shut your goddamn mouth, you filthy dog!" Elliot shoved back from the table and loomed over Thomas, who just leaned back in his chair, crossed his arms over his chest, and glared up at Elliot.

A sudden silence descended over the Green Light, and most of the heads turned their direction. Elliot stood for another moment, breathing hard through his nose, fighting the urge to punch Thomas in his sun-browned face, then slowly sat down again. When neither he nor Thomas made any further outbursts or movement, the rest of the patrons returned to their own business.

Elliot thought he'd gotten over knowing about Declan's history with Thomas. Knowing that Declan had fucked Thomas, and seeing their easy physical camaraderie when he sailed with them last year, was one thing. Hearing the sordid details was another, especially coming from Thomas.

Thomas had had Declan for five years, years when Elliot had buried how much he'd missed Declan by trying to build a normal life. Expanding the mercantile, courting Celeste. Immersing himself in the downtown business and uptown social circles, filling all the hours he could with things to do or people to distract him.

Not unlike what he'd been doing since Declan left on his current voyage and he'd decided to give Declan up for good, Elliot realized.

"Declan is free to be with whomever he wants," Elliot said. His throat closed up, and he could barely force the words out. He'd never demanded Declan give up Thomas, or anyone else. He cleared his throat and tried again. "I have no claim on him."

As stepbrothers, they at least had an acceptable explanation for their closeness and Declan continuing to live in Elliot's house when in port. But it wasn't like they could marry or be together openly.

Thomas stared at him like he'd just shifted to his other form right in front of him. "No claim on him? For fuck's sake, Bishop, I thought you was smarter than this." He jabbed a blunt finger at Elliot, an assortment of pale hash mark scars from cooking accidents standing out on his hands in the saloon's dim light. "It's been you for him since before I ever met him. It always will be. If you weren't so goddamned selfish, you'd know that already."

Elliot choked out a harsh laugh. Christ, how much he wanted to be selfish enough to keep Declan. "You don't understand," he said, swallowing another laugh before it turned into hysteria. "I'm doing this for Declan. It's better this way, in the long run. He'll understand."

Thomas opened his mouth, probably to continue berating Elliot, but Elliot kept talking, seized by a sudden inspiration. "You can have him again. You spend more time with him than I do anyway. I know how you feel about him. I won't stand in your way anymore."

Thomas's face darkened and his fists clenched on the table. For a moment, Elliot thought Thomas would lunge at him. He was a good head shorter than Elliot, and his irascible grouchiness had never tended toward violence when Elliot had sailed with the *Black Dove* last year, but he was sturdy and muscled. Elliot knew he'd no chance of winning in a brawl with him.

He kept his seat, though, probably because of his leg, and breathed heavily, his nostrils flaring. "He ain't a prize horse to trade, cabrón," Thomas hissed. "Madre de Dios, you think he's gonna just give you up? After everything that happened last year?"

Elliot froze. The *Black Dove*'s crew knew about the octopians' den, since they'd sailed there with him to rescue Declan, and Joey and Reginald had caught sight of his tentacles, but he didn't think anyone knew exactly what Elliot had to do to shift back.

"Is that what passes for pillow talk with you and Declan?" Elliot bit out. He was treading on Thomas's last strands of patience, he could tell, but maybe a black eye or a split lip would hurt more than the aching hole in his heart.

"How many times I gotta say this?" Thomas spit back. "We ain't been together since you came aboard last year. I don't go where I ain't wanted, and he don't want no one but you. If you don't want him no more, have the balls to tell him so, but don't lay whatever bee you got in your bonnet at my door. I ain't to blame for your stupidity."

All the fight left Elliot, and he was suddenly exhausted. "Of course I still want him," he muttered. He'd wanted Declan as long as he could remember, and that sense of triumphant wonder he felt every time he got to be with him never got old. Knowing that Declan was faithful to him only increased that. But then the image of Declan's still, pliant body under him flashed before him, and the erection it sparked made his guilt and shame even worse.

"Giving him up makes me wish I were dead," he said, not looking at Thomas. "But being with me is killing him, so it's what I have to do." He didn't expect Thomas to understand, and he sure as hell wasn't going to explain it, but when he risked a glance at Thomas, he was nodding as if Elliot had confirmed something he already knew.

"Figure out how to change back without fucking him, then," Thomas said. As if it were that simple.

"You don't know anything about it," Elliot retorted.

"Your mama could do it, couldn't she?" He raised his hands in surrender before Elliot could say anything. "Captain Fitz didn't tell me nothing about you two. Just a little bit about your mama and the other devilfish women in that cursed grotto." He shrugged and shoved his hands in the pockets of his coat. "Plus, I got eyes, don't I? And I know the moon phases as well as the rest of the crew."

Elliot eyed Thomas, sitting there discussing Elliot's shifting nature like it was an everyday thing. It was, oddly, a relief to be able to talk openly about it. Well, as openly as they could in a public place.

"I don't know how," he admitted.

Thomas shifted his position on the chair, and his lips tightened when his leg bumped the table's leg. Elliot's whiskey glass was still half full. He pushed it across the table toward Thomas.

"You got time, don't you?" Thomas said, after knocking back the whiskey, not bothering to thank Elliot. "Full moon ain't for another couple weeks, right?"

Elliot remembered how easily his mother had shifted back and forth, and how Celeste had told him she could teach him, too. If he'd inherited his octopian nature from his mother, perhaps he'd also inherited her ability to shift at will. He tried to tamp down the surge of hope he suddenly felt as premature, but for Declan's sake, he'd try anything.

He shoved his chair back from the table, and Thomas startled, banging his leg into the table again with a muffled curse. "Where are you staying?" he asked, gesturing for Thomas to get up.

"Boarding house down on Water Street," Thomas said. He rolled his eyes at Elliot's look of sudden concern. "Not the one run by that crimp, Edgar Sims. The nicer one, run by Mrs. Maynard. Captain Fitz paid me up for the month."

Elliot handed Thomas his crutch and left him to tuck it under his arm and get to his feet. "Well, you're staying with me now. You can fetch your belongings tonight or have them sent uptown tomorrow." He held a hand up, forestalling Thomas's protests. "I have the room. I would have offered if Declan had told me about your injury before he left."

"Doubt that," Thomas muttered, but low enough that Elliot

could pretend not to hear. He limped toward the door without further protest, though, and Elliot went to settle up with Mrs. Viola. He gave her a generous tip as a silent apology for wasting her time earlier and braced himself for a suggestive invitation to come back another night. She just smiled at him and said, "You have a good evening, Mr. Bishop."

"You too, ma'am," Elliot replied automatically. He nodded at Mariela and Bettina, still lounging near the bar, awaiting the night's customers. Some of the tension left him as he followed Thomas's stocky figure and left the saloon. At least he hadn't made this mistake.

CHAPTER 16

The *Black Dove* couldn't outrun the fog. Declan ordered full sails, and they picked up speed with the rising wind, but it wasn't enough. The fog poured over them, dropping the temperature enough to make Joey shiver despite his peacoat, and before they'd sailed more than a half dozen leagues, the fog blanketed the ship. Declan could see the wheel and binnacle in front of him, but everything beyond the quarterdeck was a shifting, dark blur.

"Should we slow down, Captain?" Joey's voice came from the steps to the quarterdeck, ready to relay his orders to the deck crew.

"Aye," Declan replied. They hadn't passed a ship in the last hour or so, but this was a well-trafficked route, and more than a few sailing ships had collided with steamships blithely carrying forward despite fog. "Hug the coast as close as we can. And I want depth soundings every mile."

"Aye, aye, Captain," Joey said and relayed the orders to Reginald, who shouted them to the deck crew, the deep bell of his voice echoing in the fog.

The fog muffled the sound of the water against the hull and

the flap of canvas as the crew furled the t'gallant and topsails.
Their speed slowed, and the low groan of the ship's wooden
timbers creaked like gunshots. Declan kept a hand on the wheel
and an eye on the ship's compass, steering her blindly. He'd sailed
in fog plenty of times, a common phenomenon in the Pacific
Northwest, and his crew was just as experienced.

Luca's voice called out depth soundings every mile, and
Declan kept them hugging the coastline as close as possible. The
shore was a faint dark shadow behind the fog, though, and
Declan couldn't make out any distinguishing features. They were
about twenty leagues from the entrance to Nance's inlet, and it
was narrow enough that they could miss it if he couldn't see
where to turn in to it. He'd have to rely on his memory of the
depth contour lines on the chart.

He couldn't even discern the bow of the ship, and Luca's body
in the starboard chains, casting the sounding lead, was only a
dark blur. And then Luca gave a strangled shout and clambered
around the shroud and back onto the deck.

"What the hell?" Declan muttered, but Reginald and Joey were
already heading forward. They huddled around Luca, then leaned
over the side. Reg pointed a finger at something, exchanging
words with Luca and Joey that Declan couldn't hear. Then the
smallest figure pushed back from the rail, and Joey hustled to the
quarterdeck.

"What's going on?" Declan demanded as soon as he was in
earshot.

"You need to see for yourself, Captain." Joey's face wasn't
scared, exactly, more bemused. Like he'd seen something he
didn't quite know how to handle. He took over at the wheel, and
Declan hustled forward to where Luca was now back in the starboard chains, staring down at the water.

"The hell's going on?" he started to ask, but Luca merely
pointed, and Declan leaned over the ship's rail, following his
finger. The sounding line dangled down past the ship's hull, the

lead still submerged. A giant octopus was wrapped about the line, half in and half out of the water, tendrils of fog curling around it. Its huge bulbous head was upside down, but its eyes were staring straight up at Declan and Luca, the rectangular pupils narrow black slits in the large amber eyes.

"What is it doing?" Declan asked.

Luca shrugged. "Hell if I know," he said. "But it ain't the only one." He jabbed his finger at three other spots in the water, close to the ship. Declan glimpsed dark shadows under the water's surface and an occasional flip of a tentacle tip unfurling, like it was tasting the air or waving at something.

"Let the damned thing go," he ordered Luca, who glared at him.

"You think I haven't tried that?" He paid out the sounding line so the portion with the devilfish wrapped around it sunk under the waves. He waited a moment, called off, "By the mark half five," then hauled the line back up. Four and a half fathoms deep.

The devilfish was still wrapped around the line. Another tentacle was slithering up the line, just past the faded calico strip marking the third fathom depth. The beast was climbing the line, though Declan couldn't imagine why.

The fog pressed down on them. A gust of wind pushed Declan against the rail, a blast of cold rain and sea spray soaking him and Luca. The devilfish seemed unperturbed, creeping another few inches up the line.

Under the usual ship's noises and roar of the wind, a faint hum reached Declan's ears. "Do you hear that?" he murmured to Luca, straining forward a little to figure out where it was coming from.

"Hear what?" Luca asked. His arms were straining at the weight of the devilfish clinging to the line, and it slipped a little through his hands. "What the fuck am I supposed to do with this?"

"Let it go," Declan decided. "Let the line trail along the ship for a while. Surely it'll give up and swim away eventually." He turned back to Reginald and ordered, "Turn ten degrees port." Reginald shouted the same in the direction of the stern, and Joey's voice repeating the order called back.

Luca paid the sounding line out again, and the devilfish disappeared under the surface. Not far, though; it kept climbing the line as Luca paid it out, its head floating just at the waterline, eyes still turned up at them.

A deep, tuneless hum filled Declan's head, louder now but still faint enough that it was barely audible over beat of the waves against the ship as she moved through the water. Declan didn't ask Luca again if he heard it. His face was set, concentrating on the sounding line between his hands, no sign of hearing anything unusual on his face.

"Give me the line," he said. Luca swiveled his upper body toward Declan and stared at him. Declan gestured impatiently. "Come on, swap places." He climbed over the rail and squeezed next to Luca on the small platform to which the shroud was attached. Luca looked at him like he'd lost his mind, but obeyed, handing the coiled remainder of the sounding line to him. Declan braced himself against the shroud so Luca could climb back on deck.

Declan hefted the coil over his shoulder and grabbed on to the shroud to keep from pitching into the drink. The water slipped below him as the ship sailed forward, and Declan felt a brief dizzying temptation to just let go and tumble into the deep.

Luca hovered behind him on deck, almost like he could read Declan's mind and was ready to grab him back on deck at any moment. Declan could understand his confusion. It had been some time since he'd been in the chains. Probably not since he was the leadsman on his father's ship when he was a boy. He'd forgotten how the spray soaked a man almost immediately. Combined with the cold damp from the fog, Declan shivered under his wool greatcoat and wondered what the hell he was doing here.

But another devilfish head breached the water's surface, and that humming sound increased. It had to be in his head rather than in the air, since Luca still didn't give any sign he could hear it. If Declan could just listen hard enough, he thought he could suss out what it was trying to communicate.

He leaned out over the water to get a better look at the devilfish swimming along the ship. The humming increased until he could hardly hear anything else—not the creak of the rigging lines, the rhythmic slap of the water against the hull, the flap of the sails overhead, or the shouts as Joey ordered adjustment to the main sail and Reginald called back in confirmation.

The devilfish wrapped around the sounding line kept climbing up it. Declan quit paying out any more length and just stood on the platform, braced against the weight of the huge beast, and let it do what it seemed damned and determined to do. The coil rested heavily on his shoulder, and the hemp line was rough in his hands.

The tip of the first tentacle to reach him was soft, though, delicately questing over his fingers and the backs of his hands. Tiny suckers flexed against his skin. It was a little like being felt up by Elliot's tentacles, though without the sexual arousal between him and Elliot. This was curiosity, he thought, or maybe verification, though he couldn't explain how he'd reached that conclusion.

Then, as slowly as it had crept up the line, the devilfish withdrew. It gave a last squeeze against the back of Declan's hand, unwound one tentacle from the sounding line, rewound it lower down, and gradually crept down the line until its body reached the water. The last tentacle uncurled from around the line, and the beast disappeared below the surface.

The other three devilfish were still swimming close to the ship. Declan could sense them just under the surface. They lined up, one after the other, the one who'd touched him taking its place at the back of the line, and Declan realized they'd made a barrier between the ship and the shore. The *Black Dove* was on a heading that would run over them if they kept to their current trajectory.

"Starboard helm fifteen," Declan shouted, and he faintly heard Reginald relay the command to Joey at the wheel over the low hum still echoing in his head. The dark, shadowed line of octopuses curved to match the ship's change in direction. The fog was still too thick to see the shoreline, and Declan's eyes strained to keep tracking the devilfish's position.

"Ease to five," he called, and the ship slowly straightened in line with the devilfish. He'd never commanded the ship from the chains, and hoped never to do so again, but if he resumed his position behind the wheel, he'd lose sight of the octopuses. He could order Luca back into position in the chains but explaining how he wanted to follow where the devilfish were leading would take too long and risk missing a signal from them.

He wasn't even sure it was necessary to follow them until a dark shape loomed ahead. As the *Black Dove* passed it, Declan realized it was another ship, wrecked on the shoals and listing on her port side. Her main mast jutted out, level with the *Black Dove*'s main sail. They'd never have seen her in this fog until it was too late.

"Shall we stop and search for survivors, Captain?" Reginald shouted.

"No," Declan called back. "There are none."

When the crew asked later, he'd tell them the tattered remnants of the sails and the barnacles encrusting the hull were what told him the shipwreck was too old to have any survivors. But that wasn't how he knew.

He knew because he saw them, not with his eyes, but in his mind, through the eyes of the devilfish swimming between the *Black Dove* and the wrecked ship. He saw the bloated bodies tangled up in the rigging underwater, more drifting amid tall kelp strands. On the land side of the ship, skeletal arms that had clung to splintered boards waved uselessly under the relentless waves that had kept them from shore until their grip slackened with exhaustion and they drowned alongside their fellows.

The *Black Dove* slipped slowly past the wreck—the *Helena Gray*, he saw now. She'd disappeared with all hands a year or so after he started sailing with Father. He wondered if her master had escaped her fate. Surely some of the crew had made it to shore, not more than ten yards away.

When they cleared the wreck, the devilfish disappeared from his view, and the low hum in his head quieted. Another league steady on course, and the fog thinned. The wind slackened and, though the clouds still loomed low and threatened more rain, at least the coastline was visible again.

Declan searched for the devilfish, squinting at the rolling waves, looking for the dark shadow of a bulbous head or the tips of tentacles peeking above the waterline. There was no sign of them now, and no glimpses of their underwater surroundings came to Declan from their perspective. If they were still nearby, they'd cut their connection to him, and he briefly felt bereft when he saw nothing around them.

He cast the sounding lead one last time, and when he hauled it back, nothing clung to the line but a few strands of kelp. He clambered back on deck, and handed Luca the sounding line and lead to be stowed away. By the time he resumed his place behind the wheel, Joey was steering them into the entrance to Nance's inlet.

CHAPTER 17

*A*s much as Elliot hated to admit it, even to himself, Thomas was right. He had to learn how to shift back without fucking Declan. Which meant he had start by shifting into his devilfish form on his own. He picked a Thursday evening, told Thomas he was attending a meeting of the railroad trustees, and arrived at the spa cavern near Point Wilson as the last glimmers of twilight were fading.

The evening was mild, but he still shivered in the cavern's cool, damp air as he lit the boiler and stripped his clothes off. Thank God the tidal pool's water was warmer than the ocean, and it didn't take long for the boiler to heat it to a comfortable temperature. He slipped into the water and submerged, then surfaced and slicked his wet hair behind his ears. The sky outside the cavern was deepening to indigo and a few stars winked into view.

The half-moon was at its highest, above the cavern's arch, out of his sight, but he could feel its slight tug against his skin. Nothing like what it would feel like at full, but it was waxing, and Elliot figured tonight was as good a time as any to see if he could shift on his own.

He stretched out and let the water buoy him, then started at the top of his head and scanned down his body. If he knew how each body part felt like while still fully human, maybe he could discern the exact places where he shifted. And if he paid attention to those places, could he develop enough control to shift when he wanted, instead of when the moon forced him to?

He should have taken Celeste up on her offer to show him how to shift outside the supermoon last year. He could try to reach out to her, the way Mrs. Jackman had reached out to his mind before, but he wasn't sure he wanted Celeste to know what he was doing. Learning to shift independently seemed like embracing his devilfish nature. He wasn't prepared to admit to Celeste that he was willing to do that. Nor did he want his efforts getting back to his mother, either.

He closed his eyes and relaxed into the gently rolling waves supporting him. His hair swirled in the water, tugging slightly against his scalp. Declan liked to tug on his hair, especially when Elliot sucked him, but Elliot resolutely turned his attention back to how his skin felt in the water. This was no time for fantasizing about Declan's cock. The whole point of this was to learn how to not need Declan's cock during the supermoon.

The water pressed against his ears, which was nothing compared to the pressure he experienced the few times he'd swum underwater in his devilfish form. His heart thudded in his throat. He slowed his breathing, inhaling for a long count of four, then exhaling even more slowly. His heart rate slowed in tandem, and the space between each inhale and exhale became longer and longer. The sides of his neck tingled, and he brushed the tips of his fingers over the spots. Three tiny slits had opened on each side of his neck, the water cool as it slipped past them.

His heart rate and breathing slowed even further, and Elliot inhaled once more before submerging his face. He held his breath in as long as he could, but when he breathed out and watched the tiny bubbles floating to the surface, his lungs didn't immediately burn with the need to breathe in again. His chest still expanded and contracted, but less so than when he breathed air, and he drifted underwater for several long minutes, waiting to see how long he could stay under before needing to surface for air again.

He sunk deeper under the water and opened his eyes. Tiny minnows zipped around him, and little flashes of panic bloomed in his mind, fading as quick as they came. Elliot realized that the panicky sensations were coming from the little fishes as they swarmed around his much bigger body. He tried picking out one from the school to see if he could catch more of its thoughts or feelings, but there were too many, and they swam too fast to track an individual. When he gave up trying to maintain focus on any particular fish, though, the chaotic senses of the school flickered in the back of his mind.

He stilled his limbs, and the panicked flitting around slowed as the minnows gradually got used to his presence. They were still skittish, darting away whenever he moved, but a few braved closer, nibbling along his leg in curious tickles.

He'd left his pocket watch at home, but figured he'd been underwater for perhaps ten minutes now. His lungs were straining a bit, and he let himself slowly float to the surface, still trying not to frighten the minnows. He took a deep breath of air and submerged again.

The warm water from the heated cavern swirled around pockets of colder ocean water piped in at the bottom of the pool. This time, he scanned his body from his toes up. He stretched each leg as long as it could go, pointing and spreading his toes, focusing on how the water slid against his skin. When the moon was full and close to the Earth, it tugged at his blood the way it did the tides, pressure building under his skin like an overworked steam engine. Shifting then was a relief, like giving over to sleep after a long, hard day.

Tonight, the half-moon's pull was weaker than it would be at full. The water swirled around him, caressing his skin. It felt like home, but his legs stayed human.

Maybe he needed a different approach. Every time he'd shifted before, the rush of shifting was sexually charged, inextricably connected with his desire for Declan. Even though this experiment was meant to find a way to stop using Declan for his needs, his feelings for his stepbrother were the only reliable way he'd been able to shift.

Elliot sighed and gave in to the thoughts that were always in his mind. Declan sprawled naked on the wide bed in his cabin on the *Black Dove*, waiting for Elliot. The freckles on his shoulders and the curve of his muscular back when Elliot took him from behind. The length and breadth of his cock filling Elliot's mouth.

Elliot's cock hardened, and he slipped a hand down to grasp it. The arousal seeping through his body wasn't as unrelenting as during the supermoon. Not the crashing waves battering the inside of his skin like a storm, more like the gentle lapping against the shore when the sea was calm.

His skin tingled from his scalp to his toes as he stroked his hand along his cock. He kept the strokes slow. This wasn't about getting off, so he concentrated on the ripples of sensation in his legs rather than his cock. Eventually, his hand stopped moving, just loosely holding his cock, while waves of sensation flowed through his legs, in time with his slowed pulse and buffered by the gentle rocking of the ocean waves beneath him.

Gradually, the pressure under his skin increased, the way it felt just before each time he shifted. He couldn't quite get there, to that place where his legs split and the shift was complete. He reached for it, stretching his legs as long as he could, muscles straining, spreading them wide enough to feel a pull in his groin. But it wasn't the right sensation, and then his cock pulsed, and the orgasm he'd been holding off rushed through him.

For a brief moment, as his back arched and he spent into the dark expanse of water, his skin expanded so much he felt bigger than the ocean itself. Tiny sparks rippled along his nerves and it almost happened, he was sure of it. But then the sparks died, and he came back to himself, still fully human, now desperately needing air.

He surfaced and gulped a few deep breaths. His legs were quivering, the aftershocks of his orgasm still rippling through him, and he used his arms to swim the few strokes across the pool to the shallow end. He lay on one of the carved stone loungers for a few more moments, soaking in the heated water, until his breathing returned to normal.

He was disappointed it hadn't worked, but Celeste had said it would take practice, so he supposed it was unrealistic to have expected to shift completely the very first time he tried it outside the supermoon. At least he'd come close. He'd try again, and again, and again, until he could shift back and forth on his own and he didn't need to hurt Declan anymore.

He pulled himself from the water and dried off, then dragged his clothes over his shivering body. He was suddenly exhausted, his mind drained and his legs still rubbery. His numb fingers fumbled with the buttons on his shirt and vest. He finally abandoned the effort halfway through and just wrapped his greatcoat around him, huddling into the thick wool's warmth.

The steps to the top of the bluff were interminable. Elliot hauled himself up and up, hand over hand on the railing, trying not to think about the long walk home. But when he reached the top of the steps, his own buggy was waiting, Mabel and Steele harnessed to it, their reins slack, Steele lipping casually at a patch of tall grass on the side of the carriage road. A dark shape was huddled in the driver's seat.

Elliot shuffled to the buggy's side and jostled the vehicle as he grabbed the edge of the seat. The figure in the driver's seat jerked upright, and Thomas blinked at him, then rubbed his eyes.

"What the devil are you doing here?" Elliot demanded, crossing his arms over his chest and tucking his hands under his armpits. His wet hair dripped down his neck, and he shivered, though he figured Thomas wouldn't be able to see that in the dark. When Thomas bent to gather the reins that had slipped off his lap, the side lantern cast enough light for Elliot to see his pale, pinched face.

"Waiting for you, what the fuck else?" Thomas grumbled. "Get in before you catch your death."

"You followed me?" Thomas should be in bed himself. His leg was barely healed, and he should be back at the house with it propped on a pillow, not napping on a hard carriage bench, waiting for Elliot.

"Fitz'd have my hide if I didn't look after you, seeing as you're incapable of looking after your damned self." He muttered further imprecations about Elliot's capabilities while Elliot climbed into the buggy and settled next to him, but also flicked the carriage robe over Elliot's lap before taking up the reins and clicking to the horses.

Elliot tucked the edges of the robe around him. "You didn't need to fetch me. I'm perfectly capable of walking home."

"Yeah, well, I was bored." He eyed Elliot sideways. "Thought of just drinking all your whiskey, but figured the sooner you got back, the sooner we can finish our game."

Elliot had started teaching Thomas chess during his convalescence, and Thomas was a surprisingly apt pupil. Elliot might even have to pay attention to win the game they'd started yesterday.

"Wouldn't mind a soak in your pool down there sometime, but figured you wanted to be alone tonight." He stared ahead at the road, and Elliot was grateful Thomas couldn't see his sudden blush.

"Did it work?" Thomas asked diffidently.

Elliot shook his head, then realized Thomas couldn't see that. He cleared his throat. "Almost, maybe. But no."

Thomas clicked his tongue at Steele, whose attention was

caught by a tuft of grass overhanging the road. "Well, maybe next time."

"I can take you tomorrow afternoon," Elliot offered, then sneezed three times in succession. "When it's warmer."

"Yeah," Thomas said, "That'd be good." They rode the rest of the way home in a comfortable silence.

CHAPTER 18

*D*eclan was pouring himself a cup of coffee from the large silver pot on the sideboard in Nance's dining room when a sudden clang of a bell broke the morning quiet. It was still early, the rising sun barely peeking over the forest that ringed the big compound on the inland side. One short clang, then a second. Declan tilted his head, waiting for the next sound.

Nance's warning system, lookouts who rang the bells when a ship entered the inlet. There was a generic warning for an unrecognized ship that posed no obvious danger, but there were also patterns for ships that stopped regularly here.

The third peal was longer, followed by three more long peals. Declan's chest tightened at the familiar pattern, the one used for his father's ship, the *Argonauta*. But it had been more than a year since Father had died. Nance must have reassigned the pattern. He supposed there was no reason for her to be sentimental about the *Argonauta*'s former signal.

He cursed whoever was coming in, though. So much for quiet and privacy to speak with Nance. The last few days had been a flurry of trading and negotiations with a captain from San Francisco and a representative from the Hudson Bay Company.

Declan knew Nance was pleased with the business, but it had taken most of her attention, and he hadn't yet found an opportunity to discuss what he'd come here to talk with her about.

The others had left yesterday afternoon, though, and the *Black Dove*'s crew—the only men quartered there for the moment—was taking advantage of the respite to lie abed later than usual. Or else they were occupied with activities Declan didn't need to know the details of. This morning had seemed like the best time to buttonhole Nance, if the old bird would ever make her appearance.

He took his coffee out on the wide porch that faced the inlet. A couple of fishing boats were out, and the *Black Dove* lay at anchor some distance from the long pier, but the water was calm, and the waves lapped gently at the beach. A great blue heron stalked along the shore, fishing for its morning meal, and a pair of gulls wheeled overhead. The forest surrounding the inlet echoed with the warbling and twitters from songbirds flitting among the leaves.

He fished the compass case from his jacket pocket and flipped the lid open. Nestled in velvet lining, the copper of the compass gleamed in the morning light. He took it from the case and held it flat on his palm, watching the needle swing around and point west. Which didn't tell him much—the vast Pacific was west of where he was standing, here at the eastern end of Nance's inlet. The devilfish women's island was out there somewhere, west of Vancouver Island, but he was still hoping to get some answers from Nance before setting off on that fool's errand.

He laid the compass on the porch railing, close enough to glance at it now and then. Having something connected with Elliot within reach was a comfort he hadn't realized he'd need on this voyage. He'd kept the key to Elliot's bedroom door in his kit while away from him those five years, but thought he'd gotten over such foolish sentimentalism. He kept it in his pocket when he was awake and on his bedside table while he slept, and he'd found himself touching it several times a day, as if reassuring himself that Elliot was still within his reach.

Twenty minutes later, a steamship puffed into view. Declan had left his scope in his room, but she seemed roughly twice as long as the *Black Dove*. She had two masts, brigantine-rigged, and a smokestack amidships for the engine. A white plume of smoke streamed behind her as she churned slowly up the inlet toward the long pier.

He was about to close the lid of the compass box when he caught sight of the needle quivering. He held it flat in his hand again and pointed it at the mouth of the inlet. He was standing a few points north of due west, but the compass needle wasn't pointing at due west anymore. It was quivering slightly and pointing northwest by west. Directly at the steamship that was sailing into Nance's inlet.

Declan tracked the steamship's slow progress toward the pier, glancing every now and then at the compass needle, which was still quivering slightly—whether because his hand couldn't keep it steady or because of the vessel's movements, he didn't know.

As the vessel approached the pier, the front door opened and Nance hustled down the wide lawn toward the pier. No one else had come running at the sound of the bells; none of Nance's longshoremen, who were usually up and breakfasting noisily by this hour. If this steamship was enough of a regular to have inherited the *Argonauta*'s bell pattern, yet met by no one but Nance, then she wasn't a cargo ship. Declan wondered what her business here was.

Nance hadn't noticed him on the porch. Declan tucked the compass away in the pocket of his coat and followed her down to the pier. The vessel slid smoothly up to the north side of the pier, and two crew members hopped to the dock to secure the ship's lines. Then a woman, tall and sturdy, stepped from the gangplank and lifted a hand to wave at Nance. Her dark hair was parted in the middle and plaited into a pair of thick, long braids, and recognition thumped Declan in the pit of his stomach.

He knew her. Or rather, had met her before, last year, when he'd been drugged, taken aboard the *Poulpes*, that eight-masted ghost ship that plied the port towns lining the Pacific Northwest straits, and dumped on the shores of the island he'd just been thinking about.

The name painted on the side of this ship was *Albatross*, but here Nance was, embracing the woman who'd skippered the *Poulpes* last year—the vessel Nance had told him last year she'd never seen—and kissing both her cheeks, like being reunited with a long lost family member.

Declan glanced at the rest of the crew swarming from the deck to the dock, duffels slung over their shoulders, heading in a straggling line toward the bunkhouse. All women, and not a word exchanged among them, even as a few jostled or smiled at each other like they were sharing private jokes he couldn't hear. He thought he recognized a couple from the crew of the *Poulpes*. Doubtless all of them hailed from the devilfish island.

And then another woman appeared at the top of the gangplank, and the lead in his stomach turned to adrenaline in his veins. He strode down the long pier toward the steamship. The lady captain slapped Nance on the back after a second hug, then gestured between Nance and the woman coming down the gangplank.

Celeste Brady, of all women in the world, arriving at Nance Carrigan's. And Nance shaking her hand like meeting octopian women was something she did every goddamned day.

Celeste caught sight of Declan approaching and called out. "Captain Fitzgerald!"

Nance swiveled around in surprise. Declan gave her a look that promised they'd be discussing this later.

"What a pleasure to see you again." She smiled at him, an open and delighted smile, looking genuinely glad to see him.

"Miss Brady." Declan gave her as polite a smile as he could muster. "I wouldn't have expected to see you here."

He cast a sideways glance at Nance, whose face had gone back to its usual impassive neutrality, and then looked directly at the third woman, whose name he'd never gotten. "Or you ever again, you don't mind my saying so."

She looked back at him and shrugged, looking supremely indifferent to his presence. "Captain," she said in a rusty voice, as if she didn't use it often. Then she nodded at Nance and Celeste and left without another word, trailing her crew in the direction of the bunkhouse.

Declan stared after her, then turned back to Nance and Celeste, glancing back and forth between them. "That's Enid," Celeste offered. "She's not much for small talk."

Neither was Declan, but where the devil to even start? Neither said anything to him, though Celeste's eyes were bright, and she was smiling as if she were greeting callers in her own parlor. Nance was having trouble meeting his eyes, and Declan wondered just how long she'd known Celeste and this particular crew were going to be arriving here.

The silence stretched into several minutes. Declan usually found silence to be a useful tool in getting information. Most people became uncomfortable with him just looking at them and rushed to fill him in on whatever he was waiting to know. It was how he got information from his crew and how he made space for Elliot to tell him things he'd otherwise keep to himself. Neither Celeste nor Nance spoke first, though.

Fine. He opened his mouth to say something, though he wasn't at all sure which of the many questions swirling around his head he wanted to ask first. Before he decided, Celeste asked, "How is Elliot?"

"He's fine," Declan said. "What are you doing here?"

Celeste cocked her head at him. "Is he?" She looked him up

and down, those amber eyes sparkling now with something other than courtesy. "And you? How are you faring?"

Declan didn't want to think about her psychic connection with Elliot or what she might know about them because of it. "I'm fine," he said sharply. "Not that that's any of your business."

"True," she said. "And neither is my business any of yours." She smiled sweetly, as if to take the sting out of her words. "I trust we can have some pleasant conversation while our stays overlap. For now, if you'll excuse me, I'd like to freshen up. It's been a rather long time since I've been on land."

"There's breakfast in the dining room, and the pink room's made up for you, Miss Brady," Nance said. "Betsy'll fetch you hot water."

Celeste thanked her and smiled brightly at Declan, then brushed past him, and headed for the big house at the end of the pier.

Nance glanced up at Declan with a resigned look. "You could eat, too, Fitz."

"I will," Declan said, crossing his arms over his chest and glaring down at her. "And then I want some answers."

CHAPTER 19

*M*rs. Terrell Jackman was the last person Elliot wanted to see this evening. She made a beeline for the empty seat next to him in the Key City Club's meeting room and settled into it with a rustle of skirts, just before her husband called the meeting to order. Elliot sighed and stifled a childish urge to sneak from the row while her attention was distracted by calling greetings to the other wives of the railroad trustees.

He had spent the morning reconciling the accounts in his office, a task that wasn't especially difficult, but required enough of his attention that he could put most other things out of his mind. He'd given Sally and the girls the afternoon and evening off, and his plan had been to lock himself in his room to somehow survive the supermoon without Declan.

But the entire town had turned out for an afternoon meeting called to address the fact that the railroad had run out of money after laying only a single mile of track, and his absence would be conspicuous. He took a deep breath, steeling himself for a long, tedious meeting, tamping down the tension already building under his skin in anticipation of tonight's supermoon.

The room was overwarm, the scents of the ladies' perfume

and the gentlemen's pipe smoke rising and combining in a harshly sweet concoction that burned the back of his throat. Judge Swan provided an update about the corporation's current financial state—dismal—and the point at which the laid track ended—nowhere useful.

Mrs. Jackman leaned closer to Elliot, her sleeve brushing against the arm of his jacket. Christ, if he couldn't get out of this room soon, he was likely to crawl out of his skin. He shuddered at the vision of his tentacles bursting through the seams of his trousers, flailing in the center aisle between the two sections of chairs hastily set up in a meeting room built for far fewer people than it currently held.

"Are you quite well, Mr. Bishop?" Mrs. Jackman's voice was soft under the rising rhetoric of Judge Swan expounding again on the benefits that having a transcontinental railroad connect to Port Townsend would bring.

"I'm fine, thank you, Mrs. Jackman," Elliot replied. His voice was steady, at least, thank heaven for small victories. "A bit warm, perhaps."

She laid a gloved hand on his forearm, and the soft pressure chafed the linen of his shirtsleeve against his heated skin. Baron Eisenbeis was now suggesting a subscription drive to raise money to lure one of the more established railroad companies to connect the track they'd already laid with an existing transcontinental line. It was an interesting idea, though one Elliot suspected Declan would never countenance.

"It's a beautiful day, is it not? Perhaps a walk along the shore after the meeting ends would be cooling?" Mrs. Jackman suggested, and her tone was quiet enough that he hardly credited what she'd said at first.

"I beg your pardon?" She was hardly proposing an illicit liaison to him, not with her husband on the other side of the room.

"Have you thought again of marrying, Mr. Bishop?" she asked, and now Elliot realized where she was heading.

He shook his head. "I have not," he said truthfully.

Mrs. Jackman sighed, a look of deep sympathy on her face that itched at him. It was hardly her business to make a match for him. He socialized with her frequently because her husband owned almost as much real estate as Joe Kuhn and Baron Eisenbeis, but Elliot's wedded or unwedded state was hardly any of her business.

He turned his attention back to the meeting. The trustees had already pledged five thousand dollars each, and Terrell Jackman pledged the same, after catching his wife's eye and Mrs. Jackman nodding magisterially at him.

"It's been more than a year since you lost Miss Brady," she persisted, her voice low under the cover of more pledges from both uptown and downtown residents, raising their hands and speaking up in turn. Her voice oozed with a simulacrum of the sympathy he was used to hearing from townspeople who'd assumed Celeste had drowned last year, but a glance at the sharp avidity in her eyes told him that she knew the truth about what happened to Celeste.

"Your devotion to her speaks well of you, but surely you must be wanting a true helpmeet to provide the comforts a man of your position should have."

The emphasis on "true" in that sentence was unmistakable. Christ, he hoped she wasn't gossiping about him and Declan uptown. The fact that Declan was his stepbrother went a long way toward legitimizing their closeness. Surely no one would question Declan continuing to live in the home he'd grown up in, at least until he married.

No one seemed to expect Declan to marry, though. Elliot supposed that was in part because he spent so much time at sea. Elliot, on the other hand, must seem a pathetic figure to most of Port Townsend's society, clinging to the memory of his former fiancée, unnaturally attached to his stepbrother, and declining all opportunities to find a wife to keep his home and bear him children.

It would be nice to have children, he thought, briefly entertaining a vision of half a dozen sons or daughters running around the grounds of the Bishop house. But that fantasy was overrun by the memory of his mother explaining her plans for Elliot and Celeste to breed a new generation of offspring that could shift back and forth between human and devilfish. Elliot shuddered in sudden and appalled arousal. His cock stiffened in his trousers, and he folded his hands in his lap, resolutely pushing away the thought of the act that accompanies breeding.

"My oldest daughter fits that bill wonderfully," Mrs. Jackman said.

Elliot swiveled in his seat to stare at her. He vaguely recalled the girl, sitting in her family's pew of a Sunday at St. Paul's. Quiet and demure, dark brown hair she'd only recently started wearing pinned up. "Your oldest?" he said, trying to remember her name. Hannah, he thought, that was it. "She's what? Fourteen? I'm not marrying a girl not even out of the schoolroom."

Mrs. Jackman's eyes were on his, flecks of amber amidst the brown of her irises, and he felt her mind poking at the edges of his. Her lips curved upwards in a suggestive smile. "She turns sixteen next month and came into womanhood last fall. She's more than ready for marriage and able to meet all your needs."

She held a hand up when Elliot tried again to politely decline. "Hear me out, please. The women in my family have a distant connection to the women in your mother's family."

He supposed it was fair to call the women living in his mother's island den "family." Mama had told him they all shared blood from the creature that had sired him.

"She'll appreciate your unique qualities," Mrs. Jackman said, raising an eyebrow slightly. "We're not as…changeable, shall we say, as your mother's family is." This was with a significant look, and she continued, "But she'll be safe with you. And she'll make you an exemplary wife."

Elliot felt his face flush hot. It was unbearable that she not only knew about him, but apparently considered him an appropriate match for her daughter. He felt a sudden desperate sympathy for the poor girl. The scene could be worse only if his own mother were here, haggling with Mrs. Jackman over the value of his stud services and her daughter's broodmare capabilities.

The price was too high, though. Thomas had been right all along. Elliot had had an opportunity to marry a woman who shared his changeable nature, and he'd given her up for Declan. If he couldn't have Declan during the supermoon, he'd figure out how to get through it on his own, but he would not—could not—be with a woman this way.

He took a deep breath, trying to craft his response. "I appreciate your...attractive offer," he finally said, grasping at the edges of courtesy. "I'm afraid I'm not ready to entertain the idea of marriage right now, nor do I expect to be so for some time." He pushed back firmly against her mind trying to worm its way past his defenses.

Mrs. Jackman leaned back in her chair, her surprised disappointment flaring briefly in his head before she gave up and stopped prodding at him. "If it's a matter of getting to know her, I can arrange a meeting. Perhaps this evening, at your home?"

"No!" Elliot's immediate protest was rather louder than he'd intended.

Baron Eisenbeis called his name, pencil poised over the ledger in which he was recording the subscription pledges.

"Ah," Elliot stumbled as he stood, then steadied himself with a hand on the back of the chair in front of him. "I pledge six thousand." He stifled a smirk at the look Jackman darted at his wife and her huff of surprise that he'd pledged the highest amount yet.

The meeting ended shortly after. Elliot gave Mrs. Jackman his hand to assist her from her chair. "I'm sure Ruby is a wonderful young woman," he said under the cover of folks gathering hats and gloves, wraps and walking sticks. "If I were inclined to marry, I would choose her. But tonight is not a good time for me to meet her."

Christ, the woman knew what would happen to her unmarried daughter if she were with Elliot tonight, of all nights, and still had no compunction of dangling her before him like a baited hook.

"And what are your plans for the evening?" Mrs. Jackman asked archly. Of course she knew. Elliot glared at her. But he absolutely would not use a fifteen-year-old girl like that, no matter how desperate he might be.

"I have some reading to do, and then I'm going to bed early." This had been a deeply inappropriate conversation to be having with another man's wife, in public no less, and he was more than ready to end it. "If you'll excuse me."

He gave her a slight bow and nodded at Jackman, who was threading his way toward them. "Please give my regards to your husband. And to Ruby, of course." He left her standing at the end of the row and strode quickly from the meeting room.

CHAPTER 20

*D*eclan held his piece until he and Nance were settled in the dining room in the big house and Betsy had served a breakfast fit for a king. He had to give it to the old girl; she knew how to put on a spread. And probably that hard conversations came easier if accompanied by good coffee and a full belly.

So, he waited until she'd sopped the last bit of her biscuit through the gravy and pushed her plate back. He forked up the remains of his eggs, and when she leaned back and lit her cheroot in its meerschaum holder, he pointed the piece of bacon in his hand at her.

"Talk."

Nance sighed. "What the devil do you want me to talk about, Fitz? I ain't a mind reader here."

Declan had a sudden image of Elliot, his head cocked slightly to one side, listening intently to things Declan couldn't hear. He'd said it wasn't quite like reading thoughts, but however it worked, it was also the way the women sailors communicated on the *Poulpes*. Something about Nance's interactions with the *Poulpes*'s captain suggested she might have a touch of it, too.

"What's she doing here?"

"Who?"

"Don't play dumb with me, woman. Celeste Brady, the woman Elliot was supposed to marry last year."

"She's the one?" Nance continued puffing on her cheroot. "She'd've been a good match for him. Shame they didn't tie the knot."

"You know damn well why they didn't." At least, he figured she knew. It was Nance who'd told him last year about the half-human, half-devilfish women who lived out in the Pacific. Nance who'd given them the compass that pointed at Elliot last year and Celeste this morning. Nance who'd sat across from him in her library when he'd worked out the connection between the super-moon and tides that accompanied Elliot's shift.

He wasn't entirely sure whether she knew he and Elliot were lovers, though she knew he liked men in his bed as much or more as women. That had been an awkward conversation when Joey had run away to join his crew.

Nance shrugged. "Her money's as good as yours here, Fitz. Whatever your beef with her, it ain't my business."

"Yeah? And where does her money come from, Nance? An unmarried woman, and young as she is?"

"Ain't my business," Nance said again, a stubborn set to her face that made Declan clench his fist in frustration.

"You know everyone's business that stops here. And from the looks of it, that woman skippering the ship Celeste came in has been here before."

"So?"

"So, the last time I saw that woman, she was at the helm of the *Poulpes*. The eight-masted schooner my father searched for for fifteen years, the same damned vessel you told me you'd never seen!"

His voice had risen loud enough that Betsy, who'd peered around the door frame, probably to clear the breakfast things, disappeared again. Declan tossed his napkin on the table and got up to close the door. Better they had this argument in private. By the time he returned to the table, he'd managed to tamp down his temper.

"Nance," he said, trying for a softer tone, though his voice still came out gruff. "Elliot's gotta go through it on his own this time, and I just..." For fuck's sake, he'd no idea how to explain this. "I need more information. You helped us last year. Isn't there anything you else you know about it?"

Nance inhaled a lungful of smoke, but turned her head and at least didn't blow it in his face. "Why ask me? Why not Celeste? Or Enid?"

"Enid and I aren't exactly on speaking terms. I only met the woman once, when she took me from here last year. This morning's the first time she actually spoke to me. Hell, I didn't even know her name until today. And as for Celeste," Declan dragged the tines of his fork through the leftover pork and beans on his plate. "For fuck's sake, Nance, don't make me talk to Elliot's former fiancée about what I do with him."

Nance chuckled dryly. "You'd be surprised about what these gals are willing to talk about. The free love movement's got nothing on them."

"Nance. Please." Declan had been trading affectionately caustic barbs with Nance all the years he'd been putting in here, and he knew she was capable of serious conversation, but sometimes, it was like pulling teeth to get her to open up.

"The hell do you want me to tell you, Fitz?" She shifted irritably in her chair, looked like she was about to push back from the table, but then stubbed her cheroot out and leaned against the chair back, crossing her arms over her chest.

"You can start by telling me how long Celeste and Enid have been coming here and what more you know about the women like them."

Nance sighed. "Just met Miss Brady today, but Enid showed up the night you disappeared from here."

It took a moment for Declan to process that. Then a wave of cold anger washed over him. "Damnation, Nance, why didn't you warn me? I didn't 'disappear' from here, that woman drugged me and took me."

Nance had the decency to look ashamed. "I didn't know that then. Didn't make the connection at first. And Elliot didn't speak with me before he left with your ship and crew. Your father told me where they were going, but my hand to God, Fitz, I'd've warned you if I'd known what she was going to do."

She leaned forward, her eyes pleading with Declan to believe her. "She didn't tell me what she was planning. And by the time I figured it out, you were already gone, and your father and Elliot went after you first thing."

Declan scrubbed his hands over his face, trying to clear away the memory of being drugged and at the mercy of the indifferent care of the women on the *Poulpes*. They didn't mistreat him; kept him fed and cleaned, but didn't let up on the opium until they were nearly to the devilfish island. He hadn't touched the stuff since, not until the laudanum-based tonic Mrs. Jackman had given Elliot for him. Which he'd dumped in the sea as soon as he left Port Townsend.

"What did she tell you?" he finally asked Nance. "About why she was here, I mean."

Nance got up then, went to the sideboard, and poured more coffee for the both of them. Declan nodded thanks and waited, keeping his eyes on her as she fiddled with the sugar bowl, stirring enough into her cup to make his teeth ache just looking at it. She finally sat down again and then muttered, low enough that he barely heard her, "She knew my sister."

"Because your sister was like them—like Enid and Elliot's mother, and Celeste? Before she died?"

Nance looked up. "How did you know she died?"

Declan took in a breath. "Joey told me."

He refrained from telling her what else Joey'd told him, about the cruel gossip he'd overheard. No need to pour salt into what was clearly still an open wound. "You never mentioned you had a sister."

Nance sighed. "There any family secrets my kid ain't told you? He sure knows how to run his mouth around you."

At least she used the right pronoun, finally. Declan stretched across the table and put his hand over hers, stilling her fiddling with the silverware. "He trusts me," he said, tilting his head to catch her eye. "You can, too, you know."

Nance sighed again, and turned her hand up to clasp Declan's. He squeezed back gently, then let her go. "I know," she said.

She gave a deep sigh. "She's been gone a long time, and ain't no one else left who remembers anything about her. Guess I kinda got outta the habit of talking about her."

She sniffled and knuckled the corner of her eye. "Suppose that's why I didn't think about anything else after talking with Enid. It'd been so long since I met anyone who knew her. Weren't no room in my head for anything that wasn't her that night."

Declan could understand that. "What happened to her?"

Nance picked up her napkin and dabbed at her eyes. The first and last time Declan seen her cry was when Joey had told her that if she couldn't accept him the way he was, he'd never come home again. He gave her a few moments to compose herself and she blew her nose, then took a sip of coffee, as if to brace herself.

"She was about to get married. To a Hudson Bay Company man, younger brother of Joey's father. Following in his brother's footsteps, you understand, and he wasn't already hitched, like my man was. Last time he came here, he brought a priest with him, to make it official-like. He knew about her and loved her anyway."

"He knew she was like them? Like Elliot?"

Nance nodded. Declan pinched the bridge of his nose and tamped down a wave of irritation. He sure as hell could have used this information from the beginning, instead of having to piece together everything from the scraps of Father's investigation and the half-truths she'd fed him last year.

She looked up at the ceiling, blinking a few more tears from her lashes, and blew her nose again. "I made her a new dress. We were gonna have the ceremony in the library. But the night before the wedding was a full moon, and they went to the hot spring when the tide was going out. He was dead by morning. Charlotte killed herself two days later."

"Shit," Declan murmured. He reached for Nance's hand again, but she waved him off, twisting the napkin between her hands. "I'm so sorry, Nance." He wished there was something he could do or say.

She nodded jerkily, then blew her nose again, and swiped her eyes with her sleeve. She took a deep breath and folded the napkin into a small square and set it on the table next to her plate. When she spoke again, her voice was calm, back to its usual smoke-scarred huskiness.

"She never told me what happened that night, but it was clear being with her was what done him. She managed to get him back to the house, naked and hardly breathing, but he never quite woke up. She wouldn't let no one tend him after we got him upstairs to her room."

She fumbled in her pocket and took out a small case. Declan pulled it from her trembling fingers and withdrew a fresh cheroot, tucked it into the meerschaum holder, and lit it for her.

She took a few deep puffs and blew the smoke out with a deep sigh. "He looked peaceful at the end. Happy, even. That was something, I guess, even if Charlotte couldn't see it. It was the guilt, you know?"

Of being the cause of her lover's death, even if she couldn't control her nature. Declan could see that. The same guilt Elliot felt for being the cause of Declan's infirmity. He'd been luckier than Charlotte's man, thank Christ. At least, so far.

He packed his own pipe full and sat with her for a time,

plumes of smoke rising and mixing over their heads, displacing the breakfast smells, until he had to ask the question.

"Why, Nance? Why didn't you tell me this last year?"

Nance shifted irritably in her seat. "The hell do you want from me, Fitz? You already took my child away from me. You come here, asking questions about stuff that ain't none of your goddamn business, demanding answers I don't fucking have. You're worse than your father, single-minded bastard that he was. He, at least, never pretended to care about us."

Declan clenched his teeth to keep from shouting back at her. He was sorry for stirring up her grief, but for Christ's sake. "You're not the only one who's lost someone, woman. And you haven't lost Joey, damn it. He's here, isn't he? He keeps coming back to you, waiting for you to accept him. The way you accepted your sister."

She shook her head. "That ain't the same, Fitz. Charlotte couldn't change the way God made her."

"And neither can Joey," Declan hissed. "It's the same in all the ways that matter, and if you quit living in the past and look around at what's here and now, you could maybe help someone the way you couldn't help your sister."

Nance's mouth fell open, and Declan felt a stab of remorse. That was a low blow, but Jesus, he was tired of having this conversation with her.

She blinked at him a couple of times, then sighed. "You're right."

Her capitulation was so unexpected that it was Declan's turn to stare at her with his mouth open. She pointed the cheroot at him.

"About Joey, anyway. He's my kid and I love him, even if I don't agree with everything he does. He's a good kid." She dropped her eyes to her plate, then looked back at him. "A good man," she said, like she was testing how the words felt.

"Like you," she continued, and damned if the woman didn't

keep surprising him today. "Glad he's got a man like you to show him the way."

A rare smile crossed her weathered face, and Declan smiled back. The warmth of her approval was nice, but not something he really needed right now.

She seemed to understand that, because the smile faded almost as soon as it came. "I wish I had more answers for you, Fitz, but I don't. If I was you, I'd talk to that Celeste girl."

CHAPTER 21

*E*lliot's irritation at Mrs. Jackman's machinations mostly dissipated on the short walk home with a fresh breeze from the waterfront. The late afternoon sun cast long shadows as he took the Taylor Street steps two at a time, already dreading the long night ahead.

He let himself into the empty house, fetched a bottle of the good whiskey from Declan's stash in his study, and locked his bedroom door, just to be safe. Sally and her girls were visiting her sister in Port Ludlow, and he'd suggested none too subtly to Thomas that he should find other entertainment tonight, perhaps at the Green Light. He had a copy of Wilkie Collins's *The Woman in White* to occupy his attention. He would get through the supermoon just fine on his own. He hoped.

Two hours later, he gave up that foolish hope. He couldn't shift out of the water, but Celeste had told him last year that the need to be in the sea during a supermoon would be unbearable. As with so many things, she was right.

The prickling in his skin that started earlier in the day increased until every change in position chafed his clothes against his skin. It was like millions of microscopic creatures worming their way under the layers of his skin, blindly seeking an unattainable goal.

He stripped down to his drawers and looked longingly at the empty ewer on the washstand. He'd left it empty deliberately, and now his skin was parched and hot, stretched too tight over bones that ached for release. He could fill the big copper bathtub in the upstairs washroom and let the shift happen there, but what if he couldn't shift back? Surely, it was better to avoid the change entirely than to have to explain himself to Sally and the twins in the morning.

But as twilight turned to full dark and the moon rose over the bay, shining its huge countenance through his bedroom windows, the ebbing tide pulled harder and harder on the thrum of blood in his veins. He tossed his book aside and stood at the window. He'd jerked off half a dozen times already, his bedsheets creased and damp.

He pushed the window sash up and let the briny scent of the night air wash over his heated skin. It was too dark to see the strip of bay visible from atop the bluff the house was built on during the day, but he could almost feel the waves lapping at his oversensitive skin. He'd checked the tide tables earlier in the day to verify when the tide would be at its lowest, but he needn't have bothered. He knew exactly where the tide was; its ebb sucked at the blood in his veins. It would be nearly dawn before it reached its height again and he could rest.

He took himself in hand again, the moonlight playing over his cock as it slipped through the circle of his fist. His mind flooded with vague images of Celeste and other octopian women cavorting under the waves, tentacles writing, bodies pressing together, the thick purple appendages of the giant octopus creature he'd met in his mother's island den slipping in and out of slick holes.

He resisted these images and thought of Declan instead, but that was hardly better. Declan on his back, legs wrapped around

Elliot's waist, as Elliot plunged into his hole over and over. Elliot's tentacles wrapped around his arms and chest, the tip of one slipping into Declan's mouth, filling that, too. Elliot working him at both ends, and Declan's green eyes smiling up at him, egging him on.

Elliot stripped his cock furiously, and when he finally spent, the white fluid spattered against the windowsill. He leaned his forehead against the cool of the window glass until his breath returned to normal. He stepped out of his damp drawers and used them to clean the dribble of come from the windowsill and wall. He'd send today's clothes and the bed linens to one of the laundries downtown, since the thought of Eugenia and Clarice laundering these items was too humiliating to bear.

Naked, he wandered around the room, pouring another glass of whiskey, trying to think of something else to distract him. The pull of the tide was relentless, but he had nothing left in him for the moment. His hands and cock were sticky, and he desperately wanted a bath, or at least a wet cloth. Maybe he could risk dampening a towel to clean himself up a bit, but as he headed to unlock the bedroom door, he heard a short knock.

"Sally, I told you to take the night off," he called. His voice was hoarse, and he hoped she couldn't guess why.

"It's Thomas. Just checking to see if you're all right." Thomas's voice sounded indifferent, though Elliot now knew him well enough to see through the stoic facade he presented to the world.

Elliot sighed. Thomas was supposed to be at the Green Light tonight. Or wherever else he found his entertainment. Elliot frankly didn't care where Thomas spent an evening, especially this one. He'd been surprisingly sympathetic to Elliot's predicament, but that didn't mean Elliot wanted him in the same house while he was desperately holding on to himself.

He cleared his throat and said, "I'm fine. Please don't let me keep you from your evening's pleasures." He knocked his forehead against the door, though not loud enough for Thomas to hear, he hoped. Christ, he hadn't meant that to sound like an innuendo.

Thomas chuckled softly on the other side, a low sound that twisted in Elliot's gut. His hand drifted down to his cock, slowly stiffening *again*, damn the mindless thing. He clenched his fist at his side, then clasped both hands behind his back. He would not jerk off with Declan's ex-lover on the other side of the damned door.

"I had a very pleasant evening," Thomas said, and Elliot closed his eyes, trying to stave off images of what Thomas might have been up to this evening. "I'm for bed. Just wanted to see if there was anything you needed."

"No," Elliot said. He cleared his throat again and tried to sound less bleak. "There's nothing you can do for me." The grandfather clock in the downstairs parlor chimed three times.

"How much longer?" Thomas asked. He sounded brisk and practical, like this was just a tedious task Elliot had to grit his teeth and get through.

Elliot sighed. "A while, still. I'm fine, Thomas, really. Thank you for checking on me, but I'd rather you just go to bed and leave me be."

Thomas, the stubborn bastard that he was, refused to just go away. Elliot heard a rustle outside the door and a soft thump suggesting Thomas was settling down on the other side of the door. Elliot opened his mouth to plead again for Thomas to leave him alone but before he got the words out, Thomas began to sing.

Elliot had heard Thomas sing before. Last year, on the *Black Dove*, when the crew liked to sing after the evening meal sometimes. Mostly bawdy songs, the type one would expect from sailors, but they also all listened raptly when Thomas sang the ballads and romantic songs he'd learned growing up in Mexico. This song had a slow, haunting melody that crept through the door like wisps of fog. The words were in Spanish, and Elliot didn't understand any of them, but there was something about it that made him feel comforted and cared for.

Elliot put his own back to the door and slid down so he was sitting on the floor. The wood was cool against his bare back, and the fibers of the rug were deliciously rough against his ass. He pulled his knees up to his chest and rested his forehead on his kneecaps, closing his eyes and relaxing a little, for the first time since he'd locked himself in his room tonight.

He concentrated on Thomas's deep and resonant voice, thick and sweet like chocolate. The moon and the ebbing tide still tugged at his blood, but the music helped distract him a little.

Thomas sang a second song, then a third, and kept singing until Elliot lost count. A few were more sprightly than the others and one was even in English—a drinking song he must have noticed Elliot tapping his foot to aboard ship last year. Most were slow and yearning. Love songs, Elliot guessed, or songs of loss and longing. Or maybe that was just Elliot projecting his own feelings on the music.

His cock was still hard, and his blood still throbbed under his skin, but the music wrapped around him and eased some of the desperate pull. He could almost imagine hands, rough with calluses like Declan's, stroking over his head and shoulders. Elliot hugged his knees tighter against his chest and pretended Declan was there, caressing him and soothing the itch in his tingling skin.

The last hour passed slowly, the minutes slipping by in beats of Thomas's songs, the imaginary hands stroking in time. The tide turned, and the desperate, aching pull slackened—imperceptibly at first—then gradually enough that his muscles relaxed and Elliot sighed in relief.

It was over. For tonight, anyway. He'd feel the effects of the supermoon the rest of the day and into tomorrow, but the worst of it was over and he'd stayed human. He'd made it. Without hurting Declan.

A sliver of dawn cracked the horizon, and Elliot lifted his head from his knees. In the hall outside his bedroom, Thomas stopped singing and cleared his throat. "Gonna go to bed now. You'll be all right?"

"Yes." Elliot unfurled from his curled and huddled position against the door and winced as he stretched the kinks from his limbs. "That was beautiful, Thomas. I don't—You didn't have to —" He felt calm and peaceful, still caught in the spell of the music. He cleared his throat and said simply, "Thank you."

"De nada, mi cabrón." Thomas's voice was hoarse, but he didn't sound resentful of Elliot keeping him awake all night. He rapped two quick knocks against the other side of the door and said, "Buenos noches, Elliot."

"Goodnight," Elliot echoed, and he listened to Thomas's footsteps retreating down the hall. He eyed his bed, the sheets and blankets still rumpled from his tossing and turning earlier that night. He was exhausted, eyelids threatening to slam shut, so despite a wish for fresher linens, he crawled into bed and pulled the covers over him.

He lay with his eyes closed for a few moments, on the edge of sleep. Thoughts of going through a night like this every supermoon for the rest of his life loomed bleakly ahead of him. Still, Declan was safe from his unnatural urges. He'd do whatever he had to do to keep him that way. After another few minutes, Elliot managed to drift off into a restless sleep.

CHAPTER 22

$\mathcal{T}$he morning after the supermoon, Declan gave up trying to sleep a few hours before dawn. A dull headache throbbed at his temple. Like he'd drunk too much whiskey the night before, when he'd only had a glass or two with Nance after supper. He'd never been afflicted with regular nightmares like Elliot, but he'd tossed and turned all night with half-remembered dreams. Vague images of a submerged threat and Elliot calling to him, reaching for him through waving kelp forests, Declan grasping at strands of his hair, which slipped through his fingers.

His whole body was sore, his muscles aching like he'd spent the night at the wheel on his ship, tossed about in a storm. The big house was quiet when he came downstairs, not even Betsy or Cook up to stoke the kitchen stove and start breakfast. Since he couldn't sleep anyway, he figured he'd head for the hot spring. Maybe a soak before breakfast would ease the soreness from his muscles.

He'd nearly reached the upper section of the chasm when he heard faint giggles coming from one of the lower pools. In all his concern about how Elliot was managing the supermoon without him, he'd forgotten the octopian women anchored in the steamship *Albatross* just offshore. He wasn't sure how many women were aboard, how they found partners to mate with during the supermoon, or even if they needed to like Elliot did. He had no particular desire to interrupt an assignation, even though he should probably warn a willing partner about the dangers of being with an octopian woman.

His men were the only sailors currently occupying the bunkhouse. Seamus and Luca were on the outs at the moment, and while Luca would slip it to anyone willing, Seamus was strictly a man's man. Reginald might be amenable, but after everything Declan been through with Elliot, he'd be damned if these women would harm any of his crew.

He peered over the rocky ledge and looked down into the chasm. The moon had set, and the eastern sky was just beginning to turn pink behind low clouds at the horizon. If there was anyone in the hot spring, he couldn't see them. Maybe it had been his imagination. There were other small settlements scattered around this side of Vancouver Island—logging camps and what-not. Maybe the *Albatross* women had found partners there. Or maybe they'd been in the pools at the lower end of the spring, and swum off into the ocean when they were finished. Elliot liked the lower pools, where the cold ocean water mixed with the hot mineral waters and the sulfur smell from the waterfall that fed the narrow, rocky chasm was less strong.

In any event, the spring appeared empty now, thank God. Declan stripped his clothes off and settled into one of the upper pools. Steam wafted from the falls and the surface of the pools. The water was hot enough to ease some of the ache in his muscles, and he closed his eyes and submerged to his chin.

Memories of being here with Elliot last year filled his mind, and he let them in. The first time Elliot changed while fucking Declan had been a desperate rush of lust and sensation, Declan letting Elliot take what he needed, but the next morning, he'd found Elliot in this spring, shying away from letting Declan see his tentacles. He'd gotten over that, as much from his instincts taking over as from Declan's reassurance that he wanted Elliot just the way he was.

He swished his arms in the hot water surrounding him and let his fingers trace the slick rocks lining the pool, wishing Elliot were here so he could explore the velvet softness of his octopian skin. He drew up the look of wondering exultation on Elliot's face when his tentacled cock pushed into Declan that morning, when they both knew exactly what Elliot was.

Fucking Elliot had held the same wonder and joy every time since, even when Elliot was fully human. And his absence now was like being in a deep, dark pit, with only the faintest glimmer of light just out of reach. Elliot wasn't lost to him permanently, but Declan could hardly bear knowing that he'd been alone last night. Not for the first time, he regretted letting Elliot talk him into leaving before the supermoon.

He floated in the pool under the shadows of the chasm's rocky sides and let the hot water lull him into a doze. He must have fallen into another of last night's dreams, because he felt rather than heard Elliot calling to him again. That glimmer of light pulsed faintly, and Declan concentrated on it until it solidified into a thin line that he could almost reach out and grasp.

He followed the light, feeling along like a rope through a dark tunnel, until he saw Elliot in his bedroom at the Bishop house.

Elliot was naked and on the bare wooden floor, huddled against the closed door, his knees pulled to his chest and his head bowed, forehead resting on his knees. Declan couldn't see his face, but his heart ached at how small and cold he looked.

He'd never been able to see Elliot in his mind like this, from a distance, and heaven knows, he'd spent a lot of time thinking about Elliot in the years they were apart. This was new and tentative. He kept losing the connection, the rope of light more like a silk ribbon fluttering out of his grasp, and he wasn't sure if

Elliot could feel him the same way. Elliot hadn't looked up from his curled-up position. Declan couldn't sense what he was feeling.

He drifted as close as he could to Elliot and tried reaching out to touch his shoulder. His fingertips grazed Elliot's skin, but the harsh caw of a raven startled him, and the connection shattered. Declan's eyes snapped open. Another raven croaked in response from a tree above the hot spring, and he floundered a bit in the warm water, scraping an elbow against the rough surface of a submerged boulder.

Now there was a whole flock of the damn birds, squawking and squabbling at each other. An unkindness or a conspiracy, weren't those names for a group of ravens, and hell if they weren't apt. Declan cursed in irritation. He scooped an armful of water into the air, hoping to drive them off, but the water just rained back down on him, and the ravens ignored him.

When they finally flew off, he tried reclaiming the connection with Elliot. The ribbon was still there, and he could feel Elliot on the other end, but he couldn't grasp it or pull himself any closer. At least he knew that Elliot had gotten through the night without shifting, even if he couldn't tell how. He wondered whether this new connection between them was similar to how Elliot communicated with other octopians.

A shaft of bright sunlight broke through the clouds on the horizon, refractions glinting on the rippling surface of the pool. The ripples changed color like Elliot's skin did when he changed, something Declan never tired of looking at. The myriad of shades from deep violet to the palest pink Elliot's tentacles were capable of were endlessly fascinating, and this was the only place they'd had sufficient privacy that he could see them in the daylight.

If he were home, they could be in the spa cavern Elliot had built near Point Wilson today, and he'd show Elliot just how much he loved all of Elliot, even the parts he was conflicted about.

Declan pulled himself out of the pool. He shook most of the water from his skin and squeezed as much as he could from his hair, then dressed quickly. He had a glimmer of an idea of how they could stay together. He just needed to figure out how to make it happen.

CHAPTER 23

When Declan returned to the big house, Celeste was in Nance's library. She had a stack of letters and periodicals spread out on the desk in front of her, a leather-bound journal at her left hand, and a pen loosely clasped between her fingers. She didn't appear to be reading the magazine spread open before her. Her dark head was turned toward the window, spectacles perched on her nose, a dreamy expression on her face.

Declan rapped his knuckles lightly at the library door as he entered. Celeste didn't seem to notice him until he leaned one hip against the end of the table closest to her. She turned her face toward him, and he smiled, but waited a few moments until the faraway look in her eyes cleared and he got her full attention.

"Good morning," he said. Interrupting Celeste while she was thinking was probably not the best way to predispose her to helping him, but he was willing to take the risk. He'd learned from the limited time he'd known her when she was still engaged to Elliot that she needed a few moments to switch from focusing on her work to a conversation with another person.

She blinked a few times, glanced at the magazine in front of her as if she'd suddenly remembered she was supposed to be reading it, then sighed and flipped it closed. *The Annals and Magazine of Natural History* was printed on the cover.

"Reading anything interesting?" Declan asked.

Celeste's hand twitched back toward the magazine, as if she wanted to open it and show him. "A paper on whether medusae exist in the deep sea. But I confess I was wool-gathering a bit just now."

She blushed a fetching rose pink, and Declan tried not to think about how she might have spent the supermoon. "And do they?"

"Do who?"

"Medusae? Do whatever they are exist in the deep sea?"

She shrugged. "Jellyfish. And of course. The author can hardly be expected to know for sure, naturally. Men have only started exploring the depths of the oceans."

The emphasis on *men* there was mild but unmistakable. "You've seen them," Declan said.

Celeste nodded. "Certainly. I've seen more things in the ocean than you can possibly imagine."

Which was as good a segue as any, Declan supposed. "Then tell me how I can become one of you."

Her eyebrows drew together, and she looked confused. "I beg your pardon?"

Declan gestured between her and himself. "Like you, and Elliot. Half devilfish. A, what do you call yourselves, an octopian?"

Now her jaw dropped. "You want to become an octopian?"

He nodded. Celeste removed her spectacles, cocked her head to the side, and looked steadily at him. He held her gaze, resisting the urge to drop his eyes. "What on Earth for?"

"Does it matter? You and Elliot suddenly developed the ability to shift. Why not me as well?"

"Because we were born with the ability to," she said. "And you weren't. If you had been, it would have manifested by now."

"How do you know that?" he asked. "I've known Elliot his whole life, and there was never any indication he was anything other than normal before last year. Something sparked the change in him. Tell me what it was."

"Why don't you ask him?" She glanced down at the pen in her hand and fiddled with it.

Declan leaned forward a little, trying to look into her face.

"I'm asking you. When did you first change? How did you know you could do it?"

She shook her head but finally looked up at him, a challenge in her eyes. "I think you know the answer to that, sir. I don't know what else you want me to tell you."

Of course Declan knew when Elliot's first change happened— he'd been there for it. He assumed Celeste's happened the night she disappeared from Port Townsend. "But why then? Why not the year before or two years from now? What was the catalyst for it?"

Celeste sighed at his dogged insistence. "I don't have any answers for you. The ability runs in families, we know that much. Passed through the maternal line, we assume, since all octopians have been women. Until Elliot. So, if your mother had been one of us, then possibly. But she wasn't, was she?"

Declan shrugged. His mother had died giving birth to him, and his father had never told him there was anything unusual about her. Then again, he'd never told Declan there was anything unusual about Elliot's mother, either.

Declan tried a different tack. "I thought you were looking for octopian men?" In his years-long search for Elliot's mother, his father had come across a parchment with a cryptic prophecy about a promised son that they'd interpreted as referring to Elliot. It turned out the prophecy was faked, drawn up by Marie's women and seeded along the Pacific Northwest coast to draw any sons of land-based octopian women to their remote island. "I'm offering here. Isn't that a win for you, too?"

Celeste snorted. "You've no idea what you're asking for, Captain."

He thought he did, actually. Elliot's mother, Celeste, all the young women who'd disappeared up and down the Pacific Northwest coast, they'd each ended up at that remote island in the Pacific with the immense devilfish he'd seen there last year. The one Marie had identified as Elliot's father. The one who his father had stabbed and been poisoned by his ink. Surely he was the key to their first shift, somehow.

"The one who made you what you are, can he not do the same for me?"

She didn't answer, just gazed steadily at him, tapping the pen between her fingers on the cover of the natural history journal in a rhythmic pattern that grated on Declan's nerves. He kept still, tamping his impatience down, willing her to acquiesce.

"Why?"

Declan cast about for something to convince her to help him. Something to trade, some way to persuade her. He hardly knew the girl, though she was clearly more than the proper young woman he'd met last year on the cusp of marrying and starting a family with Elliot. Even then, she'd had a bright mind and curious hobbies for an uptown lady. He'd liked her from the first, but he still had little idea what motivated her.

The silence between them stretched long and thin. What the hell, Declan opted for the truth. "For Elliot."

He held his breath as her eyes flicked back and forth between his. They were an unusual amber color, and when a shaft of light broke through a gap in the clouds and shined through the window on them, her pupils narrowed to rectangular slits.

Exactly like the eyes of Elliot's father.

Her eyes went a bit distant, like she was thinking through something, or listening to something he couldn't hear. "It's not working between you, is it?"

Declan shrugged. It worked just fine, it's just that the consequences were getting harder to live with. Celeste cocked her head slightly and then her gaze sharpened. "Being with him is harming you."

"Yes," Declan said.

He reached out and put a hand gently over hers, stilling her fidgeting. "Celeste, please."

She glanced out the window, and Declan followed her gaze. Joey was crossing the wide lawn in front of the big house, on his way toward the bunkhouse, Declan supposed. He felt, rather than heard, a soft sigh next to him.

Her eyes unfocused again, and it seemed like she was looking straight through him. He was about to speak again; he wasn't above begging her, when her eyes refocused on his face. She must have found some sort of answer there, because she sighed. "I don't know if it's possible. I've been studying some of the octopus species I've come across in the sea."

She tapped her pen again on the cover of the *Annals and Magazine of Natural History*, and continued, "I suppose I have some of the same questions you have," she continued. "Who are we? How are we different from them? How might we be similar?"

Declan didn't give a damn about other octopus species. But Celeste nodded as if she'd reached some conclusion and started gathering up her magazines and letters, stacking them into a neat pile that she hefted into her arms. Declan stood and reached for the stack to carry for her, but she waved him away.

"Come out to the *Albatross* later this afternoon," she said. "I can't promise that it's at all possible, but I can gather some information, and we'll see what we can see."

Declan felt the first stirring of hope in his chest. He smiled gratefully at her. "Thank you," he said simply.

Celeste snorted. "You may not feel like thanking me later. And do not get your hopes up. I highly doubt it's possible for you to become one of us unless you share our blood." She glanced out the window again. The wide lawn in front of the house was empty, Joey having disappeared off somewhere. The *Black Dove* was secured at the end of the long pier, and the *Albatross* lay at anchor some distance away.

Despite her warning, Declan was too stubborn to let go of the hope. With Celeste's help, he'd figure it out. Whatever it took to be with Elliot permanently, he'd do it.

CHAPTER 24

*I*n the late morning, Elliot dragged himself out of bed and followed the smell of freshly brewed coffee and frying sausage. He found Thomas at the kitchen stove, one of Sally's aprons tied around his stocky frame, wielding a spatula in one hand and cracking eggs into a bowl with the other. He should have slept longer, since he surely didn't get any more sleep last night than Elliot himself did.

"You shouldn't be on that leg yet," Elliot told him. "I'm perfectly capable of making breakfast on Sally's days off."

Thomas tossed him a look over his shoulder. "That right?" he said, sounding supremely unconvinced. "And what do you make for yourself when you do that?"

Elliot yawned and tried to gather his thoughts, still disordered from the lack of sleep. "All right, I usually burn the coffee and eat the leftover biscuits Sally leaves in the pantry."

"Thought so," Thomas said with a smug expression that was really unwarranted. "And I'm fine. Leg's almost good as new." He favored his injured leg only slightly as he stood at the stove, flipping the sausage and lightly scrambling the eggs. "Coffee's ready in the pot there," Thomas said, gesturing with his chin.

Elliot poured himself a cup, then refilled Thomas's. He perched on a stool out of the way and watched Thomas work. His movements were economical, all of his ingredients gathered together on the counter nearest the stove, and he hummed under his breath as he sprinkled a handful of salt over the cubed potatoes frying in a second skillet.

"Can I help with anything?" Elliot finally asked, courtesy belatedly catching up with him. It had been years since he'd spent any time in this kitchen, which Sally considered her domain. He wasn't even sure where she kept things nowadays, but it was awkward sitting here while Thomas cooked for him, and on a bad leg to boot.

"Nope," Thomas said. "Nearly done. Mrs. Jenkins keeps a proper kitchen." The admiration in his voice was more than that of one professional recognizing another, and Elliot suppressed a smile. He'd heard the two of them swapping recipes and techniques while Thomas recuperated, though he suspected this was the first time Thomas had actually done any cooking in here.

Thomas was respectful of Sally's domain, and she'd remarked to Elliot about Thomas's courtesy and politeness. They'd be a good match for each other, if either was looking for a bit of companionship. And if Thomas wasn't at sea half the year. But Sally was independent enough she might not mind that.

Thomas bent, pulled a pan of fresh biscuits from the oven, and set them on the scrubbed counter opposite the stove. Next, he fetched two plates and scooped half the eggs onto each plate, followed by crispy fried potatoes and four fat sausage links apiece.

He set the plate in front of Elliot with a thump and settled himself on the other stool across from Elliot.

"Eat up," he said, pointing his fork at Elliot's plate. "Don't want Mrs. Jenkins to come home thinking you ain't been fed while she was away."

Elliot ate. As he did so, he remembered the snatch of song

Thomas had been humming while cooking. It sounded like one of the songs he'd sung last night. "Where did you learn to sing?" he asked.

"Didn't," Thomas said through a mouthful of biscuit. His lips glistened with butter and sausage grease, and he swiped the back of his hand across his mouth, then down the front of Sally's apron. He took a gulp of coffee and glanced at Elliot. "Used to sing to mi mamá when I was a boy. She was sick a lot, bad pains that would send her to bed once a month or so. Some sort of female trouble, mi abuelo told me. She'd ask me to sing to her, said it distracted her from the pain."

He took another noisy sip of coffee and slathered more butter over another biscuit half. "Thought it might do the same for you."

"It did," Elliot said. "You have a wonderful voice."

Thomas shrugged, but he looked pleased, and the corners of his mouth lifted a little as he concentrated on his plate.

"What happened to your mother? Did she ever get better?"

Thomas shook his head. "She died the year I was twelve, along with the baby she was carrying. Then Papá and mi abuelo went later that year, in a mining accident. Lotta men died in that accident. That's when I decided mining wasn't for me and went to the coast. Signed on to the *Argonauta* as cabin boy, and haven't been back to Guanajuato since."

Elliot paused, a bite of fried potatoes halfway to his mouth. "You lost your entire family in the same year? I'm so sorry, Thomas."

Thomas shrugged again. "It was a long time ago. The men on the *Black Dove* are my family now. Family ain't always blood, you know."

Elliot nodded. He did know. He'd seen how the crew of the *Black Dove* were Declan's family, which made them Elliot's, too.

"You always have a home here, too, you know," he said. When Thomas looked up at him, surprised, he smiled slightly and repeated, "Family isn't always blood, right?"

Thomas smiled back. "True."

The rest of the day dragged on interminably. Elliot usually spent the day after the supermoon fucking Declan as many times as either of them could stand. He didn't feel as much of an imperative to shift as last night, but he could, if he were in the water. In the water or out of it, the near-constant desire for Declan made it hard to concentrate on anything else.

When the tide was low midmorning, he and Thomas played chess. Thomas won his first game against Elliot, and Elliot couldn't even use the pull of the tide against his blood as an excuse for his loss. Thomas took his queen in a series of well-planned moves when Elliot thought he was planning something else, and even though Elliot knew the game was over six moves before it became apparent to Thomas, he let the game play out to its finish.

"Checkmate!" Thomas crowed, a broader grin than Elliot had ever seen on his face. Elliot grinned back and shook his hand.

When the tide rose toward the late afternoon, Elliot lost again, this time to a gambit he should have seen the moment Thomas tried it, and Thomas set the game aside.

"Drink?" Thomas offered, and Elliot nodded. What the hell, it might dull the need coursing through his blood. He closed his eyes. Thomas pushed a glass into his hand, resting on the arm of the wingback chair Elliot was sitting in, and Elliot wrapped his fingers around its heavy crystal weight.

Thomas stoked the fire in the study's fireplace, and just when Elliot was about to ask him if he'd sing again, he settled himself on the chesterfield facing the fireplace and started a popular tune Elliot recognized from a concert he'd attended last month at the Learned Opera House.

Elliot smiled without opening his eyes and hummed along until Thomas reached the chorus. Then he joined him, singing quietly to not drown out Thomas's far superior voice. Everyone knew this song, and it was impossible to resist its catchy tune.

Elliot's own singing voice was middling at best, really. He could carry a tune, but barely, and he lacked the warm resonance that Thomas possessed seemingly without effort. Thomas launched into another popular tune, one he asked with a raised eyebrow if Elliot recognized. Elliot nodded and sang along. When they reached the chorus, Thomas changed to harmonize below the melody, which he gestured to Elliot to continue singing. Elliot did the best he could, and Thomas nodded in approval.

They kept this up until Thomas exhausted Elliot's memory for song lyrics, and then Thomas sang on alone. Elliot closed his eyes and leaned his head back against the antimacassar on the back of the wing chair. His thoughts wandered, as always, to Declan, wondering what he was doing now.

As if in answer to his thoughts, Declan's scent filled his nose, that mixture of pipe smoke, sea salt, and something else that was strongest when Elliot kissed him at the back of his neck. He felt Declan's presence as if he were in the room here, when he was supposed to be at Nance's, safe from temptation.

He opened his eyes and glanced around the study. Nothing was different than before. The fire still crackled merrily in the fireplace. Thomas was still singing and holding a piece of walrus tusk in his hands, turning it this way and that, a small knife ready to continue the scrimshaw carving he'd been working on since he'd moved into the house.

Thomas claimed he'd never had any aptitude for it, but that was clearly false modesty, because Elliot could already see the image of a giant octopus taking shape on the piece of tusk, one of its tentacles wrapped around the back, facing Elliot, beckoning him with its tip.

Or maybe that was the image in his mind. A long tentacle emerging from the sea, slim tip waving at Elliot standing at the shore. Thomas's singing faded into the background, Elliot's attention drifting between where he was, seated in his own study, and the visceral sensation of standing on a bluff overlooking a long, narrow inlet.

He could feel the gusty breeze blowing his hair from his face, at the same time his fingers were wrapped around the weight of the whiskey glass in his hand, and the stiff brocade of the chair's upholstery rubbed under his wrist. Thomas's fingers, stained with lampblack, flicked over the tusk, while the dark shape of an immense half-octopus figure swam just under the surface of the water.

The giant man-like octopus that was the source of his ability to shift. The creature his mother had referred to as his father, though Elliot still refused to think of the damned thing so. His mother may have gotten him from that beast, but Declan's father had married his mother to legitimize her bastard baby and had treated Elliot like his own son. He may not have always gotten along with the Captain, but that was who his father was.

He pushed against the questing sentience he felt from the creature in the water and turned his back on the inlet. He closed his eyes, focusing his attention on Thomas's singing to keep himself grounded in the present, in his study.

And then Declan's face was before him again, his green eyes crinkling as he smiled at someone Elliot couldn't see. He was in Nance's library, speaking to someone just out of Elliot's sight, nodding in confirmation to whatever they said that Elliot couldn't hear. He looked resolute, like he'd made a decision he'd been long considering, and Elliot felt the certainty of his conviction. Whatever Declan had decided, he'd taken his time thinking about it, and his decision was made.

Elliot lingered in his vision, if that was what this was, of Declan. He traced his eyes over Declan's broad shoulders, rise and fall of his chest as he breathed, the way his jacket and vest hung on his torso and trim waist, his strong thighs under the dark wool trousers.

With a start, Elliot realized he wasn't the only one looking lustfully at Declan. Another set of eyes—no, more than one—dozens, maybe, he couldn't tell how many. Taking in Declan's physique, lingering over his chest, his thighs, even his ass. Imagining his cock, weighing his balls in unseen hands, tracing patterns over his scarred back and around his nipples. Elliot's desire for him was amplified, magnified, by the desire of the others he sensed, until he realized it was concentrated in the searching, reaching creature swimming up the narrow inlet toward Declan.

"The hell you will," Elliot muttered under his breath, just before the deep chime of the doorbell rang.

CHAPTER 25

*E*lliot answered the door to find young Jimmy McCurdy leaning against it, red-faced and sweating, a telegram in his hand for Elliot. Elliot paid the boy and returned to the study. "It's from Declan," he said, when Thomas looked quizzically at him.

Thomas jerked his chin at the telegram. "What's it say?"

Elliot turned the yellow envelope over in his hands. He was still half in the dream, vision, whatever it was, and the doorbell had jerked him out of it so suddenly his heart was rabbiting in his chest and his hands shaking.

He'd never had a vision like that—not while he was awake, anyway. It was like his nightmares, in the constantly shifting images and the vague sense of a future threat. The same shared consciousness with the half-devilfish beast he experienced with Celeste and his mother, but someone else, too.

A different presence, out of step with his connection with the octopians, quieter and hard to pick out. It felt like Declan, even though he'd never sensed him like this before. That same confident resoluteness that he associated with his older stepbrother, with a thrum of worry underneath, probably worry about Elliot, since heaven knows Declan never worried about himself.

And now a telegram from Declan. "What the hell are you waiting for? Open it." Thomas's voice startled Elliot out of his reverie. He slit the telegram open with the ivory-handled letter opener from his desk and unfolded it.

Found a way. Home soon as it's done. D. Fitz.

"Found a way?" Thomas repeated, reading the message over Elliot's shoulder. "A way for what?"

Elliot didn't answer. A way for them to be together. He was sure that's what Declan meant. Declan had promised Elliot he'd find a way and he had. Elliot's heart swelled in his chest until he thought it might burst.

Thomas looked from the telegram to Elliot and then resettled himself on the sofa. "Ah. Found a way to change himself, eh? Figures. If Mohammed can't make it to the mountain, right?" He chuckled and shook his head. "Fitz always figures out a way to get what he wants."

Elliot's happiness faded as quickly as it had bloomed. "Change himself?" he asked. "What do you mean?"

Thomas looked up at him while he was resetting the chess-board. "Change himself into whatever the hell it is you are, no?" He shrugged, his thick brown fingers arranging the ivory pawns on his side of the board. "Come on, another game? I'm gonna beat you again this time for certain."

Elliot didn't move. He was standing in the middle of his study, his feet planted on the familiar rug, surrounded by furniture and things he'd owned all his life, but one mental step sideways, and he was back in the vision.

Of the creature that took his mother, his fiancée, and the normal life he'd planned for himself away from him. Back into that vertiginous feeling of being untethered from everything that made him himself. If Declan became an octopian, shifted the way Elliot did, then what would Elliot hold on to? Declan had been

Elliot's touchstone his entire life, what he'd clung to when his world lost all meaning.

When his mother had disappeared, Declan was there to comfort the frightened, grieving boy he'd been. When Celeste had disappeared, Declan had propped him up and kept him going until they found out what happened to her. And when Elliot shifted for the first time, Declan had held him inside his body and told him with words and his own obvious desire that Elliot was still himself, still Elliot, no matter what he looked like.

And then he connected the vision he'd had with the message in Declan's telegram. The massive devilfish that created the octopians was swimming toward Nance's inlet, heading toward Declan like an arrow in flight. The other octopian women, eyeing him the way they'd eyed Elliot when he'd found his mother. Speculating on what use they could put him to. With Elliot, they'd recognized him as one of them, and the prospect of mating with them like his mother had planned for him, fathering a whole generation of male and female octopians, had thrilled them enough to make him desirable to each of them. But it wasn't desire they had for Declan.

Or at least, not lasting desire, not an appreciation for mutual aid and purpose. It was the same short-lived interest they had in any sailor who happened upon them or who they sought out for a night. An itch to scratch, a temporary solution to a perennial problem. A man for a night, to slake their need and be discarded in the morning, with no care for any consequences.

It wouldn't work, Declan's plan. Elliot didn't know how he thought he could become one of them, but it wouldn't happen for Declan the way it had happened for his mother, or Celeste, or any of the other octopian women. Mating with the octopian women would only speed up the injury that fucking Elliot caused him. And mating with the giant devilfish? Not even Declan would go that far, notwithstanding his catholic tastes in bed partners.

Would he?

"No," he said, though he didn't realize he'd said it aloud until Thomas looked up at him.

"No, what?" Thomas asked.

"No, I can't let him do that," Elliot said. He glanced around the study, cataloguing what business he needed to take care of before leaving and what could wait until he returned.

"Why not?" Thomas asked. "If you're the same, then that solves your problem, don't it?" Thomas finished setting up the board and gestured at it.

But Elliot didn't want that for Declan. The pain and tension of shifting, the confusion and instability of being half one thing, half another, never quite what he was supposed to be. It was selfish of him, maybe, but Elliot needed Declan's rock-like stability to live with his own changeable nature.

Elliot was the water flowing along the riverbed, the waves crashing against the bluffs. Declan was the rocky gorge that held him and contained him, the cliffs standing firm, keeping him where he belonged.

Elliot suppressed a sudden urge to upend the chessboard and chuck the pieces as far as he could throw them. At Thomas, maybe, for his nonchalance about something he perceived as a quirk of nature instead of what it really was—a curse Elliot would give anything to reverse. At Declan, for his blithe readiness to give up what Elliot needed most from him. At that damned creature, most of all, for taking yet another person from him.

He clenched his hands into fists at his sides and closed his eyes. He reached out with his mind, feeling awkwardly for that quiet, faint connection to Declan. The other octopians' thoughts and emotions flooded into him, crowding his senses, overwhelming his ability to discern one from another. There were too bloody many of them, too much going on.

Thomas's hand gripped his shoulder, but Elliot shook him off.

He stumbled blindly to a chair and slumped into it, hanging his head between his knees and wrapping his arms around it. The sharp spokes of his anger pushed back against the horde of wordless chatter in his head, and he kept pushing forward, straining for the connection to Declan, feeling blindly for him.

A burst of pain flared in the back of his skull, just above the nape of his neck. It spread from center of his skull to the back of both ears, like the inside of his head was on fire. He ignored the pain and caught a fleeting sense of Declan, but it slithered away before he could latch onto it, and then Thomas had him by both shoulders and was hauling him upright.

"The hell are you doing?" he hissed. He was kneeling before Elliot, bracing him with his hands gripping hard, a worried expression on his face. "You gonna work yourself into a fit, you don't calm yourself down."

Elliot gave up trying to reach Declan and shored up his mental walls against the flood of thoughts and sensation from the octopians. The pain in his head eased, but his muscles ached like they'd been stretched beyond capacity. His limbs were rubbery and his hands shaking again, dangling limply between his knees.

"He can't, Thomas. It won't work, and I can't bear it if he tries. He'd have to," Elliot swallowed a lump in his throat and stopped. He couldn't say it, he wouldn't. Not even to Thomas. "I can't let him." His voice was thick and he ducked his head, so Thomas wouldn't see the tears burning behind his eyes.

Thomas squeezed his shoulders, and Elliot's head fell onto his shoulder like a string in the back of his neck was cut. "All right, amigo. But you gotta talk to him, sí? You can't keep this shit all bottled up inside."

Elliot nodded and lifted his head. Thomas looked into his face and must have been reassured by whatever he saw there, since he let go of Elliot and pushed himself to his feet. He went to Elliot's desk and fumbled for a pen and ink. "Should have kept Jimmy to take a message back to the telegraph office," he muttered.

"I need to get to him and stop him. Before it's too late." Elliot took the paper and pen Thomas held out to him. How long did he have before the devilfish reached Declan? His fingers shook as he scribbled the most succinct message he could think of—*Don't do it. Wait for me. E.*—and folded the paper in half.

"Thomas, I hate to ask," he began, but Thomas was already reaching for the message.

"I'll send it and make arrangements for the morning passenger steamship to Victoria. We'll find a ship going up the coast, or take a stagecoach over land, whichever's fastest."

Elliot nodded. "Thanks." His throat constricted, and he suddenly had to blink furiously to keep the tears at bay.

Thomas grasped his forearm and squeezed. "He'll listen if you explain to him, Elliot."

Elliot nodded. "I know. You're right. I just need to get to him before he does it."

Thomas squeezed his arm again and left for the telegraph office.

CHAPTER 26

*D*eclan piloted the small gig toward the *Albatross* later that afternoon. Elliot had proposed buying a steamship for the Far East route, but Declan wasn't ready to give his *Black Dove* up yet. The thought of the engine breaking down or running out of coal in the middle of the Pacific wasn't an experience Declan was interested in. That didn't mean he wasn't interested in exploring the *Albatross*, though.

Her utilitarian iron hull couldn't hold a candle to the beauty of the *Black Dove*'s wooden hull, but she was a fine-looking ship in her own right, despite the clutter of trawl nets, dredges, and tangles sprouting from her deck and dangling over her sides.

Declan came about to the starboard side gangway ladder, already lowered. Celeste was waiting on the main deck, though there was no sign of Captain Enid. He still wasn't sure he trusted the other octopian women after they'd kidnapped him from this very location last year. Hell, he wasn't sure he trusted Celeste, but if she had the answers he was looking for, he'd do whatever she asked of him.

All seemed quiet on the main deck. No sailors milling about, taking care of the routine chores needed to keep a ship in good condition, even when at anchor. Declan supposed they might be avoiding him the same way he'd prefer to avoid them.

Once he was aboard, Celeste led him forward on the main deck, past several closed doors and darkened windows in a long deckhouse. Declan glanced in a few of the windows. He wouldn't have minded a quick view of the upper engine room, but Celeste stopped at the second door forward of the smokestack. "This is the upper laboratory," she said over her shoulder as she opened the door and stepped carefully over the threshold. Declan followed her in.

The upper laboratory was the width of the deckhouse and had two windows on each side and a second door opposite the door they'd just entered through. The windows and the skylight overhead let plenty of daylight in, but Celeste flipped a switch, and electric lights flickered on, lighting the room as bright as sunlight.

"It's the first science vessel fitted with internal electric lighting," Celeste said, smiling a little at Declan's expression. "We have a Baird's evaporator and distiller that turns seawater into fresh water, as well, and provides steam heating." She gestured at a small heater on the port wall of the laboratory. Under the low hum of the filaments sparking in the lightbulbs, Declan imagined similar electric lights and steam heating on the *Black Dove*. Someday, maybe.

In the center of the room was a large square table with a lip to keep things from rolling off the surface and four sets of drawers forming the legs of the table. The aft bulkhead was furnished with built-in cases holding books and a variety of glass and metal apparatus behind glass doors, as well as a lead-lined sink in the corner between the cases and the heater.

"Science vessel?" Declan asked. She'd mentioned other naturalists and their methods in Nance's library, but Declan realized he'd no idea what had brought her to Nance's inlet in the first place.

Celeste looked warily at him, as if she expected him to mock her. "I'm conducting physical and biological investigations of the Pacific Northwest waters. Similar to the work done on the *HMS Challenger* ten years ago, though mostly focused on cephalopods and medusae."

"Like you did in Port Townsend?" Declan asked. "I remember Elliot telling me about some of your work."

She nodded and relaxed a little. "Something like that."

Celeste went to a cabinet in the starboard corner and removed several jars containing a rainbow of chemicals. Declan perused the books in the wall cabinet and pulled out a volume reporting the *Challenger*'s scientific results. He flipped briefly through its pages of illustrated specimens and wondered whether any of the volumes on these shelves described octopians such as Celeste and Elliot.

Celeste tucked the chemical jars into a wooden box and went to a hatch against the forward bulkhead, next to the chemical case. Gathering her skirts in her other hand, she descended a ladder. Declan replaced the *Challenger* report on its shelf and followed her.

The lower laboratory was even bigger than the upper lab; half again as long as the ship and probably spanning its entire width.

Worktables were installed on the port and starboard sides, and rows of brackets lined the walls above the tables, holding glass aquarium tanks filled with water and marine creatures lazily swimming in their enclosed watery homes.

The fore bulkhead had tall cabinets built in, with screened doors on the top half of each cabinet and open shelves below. The aft bulkhead had another long worktable with cabinets and drawers above and below the work surface and a sink at one end. A series of round portholes on the starboard and port sides provided plenty of light and air, but Celeste switched on the electric lights here too, which lit the room even brighter than the upper laboratory.

"That's why you have all these tanks of devilfish and such?" Declan asked. He tapped a finger on the glass, where a flock of paper nautiluses were floating in their translucent shells.

"Unlike the *Challenger* and similar missions, I prefer to keep my specimens alive, so I can observe them in as close to their natural habitat as I can recreate."

"And you just look at them?" Another tank held a pair of red octopuses with white spots. "That doesn't get boring?" Then a large reddish-brown octopus in a third tank changed colors right before his eyes, dark blue circles appearing all over its skin, and Declan couldn't stop an indrawn breath of wonder.

The octopus's skin morphed into a dark purple color, then erupted into ridges and scales that mimicked the texture of the rocks and coral of its habitat.

"Not boring, no," Celeste said, smiling. "I observe them, yes, and take notes on their behavior. What they eat, how they move, how they mate and reproduce."

She said it matter-of-factly, as if watching devilfish having sex was the same as watching them eat or move.

She opened one of the doors on the fore bulkhead cabinets and pulled out a drawer segmented into compartments, each holding an empty glass bottle or jar. "I take samples from each of them and compare them to discern characteristics that are shared or unique." She set the drawer on a worktable and returned to the cabinets.

"Samples?" Declan asked.

From a different drawer, she removed a leather case and brought that back to the worktable. She unrolled the leather case and selected a large syringe with a long needle, then a small glass vial from the drawer of empty containers.

Declan's stomach plummeted like the *Black Dove*'s anchor. Celeste caught his eye with a tiny smirk. Damn the woman, she looked like the cat who'd eaten the canary.

"I did say you might not thank me." Declan ignored that and

looked away from the needle glinting in the electric light. He focused on the large octopus crawling over the rocks in its solo tank.

"You understand that there are hundreds of species of octopus, but humans are unique among the animal kingdom. We octopians, even rarer. So, I take samples of blood, skin, anything I can get without harming the subject. Mr. Darwin talks about 'survival of the fittest,' by which he means that a species naturally preserves, through reproduction, variations of traits that give a greater advantage in perpetuating the species's survival. I'm interested in which traits we octopians share with octopuses and which we share with humans, to try to discern how we evolved to become what we are."

Despite his trepidation, Declan suppressed a smile at Celeste's earnestness. She spoke as if she were lecturing to a group of fellow naturalists, who were hanging onto her every word. He wondered what she might have done with her life had she not gone off on the *Poulpes* when it came for her the night before she and Elliot were to be married.

She gestured for Declan to sit on one of the stools tucked under the table. When he didn't move, she sighed impatiently.

"I cannot give you any answers you seek without more information."

He pulled out a stool and settled on it. Celeste took a bottle filled with clear liquid from the box that held the chemical and uncapped it. The strong acrid smell of pure alcohol filled the laboratory. She pressed a bit of cotton wool to the neck of the bottle, upended it to dampen the cotton wool, and had Declan roll up his sleeve. She swabbed the alcohol-soaked pad against the inside of his elbow, then tied a leather strap around his upper arm.

Declan turned away quickly and watched the ruby octopus in the nearest aquarium inch its way across the inside of the glass wall. Its small white suckers flexed and gripped the glass, and

Declan had a brief flash of remembering how Elliot's suckers felt against his skin. He tried not to move while Celeste held his arm. The needle pinched as it went into his skin.

"The call during the supermoon is tied to procreation, of course," Celeste said as she drew a quantity of blood from his arm. "Women with octopian blood experience the call as an inexorable pull to the water, to mate. The first time is with the male creature who contributes the traits that allow us to shift the way we do."

She blushed and tipped her head down, her eyes on the vial containing Declan's blood. She capped the vial, wrote something in pencil on a small tag she tied to the vial's neck, and tucked it into its space in the drawer. Declan could see how, after the day's work was done, she could slide the drawer back in place in the cabinet, minimizing the chance of dropping specimen containers while transporting them if the ship rolled unexpectedly.

She rose and took the syringe to one of the sinks and rinsed it with alcohol, then returned to the worktable. "Some women return to shore afterwards and give birth to children who seem human, but have the octopian blood in their veins. If they're girls, they may shift during a supermoon when they're grown. If they're boys, they may have enough of our blood that we can sense them. Elliot is the first male in generations to be able to shift form."

Declan already knew that Elliot was the first male octopian. He didn't know that there were human males out there the octopian women could sense, and he wondered what purpose that could serve the women. Perhaps it was how they found potential mates for the supermoon. He wondered if Marie had been able to sense his father.

"I can sense Elliot," Declan said. Celeste looked up at him, her expression suddenly sharp. "Does that mean I share this blood?"

"When did that start?" Celeste asked.

"This morning," he admitted.

"And not before?" She looked at him, her eyes slightly narrowed, like she was listening intently to something. It was similar to the look Elliot had when he was listening to Mrs. Jackman's thoughts. After a moment, she shook her head. "I don't sense you at all. But perhaps..." she trailed off and her gaze moved toward the aquarium with the ruby octopus, even if she didn't seem to be actually seeing it.

"Perhaps what?" Declan prompted her.

"I met your father only a few times," she said, "but Marie's told me a little about her life in Port Townsend."

Marie had lavished the same maternal love and affection on him as she'd given Elliot. He'd loved her in return, but had always known she didn't quite fit in with Port Townsend society. She was intelligent, like Celeste, and well-read, but she didn't socialize with the other matrons uptown. She spent much of her time walking along the shore, Sally had told him once, and sometimes disappeared for most of the day, coming back after supper and after Declan had tucked Elliot into bed, her dress smelling of salt spray and her hair windblown. He imagined Celeste had found a kindred spirit in Marie when she'd left Elliot for the octopians' den.

"They had a good marriage," Celeste said. "Marie said he was kinder in private, with her, than the gruff man I remember seeing occasionally at church." Declan smiled slightly. That was certainly true. His father had had little truck with religion, though he attended Sunday services when he was on shore. He'd probably paid little attention to the daughter of the rector at St. Paul's Episcopal Church. Hell, Declan hadn't recognized Celeste when he came home last year and found Elliot engaged to her. She'd been still a schoolgirl when his father had separated him from Elliot, and then it had been five years before he'd come home again.

As gruff and stern as Declan's father was to his crew and to Declan, he'd been a different man with Marie—softer, more patient. He'd smile more during his weeks at home than he did in all the months he spent at sea combined. Declan had never heard him say a harsh word to his stepmother.

He'd treated Elliot as his own son, too, despite the gossip that swirled around her about the circumstances of Elliot's conception. Even though their personalities had always grated against each other, Declan knew he'd tried to do his best by Elliot.

"They tried for more children, you know," Celeste said. "But every time Marie conceived, something happened, and she was never able to carry a child past the first few months."

"I didn't know that," Declan said. He remembered a few times when his stepmother had shut herself up in her room, and Sally had shooed him and Elliot from the house so as not to disturb her. Celeste nodded.

"I think she loved your father. She didn't say so, but she kept trying to give him more children, and we don't conceive easily, no matter who we're with. It's entirely possible that their feelings for each other created a connection that made them able to sense each other."

That would explain why Father had been so convinced Marie was still alive when she disappeared. Everyone else was sure she drowned during that terrible storm in 1873, but Declan's father had searched for her for the next fifteen years. Until he and Elliot finally found her and Celeste last year.

"Marie gave me some of her blood and told me injecting it during the new moon worked for my father, but she wasn't specific about how or why."

Celeste looked interested. "I didn't know that. Did you try it?"

"I mixed it with whiskey, but then ran out before the first supermoon this year." He looked away from her avid expression. "Elliot stuck me with some of his blood at the last new moon."

"Did it help?"

He shrugged. "Enough, I suppose. I'm back to normal now, anyway."

Celeste looked thoughtful. "I wish I had some of his blood to test. You've no idea how much I've been wanting to study him more closely. See what unique properties his blood has compared to ours."

Declan pulled the vial of Elliot's blood from his jacket pocket and handed it to her with a twinge of regret. Thankfully, Celeste didn't ask him why he was carrying it on his person, just took it from him with an avid excitement on her face. Keeping it in his pocket made him feel closer to Elliot somehow—which was disturbing, he knew—but if turning it over to Celeste helped her figure out how they could stay together, it was a small price to pay.

Celeste held the vial of Elliot's blood up against the nearest incandescent lightbulb, then plucked the vial of blood she'd taken from Declan from its drawer and held it up next to the first vial. Side by side, the difference was obvious. Declan's blood was a deep red, Elliot's darker, the color closer to magenta, almost violet.

"Now I just need one more sample from you," Celeste said, fetching a wide-mouth jar from the back of the drawer. She pushed the glass jar across the table toward him, then raised her eyebrows, and lowered her eyes until she seemed to be staring at the watch chain on his vest. He waited until she looked up at his face again.

"A sample of what?" he asked, not understanding what she was asking for.

She met his eyes, then slowly scanned down his body until she was staring pointedly at his lap. Declan suddenly realized what sort of sample she meant.

"No."

She just pushed the glass jar even closer to him. "I need a sample of your seminal fluid." She smiled slightly at his discomfort. "I did tell you that you mightn't feel like thanking me later."

"I can't just..." Declan started. "I mean, what in the hell? You can't ask a man to…" he gestured vaguely in the general vicinity of his lap.

Celeste folded her hands primly in her own lap. "Do you want my help or not?"

Declan covered his face with his hands. "Jesus, woman," he muttered into his palms.

"Oh, please," she said lightly. "There's no need for such prudery. I've never understood our cultural hostility to pleasuring oneself. If it feels good and hurts no one, why be ashamed of it?"

Declan lifted his head from his hands. "I'm not ashamed. It's just…there are some things that are private, goddammit."

Celeste stood. "I'll just adjourn to the upper laboratory, shall I?" She smiled sweetly at him, then turn to the ladder to the upper deck, skirts rustling as she climbed the steps. Declan dropped his head and let it thunk on the table's surface.

Christ almighty, what his life had turned into since getting back with Elliot. But if this was what he had to do to find a way to stay with him, well. Resting his forehead against the worktable's surface again, he snaked his hand into his trousers. Might as well get it over with, then.

He closed his eyes and called up the image of Elliot sprawled out before him, chest bare, hair wet and slicked back against his head, the pinkish red of his devilfish skin spreading into thick, muscular tentacles. His cock hardened, and a few beads of fluid leaked from his tip, slicking his hand as he stroked himself.

It didn't take long in the end, even if his warm, damp fist was a poor substitute for pushing into Elliot's tight heat. Several short, fast strokes, and he smothered a groan against the hard surface of the worktable pressing against his forehead. At the last second, he remembered to snag the jar in his other hand, shuddering as he spent into it. He cleaned his hand with his handkerchief and wiped the rim of the jar before corking it and setting it back on the table.

He took another few moments to let his breathing return to

normal and clear the images of Elliot from his mind before he pushed to his feet, tucked himself away, and tidied his clothes to look presentable. He left the jar on the worktable and ascended the steps leading to the upper laboratory, clearing his throat.

"I'm gonna—" he jerked his thumb at the starboard door to the laboratory. His face was hot, and he wanted nothing so much as to get off this vessel and away from this strange woman. "You'll let me know when you've studied your samples, yes?"

She nodded back. "Of course, Captain."

"Fine, then. You know where to find me." He couldn't think of anything else to say to her, so he turned on his heel and left the laboratory.

CHAPTER 27

"Elliot!" Someone was holding him back, keeping him from reaching his goal. The same voice snarled behind him, "Mierda, stay back, I said!"

A flurry of activity surrounded Elliot, but he ignored everything but the danger in front of him. His heart was pounding, and a surge of energy coursed through him as he lunged forward. He brought his weapon up, intent on slashing and slicing his enemy to ribbons, but his arm was caught in a hard grip, and the bones in his wrist ground together.

"Elliot," the voice at his shoulder said again, more placating than angry now. "Wake up, amigo. Whatever you're seeing ain't real."

Elliot struggled against the arms holding him, but the voice kept murmuring in his ear, and the soothing words eventually cut through the cloud of danger Elliot felt around him. He snapped his head up, intending to ram the back of his head into the face of whoever was holding him, but froze when he suddenly realized he was awake.

And cold, as a stiff breeze plastered his sweat-soaked shirt against him. His heart was still thumping in his chest, and he blinked several times to moisten his burning eyes. When he tried to bring a hand up to rub them, he realized both his arms were still held behind him. He cleared his throat, which was raw as if he'd been screaming, and croaked, "Let go of me, damn you."

The rough hands holding him tightened briefly, but then eased. "You with me, Bishop?" It was Thomas, breathing heavy next to his ear, his grip loosening enough to stop hurting Elliot, but poised to immobilize him again if necessary.

Elliot took a deep breath. "I'm fine." Thomas let go of him so Elliot could turn around, but hovered close, his weathered face creased in concern. Elliot looked around to get his bearings. He was on the foredeck of the lumber schooner they'd boarded yesterday afternoon. Thomas had arranged their passage with the lumber schooner's captain through a mutual acquaintance after they reached Victoria, as it was the fastest route up the western coast of Vancouver Island.

Nothing was threatening him, except perhaps the ring of sailors behind Thomas, glaring at him with unfriendly suspicion. The wind blew his hair across his face, and he finally had his hands free to rub at his burning eyes, when he realized his right hand held a short copper harpoon with a wicked barbed tip.

Thomas took a step back as he lifted the harpoon, and Elliot saw the bloody gash across his forearm. "Christ, Thomas, did I hurt you?" he said, letting it fall to his side to point safely at the deck instead of at his friend.

"Oughta lock you in the brig and throw that damned thing overboard," muttered one of the sailors behind Thomas.

"Better to run 'im through with it, then toss 'im overboard and keep the spear," retorted another. There was a murmur of agreement among the rest at that.

Thomas swiveled around to face them. "Ain't you lot got duties? The hell kind of vessel your captain runs with the whole damned crew gawking at a paying passenger?" He waved a hand at them, not the one attached to his injured arm, and Elliot opened his mouth to—well, he wasn't quite sure what. Apologize, maybe. He'd been sleepwalking, he realized that now, and having a nightmare.

Thomas managed to convince the crew to return to their stations, a few still casting black looks at Elliot, and then returned to Elliot with a tattered wool blanket.

"What happened?" Elliot asked him. He was in just his shirt, untucked from his trousers, his vest and jacket who knew where, and he shivered against the damp fabric clinging to his still-clammy skin.

Thomas wrapped the blanket around his shoulders, and Elliot held the harpoon carefully away from him, barbed tip pointing down. He couldn't let go of it yet, and Thomas seemed to understand that, because he didn't try to take it away from Elliot. "You tell me," he said. "You been tossing and turning all night, muttering nonsense in your sleep." He fidgeted with the blanket, tugging the edges of it closer together, but then stepped back and leaned against the rail.

"You finally seemed to calm down just before dawn and I got a few winks in, but then got woke by a commotion on deck. Came up to find you swinging that damned thing around like the hounds of hell were after you." He jerked his chin at the harpoon still clenched in Elliot's hand. "Who was after you?"

The details of the dream were lost in the confusion of waking from his sleepwalking, but the sense of danger stalking him, or someone he loved, still weighed him down. He glanced up and down the schooner's deck. Stacks of lumber planks were piled high on each side of the deck, and the crew had finally stopped staring at him and returned to their work. There was nothing out of place, no obvious danger, and he shrugged and turned to face the horizon.

"I don't remember." At Thomas's skeptical snort, he tried to sound convincing. "No, really, I don't. I know I was in some sort of danger, but I don't recall the details."

"The hell you brought that thing for, anyway, other than to cut me to ribbons?" Thomas didn't sound terribly concerned about that prospect, but Elliot felt a stab of guilt.

"It's not for you," he said. He felt better holding the harpoon, safer, more prepared for whatever was coming, but also distinctly uncomfortable. Touching the copper shaft with his bare hand gave him an unpleasant sting, like grasping a handful of nettles. He bent and laid it on the deck, then stepped one foot on it, to keep it from sliding along the deck. And to keep it near to hand if he needed it.

Thomas swiveled and rested his elbows on the rail next to Elliot, his hands loosely clasped. Blood from the gash in his forearm dripped sluggishly along his skin and off his arm into the ocean. Elliot took his handkerchief from his pocket and turned to face Thomas. "Let me see your wound," he said.

Thomas stood stolidly next to him while Elliot dabbed at the wound with his handkerchief. The wound wasn't as deep as Elliot had feared, and the blood was already slowing. He folded the handkerchief into a thick rectangle, pressed it firmly against the wound, and stood there for a few moments, holding Thomas's warm arm sandwiched between his hands, listening to the gurgle of the rushing sea beneath them.

"I'm sorry for hurting you," he finally said, not looking at Thomas. He felt Thomas shrug.

"It's just a scratch, Bishop." He let Elliot wrap the handkerchief around his arm and tie the ends in a small knot to keep the wound covered. When Elliot was done, Thomas leaned his back against the rail and looked up into Elliot's face. He was several inches shorter than Elliot, but a reassuring presence. He didn't smile much, but at least he wasn't afraid of Elliot, even though Elliot had tried to harm him. After a few moments of quiet, he said, "Who's it for, then?"

Elliot glanced at the harpoon at his feet, then the dark waters of the Pacific. The threat from his nightmare rose in his mind, but he pushed the dread back. It wasn't after him, he realized now. "My father," he said, suddenly too tired to come up with a lie.

"The senior Captain Fitzgerald?" Thomas's voice held a note of surprise. "Ain't he dead, a year ago now?"

Elliot couldn't remember what he and Declan had told the *Black Dove*'s crew last year when they left the cavern where his stepfather had died, poisoned by the ink of the creature that made Elliot what he was, but killed out of mercy by Elliot's mother. He supposed Declan must have told Thomas and the rest something, since the *Black Dove* had carried Elliot and the Captain to the octopians' island den to rescue Declan, but only Elliot and Declan had returned.

"Not him." He glanced at Thomas. "You do know I'm not related to Declan by blood?"

Thomas shrugged. "'Course. Captain Fitzgerald raised you, though, didn't he?" He had, and for the first time, Elliot let himself feel a measure of grief for the man who'd taken on the responsibility of a bastard boy not his own. Which only heightened his desire to take his revenge. "This other father you're after," Thomas continued, "You expecting him to suddenly appear on board a schooner at sea?" He didn't sound skeptical, just curious. Like he'd believe anything Elliot told him. Which, come to think of it, so far he had.

Elliot shrugged. He wasn't ready to explain who his real father was, though. Not even to Thomas, who'd been so far impossible to shock, but knowing Elliot shifted into a half-devil-fish was one thing and seeing the creature that his mother had described as his father was another. Even Elliot had a hard time crediting how his mother had become pregnant with him.

When Elliot didn't answer, Thomas pushed off the rail. "Sleepwalking again, like you did on the *Black Dove* last year? We maybe should have gone over land after all."

"Maybe," Elliot said tiredly. He'd woken a few times during

last year's voyage, on deck with no memory of how he'd gotten there, clinging to the *Black Dove*'s shroud and about to jump into the sea.

Thomas turned his gaze forward, past the schooner's bowsprit. "Well, we'll be at Nance's in a few hours. At least tonight you can sleep in a proper bed." He raised an eyebrow at Elliot. "Maybe tie yourself to it, eh?"

Elliot nodded. The nightmares he could handle; he'd had them off and on since he was a boy, though nothing kept them at bay better than sleeping pressed against Declan's warmth, which he missed like the ache of an amputated limb. A few more hours and he would be at Declan's side, and he'd make sure nothing harmed Declan.

Thomas slapped him on the back and left Elliot staring down at the water rushing past the hull, alone. He couldn't see any devilfish under the surface, but he knew they were there.

CHAPTER 28

*D*eclan spent the next several days in an agony of waiting. Waiting for the new moon and another injection of Elliot's blood because Celeste wanted to see what difference that made to the samples she took from him. Waiting for Celeste to explain what the devil she was doing with all the samples he gave her. Waiting for answers that would allow him to go home to Elliot.

Declan hadn't seen Celeste in those days, either. To collect her samples from Declan, she sent a member of the *Albatross*'s crew, a small woman with deceptively delicate hands that wielded her syringes with practiced ease, but gripped his arm with wiry strength while she was pushing the needle in. She spoke little and had a no-nonsense air about her that made it somewhat easier to comply. She took scrapings from various sections of his skin and the inside of his mouth, what seemed like an endless quantity of his blood, and more samples from places he tried not thinking about.

As the days passed, he tried to keep himself occupied with things other than missing Elliot. He joined the rest of the crew in careening the *Black Dove* on the beach and scraping barnacles off her hull, then giving her a fresh coat of paint. Reginald had looked askance at him when he suggested it, but for fuck's sake, he was going out of his mind with boredom, and if he couldn't go anywhere or conduct any business for the next few weeks, at least his ship would be in tip-top shape when he could.

He read a selection of books from Nance's library, went for walks along the shore, bathed in the hot spring in the mornings, and drank whiskey with Nance in the evenings. This afternoon, he was sprawled on a sofa in the library, smoking while he listened to Nance play piano, when a soft tap came at the door.

"Captain Fitz?" Joey's blond head peered around the open door. Nance's fingers fumbled to a discordant end.

"Joey!" she said, hustling to the door and drawing Joey inside. "Haven't seen you in days, love. Just because you sleep in the bunkhouse don't mean you can't have a meal with your old mam now and then, does it?"

Joey's cheeks pinkened, but he submitted to Nance's coddling as she tugged his jacket straighter and licked a thumb to smooth a strand of hair off his forehead. "I'll fetch something from the kitchen," she said. "And then I want to hear what you've been on about lately." She bustled from the library, calling for Betsy to put the kettle on.

Joey came all the way into the library and set the now-familiar small leather valise on the edge of the big table in the middle of the room. "When the hell did you become her assistant?" Declan demanded.

Joey shrugged, and the tips of his ears turned pink. "Everyone else was busy, and I wasn't doing nothing, so I offered."

Declan snorted. "Clearly, I need to find more work for you to do. Other than jabbing me with needles."

Joey's expression turned earnest. "She showed me how. I been practicing, and she says I got a natural aptitude for it."

He glanced between the valise and Declan with an apologetic smile, and Declan sighed. He swung his feet from the sofa and straightened up, then knocked the ashes from his pipe bowl before laying it next to the book he'd abandoned and joining Joey at the big table. "What the devil is she doing with all these samples?" he grumbled, not expecting Joey to answer him.

"Looking for signs of compatibility," Joey said. "She's looking to suss out what makes humans and octopians different and what's same-like."

At Declan's surprised look, he shrugged. "Well, there gotta be some things that are the same, yeah? I mean, you and she both got two arms, a head, and a heart that beats inside your chest, don't you? Folks like her look just like people on their outsides. When they're on their two legs, anyway. She's looking at what makes them same or different on their insides."

Joey took a selection of small vials and jars from the valise as he spoke and lined them up on the table next to it. Then he brought out that damnable syringe, big needle already affixed to it. Declan looked quickly out the library windows. He still didn't like being stuck with the damned thing, but it was easier if he didn't look at it or watch when blood was taken or injected in his arm.

"What's she found, then?" Declan asked, staring fixedly at a copse of cedar trees visible through the window, some yards from the house.

Joey tied the leather strap around Declan's upper arm and squeezed his elbow as he stuck him with the needle. "She says that Elliot's daddy—you know, the one who made them?" Declan could hear the question in Joey's voice. He wasn't talking about Declan's father, Elliot's stepfather. Declan nodded.

Joey continued, "He's got some sort of chemical in him that he probably got from his ancestors. It's like the ink regular octopuses—the ones as don't shift—shoot out to paralyze their prey. Just like with fish or crabs or whatever, this chemical in Elliot's daddy affects a regular man's nerves. Makes his arms or legs not work right." Declan was familiar with that phenomenon. "Too much of it can stop a man's heart from beating."

"And the octopian women have this chemical, too?" Declan asked.

Joey nodded. "They gotta, else they wouldn't be able to be with him, you see? But Celeste says the chemical is probably different in them, because part of them's human too. So they inherited a little bit of something from their daddy and a little bit of something else from their mamas, and that mixes into something unique in them."

He'd finished taking Declan's blood and tucked the vial away in the valise. Declan felt a little less squeamish with it out of sight. "You're on a first-name basis with Celeste now?" Declan asked.

A dreamy expression crossed Joey's face. "She knows so much about all kinds of things, Captain. You saw the books in her laboratory. She's read nearly all of them. And she writes stuff, too. Letters to other naturalists and important men at universities, telling them about her studies and asking them questions about theirs. She's the smartest person I ever met." He ducked his head and fiddled with the strap of the valise.

Declan tilted his head to catch Joey's eye. "Joey, you haven't been with her, have you?" He'd heard those telltale giggles from the lower pools the morning after the supermoon and assumed some of the octopian women on the *Albatross* had found willing partners. But he'd not thought about who Celeste might have been with. Not wanted to think about that, truly. He'd no desire to be speculating on Elliot's former fiancée's taste in bed partners. Damnation, she hadn't gone after his first mate, had she?

Joey, though, Joey'd said he liked girls. Told Declan flat out he'd like to find a nice girl someday and marry her. "Nice" might not the first word Declan would use to describe Celeste, but she was pretty enough, and around the same age as Joey. He could understand the lad's attraction to her; for Christ's sake, he'd seen firsthand how the supermoon enhanced an octopian's sexual desire.

But Joey deserved a woman he could be with long term. Marry, even, as long as his birth record wasn't found out. Not a brief interlude with a woman who'd already abandoned one fiancé and who'd picked him because he was convenient and she was desperate.

He glanced at the library's open door. Nance hadn't returned yet, and he couldn't hear her voice or footsteps from the kitchen, thank God. Better she not find out her only child had fallen for an octopian woman yet.

"Joey, you know you can't be with her forever. Once our business here is finished, she'll sail off, and chances are, you'll not see her again."

Joey took a long stick with a bit of cotton wool stuck to the end and gestured to Declan to open his mouth. He did, and Joey stuck the stick inside, twirling the pad against the inside of Declan's cheek. It was one of the routine samples that had been taken from him each time, but this time, Declan got the distinct impression Joey had chosen this moment to keep Declan from speaking further.

When he pulled the stick out and upended it into a clean vial, Declan tried again. "Jo-Jo, listen to what you just told me about how humans and octopians are incompatible. You said she told you being with an octopian woman can stop a man's heart. That could happen to you."

Joey looked unconcerned about that prospect. "Could happen to you, too."

Declan snorted. "I'm well aware. All the more reason for you to not replicate my mistakes." Joey was the nearest thing to a son Declan would ever have, and he'd be damned if he let Celeste hurt Joey. If Joey was with her for just one supermoon, perhaps he'd be all right, but he should end it before what had happened to Declan happened to him, too.

When Joey didn't say anything, he tried another tack. "You've just met her, lad, you can't possibly be in love with her. There's plenty of other women out there. You can find one who's more compatible."

He could order the lad to stay away from her. Joey had never challenged his captain directly, not even off-ship and on a subject unrelated to their working relationship. And Declan cared about the lad too much to lose him to Celeste Brady, of all women. Couldn't she have found someone else to meet her needs?

"She's the only one I've found who likes me the way I am," Joey said flatly. His face took on a mulish expression. "I ain't giving that up without a fight. Ain't that why we're here? To find a way to make it so you and Mr. Elliot can be together without anyone's heart stopping?"

Declan shook his head. "It's different with me and Mr. Elliot. We..." He stopped, unable to explain what was different about him and Elliot without revealing too much. "We've got a lot of history, that's all." He took a breath and tried his last card. "What would your mam say, Jo?"

"About what?" Nance took that moment to stroll back in the library, damn her. But if that's what it would take to convince Joey, so be it.

Joey beat him to it, though. He lifted his head and looked his mother in the eye. "Me stepping out with Miss Brady, mam. The captain thinks she's dangerous. But I don't care, because I love her."

Betsy bustled in just after Nance with a tray laden with dishes, a pot of coffee, and three ceramic mugs. Nance cast her eyes between Declan and Joey, saying nothing while Betsy set the tray down on the table and poured the coffee. When Betsy finally left, Nance took a seat at the table, stretched her legs out, and tugged at the fabric of her trousers. She lit a cheroot, blew a few lazy smoke rings, and took a noisy sip of her coffee. Then she leaned back in her chair, and said, "Ain't a one of those women that's not dangerous, Fitz. Miss Brady seems smarter than most, though."

Joey smiled at his mam so wide, Declan's heart broke a little to see it.

"She's the smartest person I ever met, Mam. You won't believe all the things she knows."

Declan held his hand up to prevent Joey from launching into another list of things his lady love knew. Nance glanced at him, a twinkle in her eye indicating she knew the flood Declan had prevented. "But she's an octopian. And not to be indelicate, but she ain't right for you."

He turned to Nance, hating himself even as he said, "You, of all people, know this, Nance. Look what happened to your sister. You don't want the same thing to happen to Joey."

The twinkle in Nance's eyes disappeared, and grief clouded her face. Before she could say anything, Joey interjected. "Aunt Charlotte was one of them. Which means I got a touch of it myself. Celeste showed me under her scope thing how our blood looks similar enough that she thinks it's going to be okay."

"She thinks?" Declan protested. "That's hardly reassuring, lad. And what if she's wrong?" He addressed Nance again. "It's too risky."

He knew it was futile even as he said it. Joey'd left home in large part because his mam resisted letting him make his own decisions and be the man he wanted to be. He'd hardly do as she bid now, especially against the lure of a woman like Celeste.

Nance looked at Declan, her weathered face showing more than her age, and shook her head. "Charlotte made her own choices, and I couldn't stop her then any more than I've been able to stop this fool from doing anything he wants to do."

She leaned forward to grasp Joey's hand, her eyes soft. He was surprised enough that he let her take it, and Declan saw the dawning of something in his eyes. Disbelief, maybe, or the faint beginnings of hope. Nance squeezed Joey's hand. "You gotta be who you are, son, and you can't help loving who you love. Ain't that right, Fitz?"

Declan gave up, for now. He'd speak to Celeste later, perhaps, ask her for more information about—what was the word Joey'd used?—compatibility. Appeal to her better sense, assuming she had any, if she couldn't convince him that Joey would be safe with her.

Declan submitted to the rest of the indignities Joey subjected him to with as much grace as he could muster. Joey stabbed him that infernal needle again, this time filled with Elliot's blood, since tonight was the new moon. He handed Declan a jar, and Declan adjourned to his room upstairs to provide the last sample. When he returned to the library, Joey and Nance were chatting with each other more comfortably than they had in years.

Declan handed over the jar, his face hot, and tried not to look at Nance. Thankfully, Joey tucked it away quickly in the valise and closed it, flipping a wide strap over the top and buckling it down. Declan cleared his throat. "When will Celeste be done studying whatever she's studying?" He'd tried to be patient so far, but he needed some goddamn answers and he was tired of waiting.

Joey swung the valise off the table and went to kiss his mother's cheek. "Couple more days, I think. She's waiting on one more thing."

Declan groaned internally. Not more samples from him, he hoped. "What's she waiting on?"

Joey shrugged. "Dunno. She doesn't tell me everything. I'll tell her you asked, though."

"Bring her 'round for supper some night, won't you, Jo?" Nance smiled back at the great beam on Joey's face.

"I will, Mam. Promise."

She walked Joey to the front door, leaving Declan, frustrated and worried, in the library alone.

CHAPTER 29

*S*hortly before sunset, Declan set out on a walk. He told Nance he'd be back in time for supper, but he needed to clear his head, and there was only so much of Joey's lovestruck mooning over Celeste he could take. Of all the women in the world for him to fall for, it figured it'd have to be her. The lad just couldn't help but make his life as complicated as possible, apparently.

He hadn't set out intending to visit the hot spring, but found himself less than half a mile from the ocean's edge of it, almost without noticing where he'd been going. He quickened his pace toward it. He'd have a soak, maybe, while the sun set behind the low clouds gathered at the mouth of the inlet, then head back to the big house, hopefully in a better mood than when he'd left. Joey was his own man, and as much as Declan wanted to protect him, he couldn't very well keep them apart, especially since he understood what it was to love an octopian.

Before he reached the cliff at the end of the beach that formed the chasm where the hot spring flowed to the cold ocean, he caught sight of a familiar figure standing on the rocks at the ocean's edge. He blinked against a sudden gust of wind that tossed a spray of seawater in his face and squinted his eyes at the figure.

It looked like Elliot. But it couldn't be, of course. He knew that, even as he quickened his pace toward the cliff. Elliot was safely home in Port Townsend. And no vessels had arrived in Nance's inlet; he'd have known if one had.

Still, the figure on the rocks had Elliot's build, and the shape of his head. The waning light made it impossible to discern the color of his hair or to see his face clearly. It could be anyone, of course. A man from one of the logging camps farther north and inland on Vancouver. A native from one of the remaining Nootka tribes that had populated this coast before contact with whites had decimated their population. A sailor staying in Nance's bunkhouse, except that the only sailors staying in Nance's bunkhouse now were his own crew.

And something about the figure on the rocks tugged Declan toward him. Something like, yet not like, the connection he'd felt the night of the supermoon, that ribbon of light he'd used to see Elliot in his bedroom in Port Townsend.

If it was Elliot, somehow here without warning, he'd picked a damned inconvenient place to take in the sunset: at the base of a tumble of boulders, nearly in the water. Declan lost sight of him a few times, clambering over and down the boulders, scraping his hands on sharp edges, twisting his damn ankle when one foot slipped between two rocks.

He'd opened his mouth when he came within earshot of Elliot to chastise him for putting himself in danger, but before he could get the words out, the figure disappeared. Declan scrambled over the boulder he'd been standing on and peered down into the swirling ocean below. Tonight was the new moon. Elliot might have taken the risk of swimming during a new moon, when he was unlikely to shift, but neither of them knew this was for certain, and he'd never done so before. At least, not to Declan's knowledge.

The ocean's current swirled around the boulders at the base of the hot spring. The sun had dipped below the horizon, and twilight was settling over the path back to Nance's compound. It must have just been a trick of the light. It wouldn't be the first time the ocean had made a man see something that didn't exist.

Declan dipped his hand in the cold water and wiped it over his face. He was tired and no longer in the mood for a soak in the hot spring. The light was fading fast, and the clouds obscured any stars that might light his way back to Nance's. It was time to head back.

Before he could push himself to his feet, a cold wetness coiled around Declan's wrist, and he jerked his arm away instinctively. It didn't release him, though, and he looked down at a thick tentacle, thicker than his own arm, wrapped around him from wrist to elbow. In the fading light, it was a dark purple, and he pulled back against it, to no effect.

Another tentacle broke the water's surface and grabbed his other arm. His hand closed into a fist, and he jerked back, but the thick muscle tightened around his wrist like a vise until his fingers went numb.

Not Elliot's. He knew that. Elliot's tentacles were slimmer, a rose color that lightened to pale pink at the tips. These were thicker, stronger, and Declan barely had the presence of mind to inhale a lungful of air before they pulled him under the water's surface.

More tentacles wrapped around his body, snugging him up against a firm but giving presence. Declan struggled against them, but they tightened steadily until he was squeezed hard enough against whatever was holding him that he couldn't move anything. His chest started to ache, his ribs compressing and his lungs burning with the need to breathe in more air.

He twisted and squirmed as much as he could, which wasn't much, and another tentacle wound around his neck, squeezing even tighter. He was desperate for air now, turning his head from side to side, futilely seeking a spot loose enough to gasp for breath. Bubbles swam before his eyes, the last of his air releasing through his nostrils.

And then an inky, dark cloud obscured everything in front of him. Thicker than the ocean water, a viscous fluid that swirled around his head and coated his face. It was warmer than the water surrounding him, and despite his brain shrieking at him not to breathe it in, some got up his nose.

It was like taking a deep draught of opium, hitting the back of his throat and spreading through his body. His fingers and toes tingled and went numb, and he felt his muscles go slack within the tentacles holding him. The tentacle around his neck loosened and withdrew, and Declan could feel his body being turned around in the creature's hold.

It pressed his face against something firm and rubbery. A funnel or tube, the opening of which spread wide enough to cover his nose and mouth. Cool air brushed against his lips, and Declan breathed in precious oxygen.

He still couldn't control his arms or legs, but he could breathe as long as he stayed still. The muscles of the creature holding him shifted, and he realized vaguely that they were swimming now, though he couldn't see where they were going. His mind drifted, and a blank fog washed over him. He struggled to remain conscious as long as he could, but the swift undulations of the creature carrying him, the soft puffs of air against his lips and nose, and the effects of the ink cloud lulled him to slumber.

When he woke, he was lying on a cool, hard surface. He slipped in and out of consciousness, the fog of confusion in his mind clearing slowly, like clouds drifting apart reluctantly. His head throbbed, with a dull ache in his temples. His mouth wasn't the same cotton-dry that came after a night of too much whiskey, but the sluggish heaviness of his limbs was far too reminiscent of taking opium.

He pushed up on one elbow and took in his surroundings. He

was alone, or at least he couldn't see anyone or anything in his immediate field of vision. Stretched out on some kind of stone, uneven with dips and small depressions, but smooth under his fingertips. Worn smooth, maybe, like water does to stone. Water definitely nearby; he could feel a damp coolness in the air and hear the muffled ripple of gentle waves nearby.

He turned on his side and looked down his body to assess its condition. Two legs still, stretched out akimbo as if they didn't belong to him anymore, and he couldn't feel the waterlogged fabric of his trousers clinging to them. Christ, what his life had come to that he could look at his own two legs and feel a slight surprise there weren't more.

Two arms, also, which functioned somewhat better than his legs. He got himself seated all the way upright and looked around him. A cavern, dark and close at the back of it, where he was. A wide pool of dark water in front of him and a shaft of weak sunlight on the other side of pool. Which at least meant he wasn't going to run out of air in here. The walls glittered with phosphorus, and answering glimmers winked in and out in the water. The smell of sulfur was strong enough to clear the remaining haze from his mind, and Declan was finally able to place himself.

He had to be somewhere near the hot spring, and therefore, no more than a couple of miles from Nance's compound. This was far better news than the last time he'd been kidnapped by octopians, when he'd awoken on a ship in the middle of the Pacific Ocean. Once he got some answers and figured out how to get out of the cavern, he could get back to Nance's quickly and easily.

He was still wearing his shirt and vest, as sodden as his trousers, and he patted at the pocket that held his watch. Still there, by some miracle—the chain hadn't detached from its button—but stopped. He shook it a little and tapped at the glass face. Stopped at a few minutes before eight o'clock, but impossible to tell whether it had stopped in the morning or evening.

He tucked the watch away and eyed the cavern's opening. The ledge he was sitting on petered out a few feet away, and the only way to get to the entrance was to swim across the pool. He eyed his own legs, the feeling starting to return in pins and needles down his calves, and wondered what it would take to shift into a devilfish form like Elliot.

As if in answer to that question, the pool's surface rippled, and an astounding sight emerged. First, the head of a giant octopus, bigger than any Declan had seen before, yet vaguely familiar. Also unlike any octopus he'd seen before, its flexible, oblong body stretched and firmed as it rose above the waterline, lengthening and expanding into a shape that was distinctly man-shaped, with a broad torso, thick neck, and head only slightly disproportionately larger than its body. That is, if any man had deep purple skin, huge amber eyes, and a pair of tentacles in place of arms.

"Son of a bitch," Declan whispered to himself. The head of the figure before him nearly brushed the ceiling, and his body blocked Declan's view of the cavern's entrance. His skin paled to the color of the lilacs Declan remembered Marie used to tend in her garden at the Bishop house, and his eyes gazed at Declan with human-like intelligence. This must be Elliot's father.

Declan had only gotten a brief look at him last year in the octopians' den, and that of him in his octopus form, tentacles joined to his massive mantle with a sprawling web in between. It stood to reason that he could shift as well, from octopus to human-like, if his offspring could shift from human to octopus-like.

"It was you who brought me here?" Declan asked. His voice was rusty and his throat sore, whether from swallowing seawater or the remnants of whatever had drugged him, and he coughed a couple of times into his damp shirt sleeve.

Elliot's father didn't answer, and Declan wasn't sure whether that was because he didn't speak English or couldn't speak at all.

He had a semblance of a mouth, along with a small protuberance with two slits under those huge, liquid eyes, which must function as a nose. And his chest rose and fell just like Declan's, so he clearly breathed air.

"There must be some way you have of communicating, eh?" Declan said. He pointed at himself, jabbed a thumb at the cavern entrance, then pointed at Elliot's father with raised eyebrows to indicate his question. He'd used gestures and simple sign language to communicate with sailors and merchants in some of the ports he'd been to where English wasn't spoken, but this was the first time he'd tried communicating with someone who couldn't speak.

Elliot's father nodded that massive head, and Declan realized he needed something to call him. "Guess you can't tell me your name, if you have one," he said. He tapped a finger on his lips and then quit when he realized his habitual gesture while thinking might be misunderstood as some effort to say something specific. "I'll call you...George."

He looked up and down at the figure before him, from his huge head, past his broad shoulders and massive torso, to where his lower half, presumably tentacles even thicker and longer than Elliot's own, were under water, keeping him upright. "Don't know that you look very much like a George, but it'll do, eh?" He chuckled to himself, and an answering merriment seemed to glimmer in George's eyes.

"Still wish there was some way to talk with you," Declan said, mostly to himself. Sign language wasn't going to be sufficient to find out what he really wanted to know.

Something nudged at him while he thought about what the hell to do now. Not physically, but a foreign presence in his mind, tentatively probing. Declan recalled that the octopian women seemed to communicate without words and that Elliot had something similar with Mrs. Jackman at home. He didn't quite know how to participate in that, but he tried opening his mind, the way a medium he'd once seen performing a séance had said to do.

A flood of images poured into his mind, a kaleidoscope of sea and sky and stone flashing before him. The images stabbed like needles behind his eyeballs, and a cacophony of sounds pressed against his eardrums from the inside. Declan winced and closed his eyes. "Whoa, there," he said and wrapped his arms around his head. "Too much, man, too much." The flood cut off as suddenly as it had started. Declan took a couple of deep breaths, his headache worse now, like a vise clamped around his temples.

He cracked an eye open and looked up at George, who had the same stricken expression on his strange yet beautiful face as Elliot got when he thought he'd hurt Declan. "I'm all right," he said, and damned if it wasn't the strangest thing to be reassuring Elliot's father the same way he'd spent his life reassuring Elliot. "Just take it easy, okay?"

George nodded and gingerly poked back into Declan's mind. This time, the images came in a trickle, starting with a vision of Declan himself, picking his way over the rocks toward the sea. Before Declan's eyes, George's appearance changed again, his skin lightening even more until it was a pale pink, almost the color of Elliot's skin. His facial features shifted to look even more human; he even had a red slash that looked rather like Elliot's mouth. His body shrank down to a more human-like size, and his torso compacted to a very attractive set of pecs and abdominal muscles. His resemblance to Elliot wasn't perfect; up close, it was obvious that he wasn't all the way human. But Declan now knew George was the figure he'd seen on those rocks.

He also felt the same shadow of his connection to Elliot, the ribbon of light and love that tethered him to Elliot. It was fainter here, between him and Elliot's father, a simulacrum of the real thing he felt for Elliot, but it was definitely what had drawn him out in the first place.

George's appearance gradually shifted back to how he'd

looked before taking on Elliot's and the images in Declan's mind were now of how he'd swum in his octopus form, Declan wrapped in his arms, through kelp forests and along the rocky shore until they'd squeezed through an impossibly narrow crack in a seamount and surfaced in this cavern.

CHAPTER 30

*E*lliot was the first one off the lumber schooner when it finally docked at Nance's long pier. The *Black Dove* was floating at anchor some yards away, and a steamship with the name *Albatross* painted on her hull was docked on the other side of the pier.

Elliot set off toward Nance's house at a rapid clip, weaving around Nance's longshoremen hustling to help unload the lumber, and leaving Thomas to make his courtesies to the schooner's captain and arrange for their baggage to be taken to the big house. The only thing on his mind was finding Declan and seeing for himself that he was safe.

As he passed the *Albatross*, something caused him to glance at her. A dozen or so women were arrayed along the main deck rail, and Elliot nearly tripped over a dock cleat, catching himself by the line tying the steamship to it. He shaded his eyes with his other hand and surveyed the women staring down at him.

Octopian women. Dressed in loose robes in browns and greens, the color of seaweed because that's what they were made of, with side slits that allowed their legs to split when they shifted. The same robes the octopian women made and wore at his mother's island. What the devil were they doing here?

A tall, dark-haired woman with thick braids draped over her bosom stood with her legs braced wide, the rest of the women flanking her on either side. Her stance reminded Elliot of Declan, standing on the *Black Dove*'s deck, radiating command and always the center of his crew's attention. He guessed her to be the captain of the *Albatross*, and she stared down at him with steady dispassion.

Elliot let go of the mooring line and resumed his trek up the long pier. He could feel the octopian women's eyes boring into his back, but the farther he got away from them, the less likely they'd be able to get into his head. Whatever they were doing here, his priority was still finding Declan.

But Declan wasn't in Nance's house. Nor was Nance herself. He searched the crew's bunkhouse next and recognized some of the personal items strewn around the bunks as belonging to the *Black Dove*'s crew, but there was no sign of Joey, Luca, Seamus, or Reginald.

He returned to the big house, calling Declan's name, then Nance's. It wasn't until he reached the back of the house, where the kitchen and scullery was, a section of the house he'd never been in, that he found anyone. He slammed open the kitchen door, and a small woman in an apron and white mobcap bolted up from shoveling coal into the big cast iron stove and shrieked.

"Betsy," Elliot said. He halted just inside the door, and held a placating hand out to her. "I'm sorry if I've frightened you."

Betsy clutched at the apron's fabric over her chest and stared wide-eyed at him. "Lord, you gave me a fright, sir." She blinked at him owlishly and then squinted. "Mr. Bishop, ain't you? I didn't know you'd be arriving here. Mrs. Carrigan didn't say anything..." Her nervous chatter trailed off and she swallowed hard. "Is there something you need, sir?" Her other hand lifted to tuck a bit of hair under her cap, and he saw that it was trembling.

The fingers still clutching her apron were white at the knuckles even with her work-reddened hands.

Elliot tried to smile at her to calm her fright. "I'm so sorry, Betsy. I shouldn't have burst in on you. I'm looking for Captain Fitzgerald. Or your mistress. Would you know where they are?"

Betsy swallowed again, and Elliot tried to rein in his patience. It was his fault the girl was flustered and if he wanted any answers, he'd do well to look less threatening. He let his arms dangle loosely at his sides, turning his palms toward her to show he had nothing in them to hurt her with. He couldn't help his height, but he took a couple steps sideways, not crowding her and leaving the doorway open so she didn't think he was trying to block her escape.

"Captain Fitzgerald?" she stammered. "He's dead, ain't he? I know I heard Mrs. Carrigan say so, didn't I? She gave the bell signal for his ship to another one, months ago."

Elliot tamped down the frustration that was building under his skin like a storm. Of course. To Betsy, Captain Fitzgerald was Declan's father. He opened his mouth to correct himself when the line between Betsy's thin eyebrows cleared. "Oh, you mean the younger Captain Fitzgerald. Of course, sir, sorry." She let go of her apron and flapped a hand in front of her face. "I'm all flustered, sir, and sorry about it. Captain Fitz went for a walk last night but never came back. Mrs. Carrigan and Miss Brady and everyone are out looking for him."

Elliot stared at her. Not again. Declan had disappeared from Nance's compound last year, taken to the octopians' den on his mother's orders, a ploy to get Elliot to comply with her plans for him.

But the octopian women's ship was still here. And now he realized who else had been aboard it. "Miss Brady?" He could barely speak her name aloud. "She's here?" Without waiting for Betsy's answer, Elliot spun on his heel and left the kitchen.

He found Celeste and Nance huddled together on the pier,

next to the *Albatross*. The octopian crew had dispersed, but Joey was chatting with Thomas a few steps away from the women, like nothing was wrong, when everything imaginable was falling apart. He nearly ran across the big lawn from the house to the pier and, for a change, let his mind open to Celeste's and the other devilfish women's thoughts, not bothering to keep his civil or conciliatory.

"Where is he?" he demanded without preamble when he reached them.

"He's with your father," Celeste said promptly. As if this were a trifle, a social call upon a neighbor, or a planned visit to a family member. "He fetched Declan last night, around sunset, but none of us have been able to reach him since."

An image from Elliot's nightmare flashed through his mind. "I telegraphed him before I left Port Townsend. To wait for me."

"Waiting doesn't appear to be Declan's strong suit," Celeste commented, and Thomas snorted in agreement behind her. "He insisted I call him. 'Going to the source,' I believe is how he phrased it."

Elliot took a menacing step toward Celeste. He'd never hit a woman in his life, but damned if this last year hadn't had a number of firsts. He loomed over her, his shadow from the late afternoon sun covering her like a shroud, but he didn't care. "What have you done?" he demanded. He clenched his fists at his sides to keep from throttling her.

She didn't cower before him, but Joey pushed in between them anyway. "Calm down, Mr. Elliot," he said. Thomas stepped forward as well, the copper harpoon clasped loosely in one hand. Elliot glared at both of them.

"Calm down?" he nearly shouted in their faces. He fixed his eyes on Celeste, half hidden behind Joey but still holding her ground. "I will kill him, you, and everyone descended from him before I let Declan become one of us."

Elliot switched his attention to Joey, who still had a placating hand stretched toward Elliot, his other arm behind him, hand brushing Celeste's waist. "I'm surprised at you, Joey. He thinks of you like a son, and this is how you repay him?"

Joey's eyes were steady, gazing back at him, though a tinge of pink colored his cheeks. "It's his choice," he said simply. "He'll do whatever it takes to be with you."

"And if that beast kills him?" Elliot shouted. The last time Elliot saw the immense octopus that fathered him, it released a poisonous ink that would have killed Declan's father if Elliot's mother hadn't killed him first. She said it was to spare him the agony of dying from the ink's poison, and Elliot had no reason to doubt her. Not on that score, at least. The same ink could kill Declan. Or he could drown. Either option seemed far more likely than Declan's plan succeeding.

"He won't kill Declan," Celeste said calmly. "At least, not on purpose. He'll—"

Elliot put a hand up to stop her, and Joey advanced another step toward him, Celeste completely behind him now. "Do not tell me what that monster will do to Declan." He scrubbed his hand over his face, feeling the hot prick of tears behind his eyes, but held them off. "For Christ's sake, Celeste, if you've ever cared for me, there has to be another way."

"Do you think I haven't tried to find one?" Celeste's calm finally broke. "There's so much about us that I still don't know. I'm working off my own observations, the limited information your mother's people have shared with me, and writings from naturalists and sailors who know even less than I do. I agreed to call him here because it's the only way to get answers I don't have."

Elliot started unbuttoning his jacket and vest and removing his collar. He stopped, collar studs cupped in his hand, and looked at her, a bright flash of hope warring with the fear and anger flooding through him. "So there is a way?"

"Maybe," she said. She stepped around Joey, toward Elliot, and stretched her hand out, palm up. Joey kept a hand on her shoulder, ready to yank her behind him again if Elliot made a move toward her. "But I'm telling you, Elliot, it's just a theory. I have no idea if it will work."

She wiggled her fingers slightly and he dropped the collar studs into her palm. "It won't turn Declan into an octopian—at least, I'm fairly certain it won't—but it might kill the both of you."

"I don't care," Elliot said promptly. "I won't have him change because of me. Not like this, anyway." He stripped his jacket and vest off, dropping them in a pile on the deck. He yanked his boots off and hustled out of his trousers. He kept his shirt on, since he absolutely would not disrobe entirely in front of his former fiancée, Nance, and half the crew of the *Black Dove*. He snatched the copper harpoon from Thomas with his right hand and gripped the ship's rail with his left.

"If anything tries to stop me down there, I'll kill it," he promised Celeste without looking over his shoulder. "You communicate better than I do with them. If they won't help me, tell them to stay the hell out of my way."

He didn't wait for her response, but took a deep breath, bent his knees, and dove headfirst from the side of the pier into the water.

CHAPTER 31

*E*lliot dove down into the depths, water pressing against his ears. Startled fish scattered before him as he kicked his legs as hard as he could. He floundered a bit, treading water until his legs lengthened and divided into the strong, sleek tentacles that made it effortless to keep his place in the water. He realized he hadn't even considered whether he'd be able to shift this far from the full moon. He'd just done it, hadn't needed to concentrate on the rhythm of the waves or harness the lust the full moon brought on. His fear for Declan's safety overrode his anxiety about shifting, or his fear of being unable to shift back. He would deal with shifting back after he found Declan.

He swiveled his head around to get his bearings in the vast expanse of the sea. There was the *Black Dove*'s hull ahead of him, and the dim shadow of the larger *Albatross* over his left shoulder. Sunlight trickled several feet below the surface, and Elliot could see a wide variety of marine life swimming around. Schools of fish in a rainbow of colors darted around, ignoring his presence, occupied with their own business. A sea slug floated past, strange and beautiful, its soft body white with colorful protrusions, wiggling in the water independently, seeking food or prey, or just enjoying the feel of water swirling around its extremities.

Elliot surfaced for air and slicked his hair back from his face. He was already leagues from the *Black Dove*, close to the entrance of Nance's inlet. He submerged again and swam around it, his tentacles bunching and extending behind him, his fear for Declan's safety propelling him faster than he'd swum before. As he swam, hugging the coastline, the kelp forest thickened, tall towers of thick green-brown blades gently drifting in the current. The light changed to a golden hue, reflecting off the brown kelp, and even more colorful fish swam through and around the long strands.

A seal peered at him from behind a thick kelp column. Elliot paused, his tentacles rippling to keep him steady in the water, the copper harpoon held loosely at his side, spear tip pointing down. The seal's large, liquid eyes gazed at him, and Elliot gazed back. He tried to tamp down the anxious fear pushing him to tear the kelp forest apart until he found Declan, and made himself listen. A prickle of something external tickled his mind. A sense of curiosity that wasn't Elliot's. The seal moved a little closer, and Elliot stayed still, tentacles barely rippling to keep him where he was.

He thought about Declan as he might appear to an underwater creature and projected that image in answer to the seal's overture. The seal swam even closer, nosing along Elliot's body, like a dog catching a person's scent. Elliot let it, but kept asking wordlessly about Declan. Had the seal seen him? Did it know where Declan was?

After what felt like ages of the seal snuffling and sniffing around Elliot, getting tangled up in the billowing folds of his wet shirt, the seal nudged its head against Elliot's hand. He moved his hand out of its way, but the seal followed him and nudged his hand again. Elliot kept his hand still, and the seal pushed into his palm. Elliot got the hint and petted its head, then ran his hand along its back. The seal arched into his hand, and Elliot couldn't help smiling as he petted and rubbed the seal's spotted skin.

You like that, don't you? he thought at it, and the seal twisted and turned over, exposing its underside, looking for all the world like a dog wanting a good belly rub. Elliot complied, and the seal closed its eyes and squirmed beneath his hand. Elliot projected the image of Declan again. *Man,* he thought. *Somewhere here. Needs help. Where?*

The seal corkscrewed under his stroking hand once more, then swam up his body and stuck a nose in Elliot's armpit. He flinched away from the tickle and then got the distinct sense the seal was giggling at him. The seal flicked its back flippers and shot a few feet from Elliot. It looked over its shoulder at him and then swam forward a few more feet. Paused, looked over its shoulder again, then pointed with its nose toward a spot where the seamount rose to the surface, towering over him, its rocky surface covered in anemones and star fish, its cracks and crevices dark mysteries holding who knew what dangers.

The seal gestured with its nose again. Elliot nodded and swam after it. It raced off toward the seamount, Elliot following. It stopped at a narrow crack in the rocky cliff, barely wider than Elliot's shoulders. He looked dubiously from the crack to the seal and back. The seal nosed into his hand again, and Elliot rubbed its head, scratching lightly just behind where its ears would be, if it had ears. It purred and wiggled against his hand, then twisted around and shot away through the water, its pleased satisfaction at its ability to help him filling Elliot's mind.

Elliot peered into the dark crevice. It was impossible to see more than a few inches inside, and he wished the seal hadn't left him. He didn't need to surface to breathe just yet, but he had no idea how far into this cavern Declan was. He presumed—he hoped—there would be a pocket of air inside to keep Declan alive, and he resolutely pushed out of his mind the thought of

Declan trapped inside, drowning in the dark, alone. Or worse, maybe not alone.

He squeezed through the crack in the seamount. Christ, how had Declan fit? After a lifetime of hauling lines on ships, his shoulders were wider than Elliot's own, and he didn't lack bones in his legs the way Elliot did at the moment. The light faded fast, and Elliot groped his way along a narrow tunnel. It seemed to be angling upward, more or less, and he hoped to God there wasn't anything spiny or poisonous clinging to the rough walls.

The tiny slits on either side of his neck fluttered. He'd displaced most of the water in the tunnel, and he was going to need breathe air soon. He kept going, pulling himself hand over hand along, and eventually realized he could see the shape of his hands. Either his eyes had adjusted to the dark, or there was some light ahead.

He was getting a little light-headed from lack of oxygen when he finally fell through the other end of the tunnel into a dimly lit cavern. The light came from millions of tiny bioluminescent creatures glowing and sparkling in the water. His head broke the surface, and he sucked in a deep breath of air.

He combed his wet hair back from his face with his fingers and looked around the cavern. It wasn't very large; about the size of his parlor at home, the ceiling no more than ten feet above him. The water was warmer inside it, maybe because it was sheltered from the open ocean, maybe due to another hydrothermal vent under the ocean floor, like the one his mother's island sat atop. More bioluminescent plankton clung to the cavern walls and ceiling, dotting the surface like constellations of stars.

A massive pale shape was half in, half out of the water in the center of the cavern. Shaped like a man, but wrongly so, with shoulders sloping to a pair of thick tentacles instead of arms, tapering to three slim digits at the ends, like rudimentary fingers. Its torso was as wide at its middle as at its shoulder, then spread wider still, and Elliot caught a glimpse of thick tentacles swirling and thrashing below the surface. Its head was bent down, focused on something lower than its eye level.

Elliot slipped around the edge of the cavern. Declan was huddled in a corner farthest from the tunnel Elliot had come out of. Alive, at least, thank God, though he looked cold and small, and his pale face shone in the dim light. He smiled at the beast before him and said something too low for Elliot to hear.

As if in response, the monster moved closer to Declan and stretched one of his tentacle arms toward him. Declan stretched his arm out to meet it, and that was all Elliot needed to see. He changed his grip on the copper harpoon and swam toward the beast, streaking silently across the width of the cavern's pool, streamlined and ready, keeping just under the surface to avoid getting caught by the monster's tentacles swirling in the dark depths below.

He thrust the harpoon into the monster's side, then slammed his shoulder into its body, catching it off guard and thrusting with his own tentacles, twisting the harpoon in its flesh, shoving against the beast's body to get it as far away from Declan as he could.

CHAPTER 32

*A*n unearthly scream rent the air, and George's body jerked as if shot. The water erupted into a swirling whirlpool of crashing waves and flashing tentacles. George swiveled to face his attacker, and Declan struggled to his feet. He leaned forward over the water, trying to figure out what the hell was going on. Something had come up from behind or below and stabbed George. Declan could see a barbed tip of some sort of weapon sticking through his side.

George twisted away from it, and the weapon tore free from his body. Blue blood welled from the wound in his side until George slapped a tentacle against it, still spinning and turning to find who had attacked him.

The water around him clouded with swirling darkness, far more than the inky cloud that had drugged Declan last night. Declan recalled the last time he'd seen this, when his father had stabbed George in his octopus form, and his stepmother had strangled him with her tentacles to spare him the pain of dying from the poisonous ink. Elliot's head surfaced above the water, then submerged in the cloud of ink.

"No!" he shouted, although he didn't know how Elliot would hear him underwater, in the midst of such a melee. "Elliot!"

Elliot surfaced a few feet away from George, still thrashing about. He stilled when he caught sight of Elliot, and Elliot paused in the motion of lifting his arm with the harpoon clenched in his hand, ready to thrust again.

"Elliot, stop!" Declan shouted, but Elliot didn't look at him.

"Stay out of the water, Declan," he said, a steel note in his voice that Declan had never heard before. "Once I kill this bastard, I'll get you back to Nance's."

"Damn it, Elliot, no. He's your father, and he hasn't done anything to hurt you." Except release poisonous ink into the water that could kill Elliot, but for fuck's sake, Declan could hardly blame him for acting in self-defense.

"Get the hell out of the water before the ink poisons you," Declan shouted.

Elliot ignored him, clutching the copper harpoon Declan's father had once stabbed George with, and cocked his arm back, ready to throw it. The two of them hung in the water, tentacles churning underneath to keep them afloat, and damned if that wasn't something, watching father and son face off against each other.

The wound in George's side had closed with only a small smear of blood on his skin. He was staring at Elliot, halfway between his octopus and man forms, and Elliot was staring back at him. Declan couldn't hear their thoughts, but when Elliot's face darkened and he pulled his arm back to throw the harpoon, Declan launched himself into the water between them.

Which was a damn fool thing to do, he knew even as he did it. The harpoon grazed his arm before plunging into George's upper tentacle arm. Declan plummeted down, water closing over his head, his boots and waterlogged clothes dragging him to the bottom.

He held his breath as he sank through the cloud of black ink. A flurry of grappling tentacles whirled above his head, and he kicked as hard as he could to get away from the ink and the long, whipping, muscular limbs. His arm was on fire, but he couldn't focus on that right now. He had to get to the surface before he ran out of air. He should fucking learn to swim sometime, if he was going to spend half his life in the goddamn water, instead of just sailing on it.

He churned his arms and legs, straining desperately to reach the surface, and managed to keep himself from sinking any more, but the faint light above him didn't seem to get any closer. Until a strong tentacle wound around his flailing arm, the uninjured one, and dragged him upward. His head cleared the water, and he gasped a mouthful of water and air, then slipped back under the surface.

When he was pulled up again, Elliot wrapped an arm around him and held him to his chest. Declan coughed a stream of water down Elliot's back and held on, struggling to get his breath back. He tucked his face into Elliot's neck, but after only a few moments, Elliot grabbed him by the shoulders and shook him hard. Where he got the strength from, Declan had no idea, because he still felt dazed from the lack of air and George's ink.

"What the hell was that, Declan?" Elliot didn't sound out of breath at all, damn him, but he was furious. So was Declan. Or he would be, once he got enough breath back to give Elliot what for.

"The fuck?" Declan managed to get out when Elliot stopped shaking him. His brain felt like mush inside his skull, and he struggled to get his thoughts together.

Elliot shook him once more, and despite his wooziness, Declan had had enough. He braced his feet against Elliot's thick tentacles under the water, shrugged one shoulder out of Elliot's grip, hauled back and clocked Elliot in the jaw. He couldn't get much leverage behind the punch—and he didn't usually solve his problems with fisticuffs—but he'd been in more than his fair share of bar fights and he knew how to throw a punch even in tight quarters.

Elliot's head rocked back, and he lost his grip on Declan, who pushed away from him and turned onto his back. He let the water buoy him, and the waves washed him to the side of the pool, where he pulled himself onto a large, flat boulder.

He settled himself on the boulder, legs still dangling in the water, and pushed his wet hair out of his eyes. He searched for George, who was nowhere to be found. The harpoon was stuck fast between two rocks, pinning a limp, pale appendage against them.

"What the fuck did you do, Elliot?"

"Me? What about you? What the hell are you doing here, Declan?" Elliot's face was pale with anger, except for a red splotch where Declan's fist had connected with his jaw, and his eyes were colder than Declan had ever seen.

Declan wiped his wet hand down his wet face and then on his wet shirt. His arm still stung where Elliot's harpoon had sliced through him. He plucked at the tear in the wet fabric of his shirt and craned his neck to look at the wound. It wasn't nearly as bad as he'd thought. Clean edges, not a lot of blood. Thank heaven for small mercies.

He stretched his other arm up over his head and pointed and flexed his feet, testing the feeling in his limbs. Everything seemed in working order, so maybe he hadn't been affected by the ink in the water. Elliot didn't seem to be, either. Maybe George hadn't released enough to harm either of them.

"Answer me, damn it," Elliot demanded. "What are you doing here?"

"Met your father," Declan said, and Elliot's face paled even more.

"So, he brought you here? For Christ's sake, Declan, you should be more careful. Why were you out where he could get at you in the first place?"

"Stow it, Elliot. He didn't hurt me."

"What did he do to you?" Elliot asked. "Did he fuck you?"

Declan stared at him. "No! Jesus, Elliot, what the hell would make you think that?"

Elliot looked unconvinced. "If he touched you, if you let him do that to you, I swear to God, I *will* kill him."

"He didn't," Declan snapped. "And jealousy is not a good look on you, Elliot. Especially not of your own father."

"Stop calling him that," Elliot snarled. "He's a monster, and if I hadn't had to save you from drowning again, I could have sent him back to hell where he belongs."

Declan felt a cold numbness seep through him, despite the warm water lapping at his legs. The look in Elliot's eyes chilled him more than the air cooling the wet shirt on his back. "You can't change who you are and where you came from, Elliot. And you might try getting to know him so that you can understand more about yourself."

"You didn't see how he looked at you and what he wanted from you," spat Elliot. "I will not let him turn you into one of us."

"Would that really be so bad?" Declan asked.

"Yes!" Elliot's voice echoed off the cavern walls. "He has taken *everything* from me. My mother. My fiancée. The life I could have had before he made me what I am now." He gestured at the tentacles Declan couldn't see below the water line, a look of disgust on his face that he'd never shown to Declan before. "I won't give you up to him, too."

Declan sighed. "That's not going to happen, Elliot." He was suddenly exhausted. He was the one who'd lost a night of proper sleep, been drugged with George's ink. Still, it was his job to reassure Elliot. As always. "He didn't try anything like that with me," he said, as soothingly as he could manage.

"You didn't see the way he looked at you," Elliot said again, a stubborn set to his jaw.

"Oh, for fuck's sake, Elliot." He set aside his irritation and groped for the connection that tied him to Elliot. He gave it a sharp imaginary tug, and Elliot actually jerked forward as if caught on the line. He held Elliot's eyes and did it again. "Don't you feel that?"

Elliot drifted closer to him, though still not close enough to touch. Declan tugged on the thread a third time, and Elliot swam up to him in a rush of water cascading over his legs. Declan put his hand on Elliot's head and slid it down his face to cup the side of his jaw, where he'd punched Elliot. "Don't you know by now that you are it for me?"

Elliot closed his eyes and leaned his forehead against Declan's knee. Declan stroked his hair. "I know I've had others before, Ellie, but no one else has ever mattered as much to me. You're mine, and I'm yours. Everything else is just shit we'll have to deal with. Together."

He looked across the pool to where George had disappeared. "I thought maybe this way, I could prove that to you." He hadn't gotten the answers he was looking for, but now that he knew how to communicate with George, he'd think of some other way of finding him again. If he could convince Elliot to stand down.

Elliot turned his face away, still leaning against Declan's knee, and sniffled. The sound echoed in the cavern. Declan kept stroking his hair. "I'm sorry," he said, his voice a little muffled. "It scares me sometimes, the things I'll do to be with you. I know that being with me is eventually going to kill you, and yet, I can't stop."

Declan glanced at the amputated tentacle still pinned to the rocks by Elliot's harpoon. "I know, Ellie. We'll figure it out. Celeste will help."

Elliot finally looked up at him but the bleak expression on his face tore at Declan's heart. "How can she, though? Every time we're together, something terrible happens to you. But I'm serious, Declan, I don't want you changing into a monster like me."

Declan socked him lightly on the jaw, careful not to press too hard against the bruise forming there. "You're not a monster, Elliot, and I don't want to hear that again from you." He smoothed a wet strand of hair from Elliot's cheeks and tucked it behind his ear. "Besides, nothing terrible's happened to me."

Elliot snorted. "That's not true. I stabbed you." He lifted his head and took Declan's arm in one hand, turning it to inspect the wound from when he threw the harpoon at his father. "I didn't mean to hit you. If you hadn't been the damn fool who jumped in front of him," his voice trailed off as he parted the rent in Declan's shirt sleeve. Declan craned his neck and looked where Elliot was running his thumb over Declan's upper arm. There was no wound, just a faint red line about six inches long.

Elliot grabbed Declan's other arm and twisted it this way and that. No wound on that arm, either, and no tear in his sleeve, so the left was definitely the one the harpoon had gone through. "What the devil?" Elliot murmured, but then Declan remembered.

"Your father," he said. "When you stabbed him the first time, I saw a big gash in his side, and blood running into the water. But then a few minutes later, it healed on its own." He poked a finger at his own arm, prodding here and there to see if it hurt. It was a bit tender, like a three-day-old bruise, but otherwise looked as if he'd merely scraped himself on a bit of rusty nail or something. "The blood," he said. "Of course."

"Whose blood?" Elliot asked. "What about it?"

"Your father's blood," Declan said. "It must have healing properties." He glanced at George's tentacle, still pinned to the rocks near him and leaned across to tug at the harpoon. He couldn't get enough leverage to pull the damn thing free from where he was sitting, so he gestured to Elliot. "Fetch that for me, eh?"

Elliot's face reflected his distaste, but for once, he didn't argue. He swam around Declan's knees and pulled the harpoon free. The severed arm fell into the water with a quiet splash, but he grabbed it before it sank and brought it to Declan.

It was one of George's upper arms, longer than Declan's leg. Its cool weight draped across Declan's lap, the tip dangling into the water, while Declan inspected the severed end. Instead of a jagged tear with blood leaking from it, the end was smooth and pink, closed over in an irregular shape.

"I had him," Elliot said. "I had him pinned there. But then you didn't surface and I had to find you. So, I took my eyes off him for long enough to get you and..."

"And he must have pulled against the harpoon hard enough to tear his own arm off." Declan winced. That surely hurt like a son of a bitch, but he could hardly blame George. He ran his fingers lightly over the closed-over end. "And yet, it's healed. See?" He showed Elliot, who shuddered and retreated a little. Declan kept stroking the smooth muscle of the severed tentacle in his lap, thinking, until he noticed Elliot's expression. He stilled his hands, folding them atop the tentacle.

He glanced from the arm in his lap to his own bicep. "There was blood on the harpoon when you stabbed him the first time," he said, working it out. "Which got into my arm when the harpoon went through me the second time."

"And healed you?" Elliot said skeptically. "That's impossible."

Declan looked at him, treading water with six tentacles below the waist instead of two human legs. "You're one to talk about being impossible, Ellie."

Elliot's face turned a bright red, which spread down his neck and chest. Declan tried to keep himself in check, he really did, but the stress of the day and Elliot's expression were just too much. He threw back his head and laughed until the cavern echoed. Elliot didn't join in, but his blush faded a bit and his lips twitched until a small smile crossed them, which lingered a while after Declan stopped laughing, even if it was a little bitter.

"Come on, Ellie," Declan said, slinging the heavy weight of George's tentacle over his shoulder. "We need to take this back to Celeste."

CHAPTER 33

*C*eleste was far more excited about the severed tentacle than any woman should be, in Elliot's opinion, as was Joey. He could barely stand to look at the thing himself, but Celeste fluttered about it as if it were the Holy Grail. He and Declan had made it back to Nance's on foot. The cavern turned out to be just behind the waterfall above the hot spring, so it was just a matter of towing Declan, still clutching the cursed tentacle, to the cavern's entrance, where Elliot had somehow managed to shift back without even thinking about it.

Declan had crowed delightedly and slapped him on the back, as if Elliot were a baby taking its first steps. He'd only barely resisted the temptation to snap something hurtful and cruel at Declan's shining face. It wasn't Declan's fault that Elliot couldn't manage shifting on his own before. None of this was Declan's fault.

And still, it was Declan who'd borne the brunt of everything since Elliot had learned what he really was. Declan, who'd accepted him and loved him, who'd let Elliot fuck him until he passed out, who'd been taken and drugged twice now by Elliot's own kind, and who still seemed excited rather than terrified to have met the monster—he absolutely refused to think of that beast as his father—who made Elliot what he was.

They'd arrived back at Nance's in a state of deshabille that would have been humiliating if Elliot had been less fatigued and frustrated. Declan had wrapped his coat around Elliot's bare hips to protect him from the worst of the brambles on the overgrown path from the hot spring to the back of Nance's big house. He'd still cut up his feet and barked his shins on the rocks scrambling down from the cavern's rocky entrance, and the underwater fight had left him quivering with exhaustion.

He submitted to Declan's cleaning his scrapes and bandaging his feet with less grace than he should have, but flatly refused Declan's suggestion that he rest while Celeste examined the severed tentacle. If Declan could manage to still be awake and coherent after his ordeal, Elliot could at least sit beside him, even if his attention kept wandering from the discussion happening in Celeste's upper laboratory on board the *Albatross*.

"I think we need to do it today," she was saying when his attention finally focused. He'd been watching the small ruby octopus meander across the inside of her glass tank home in the aquarium bolted to the port bulkhead. Her white suckers grasped and flexed against the glass as she extended her tentacles wide, as if she were testing the confines of the tank. Her entire underside was revealed, all the way up to where her suckers met at the mouth under her web.

Elliot averted his eyes. It seemed indecent to stare at her, which made him realize he'd been thinking of her as female and not as a thing. He turned his attention back to Celeste and Declan so he didn't have to think about what that meant.

"The new moon was last night, and I don't know how much that really matters, but Marie must have had a reason for advising you to do it then." Celeste was seated across from Elliot at the lipped table in the middle of her laboratory, Declan at his right and Joey on his left. The severed tentacle was on the table in front of them in a shallow pool of seawater, the thick end resting across the mouth of an open jar. The jar was half-filled with a thick, viscous, blue fluid, and more was trickling from a slit she'd cut in the tentacle's rubbery skin. The cut was closing up again; Celeste had already used her small, sharp scalpel on it a couple of times, since the wound kept healing itself.

"Might as well get it over with, eh, Elliot?" Declan said, then nudged Elliot when he didn't respond.

"Ah, yes, of course," Elliot said absently. But then, "Sorry, what are we getting over with?"

Celeste flicked her eyes up at him, but kept her attention mostly on her work. Declan sighed with impatience, but his voice was level when he said, "The transfusion. Haven't you been paying attention?"

Elliot looked from Declan to Celeste to Joey. Declan had his arms folded on the lip of the table. Joey was leaning toward Celeste, holding the jar steady while she drew the scalpel along the healed incision and squeezed more blood into the jar. They'd obviously reached some conclusion about what to do next while Elliot had been wool-gathering.

"Transfusion? What transfusion?"

Declan sighed again, but it was Celeste who answered, still deftly manipulating her scalpel and the severed tentacle. "I've agreed to try transfusing a mixture of your blood with your father's into Declan, in the hopes that will make the two of you more compatible without Declan changing into one of us."

She leveled a look at Declan. "The operative word being 'try' here. I've never done this before, the transfusions I've read about have had decidedly mixed success, and one or both of you could very well die during or afterwards. This is against my better judgment, but it's the best idea I've been able to come up with in the face of Declan's badgering." Her voice was acerbic, but her face softened as she continued to look at him, and Declan smiled at her, then Elliot.

"I have faith in you, my dear," he said cheerfully, then looked expectantly at Elliot. "What do you say, Elliot?"

"I, ah," Elliot started, then ran his fingers through his hair. It was mostly dry now, but his mind was still half back in the cavern and the conflicting swirl of feelings he hadn't had time yet to deal with. "Explain it to me again, please?"

"I told Celeste about how George—"

"George?" Elliot interrupted.

Declan gestured at the tentacle. "Your father. Needed something to call him, didn't I?" He cocked his head to the side. "I suppose I could have called him Mr. Bishop, but that ain't right either, is it?" He turned to Celeste. "What do you call him, then?"

Celeste shrugged, still gently squeezing the tentacle, her eyes on the trickling spurts of blood dripping into the jar. "Um, we don't, really. There's no confusion about whom we're addressing in the way we communicate with one another." She gave one last squeeze, set the scalpel down, and gently curled the tentacle around itself in the pool of seawater on the lipped table. She looked off into the corner, thinking. "He has a name, but it's hard for humans to pronounce." Her lips moved like she was sounding something out under her breath, but she shrugged again and smiled at Declan. "George works just fine."

"All right, then." Declan turned back to Elliot. "So, I told Celeste about George's ability to heal himself and how getting George's blood into my arm healed that scratch." Elliot opened his mouth to protest that it wasn't a scratch—he'd sliced Declan's arm nearly in half—but Declan quelled him with a stern look, and he subsided.

Declan went on. "We already knew that a bit of your blood helped me, the way it helped Father stay with your mother. So, Celeste here just put two and two together and came up with the idea of combining your blood and your father's."

"The problem with the way you've been doing it—and the way your father and Marie did it—" Celeste said, cleaning her scalpel with a wash of alcohol and putting it away. "I *think*," she emphasized, "because heaven knows I am not an expert in this—"

"Don't sell yourself short, miss," Declan interjected. "You're the most expert person we have on the subject of octopian biology."

"But not of human biology," she countered. "I'm not a physician. I'm just a naturalist, and all my knowledge comes from observations, not experimentation."

"You know more about everything than anyone else I've ever met," Joey offered, then blushed bright red when Celeste smiled at him. Elliot had nearly forgotten the boy was there, and the expression of puppy-dog adoration on Joey's face was matched by a soft affection on Celeste's. Elliot looked at Declan, who met his eyes with resigned acknowledgement. Trust Declan to have already noticed Joey was smitten with Celeste. Despite Elliot's own worries, he felt a small stirring of happiness for them. If anyone deserved love and acceptance, it was Celeste and Joey.

"What I was saying," Celeste continued, "is that your father used only a bit of Marie's blood, and it helped a little, but didn't solve the underlying problem." She nodded at Declan and Elliot. "Same with you two."

"So, Celeste initially thought that more of your blood might help more," Declan took up the explanation. "But there's a limit to how much of your blood she can take at once."

"I thought about mixing your blood with mine," Celeste said, as if she were discussing her favorite recipe for sponge cake. "But I'm not the one who's..." she trailed off and looked meaningfully at Declan, then Elliot. Elliot felt his face flaming with embarrassment.

Declan, on the other hand, seemed to hardly ever suffer from that condition. "When I saw that George's arm healed over by itself and that getting his blood into the cut on my arm healed it too, I figured there must be something Celeste could do with it."

He smiled at her like a proud parent. "She's the one who came up with the idea of mixing your blood together."

Celeste rose and went to the wall of tall cabinets. She knelt and opened the doors to one of the lower cabinets, rummaging amid clinking glassware. "It will make you weak," she said, looking over her shoulder at Elliot. "The amount of blood I'll have to take, though you should recover with a few days of rest. But I have no idea what effect it will have on Declan. My hope is that George's blood heals whatever internal damage he's experienced in being with you, and that a greater quantity of your blood mixed with his inoculates him against further damage. But, as I said, transfusions are risky, so you must understand that I can't promise anything."

"We'll take the risk," Declan said immediately. "Won't we, Ellie?"

"It won't turn him into one of us?" Elliot asked Celeste. He didn't think Celeste would be suggesting this if she really believed Declan was likely to die during the transfusion, but he would not countenance Declan turning into an octopian.

Celeste sat back on her heels and closed the cabinet doors. "I highly doubt it," she said, rising to her feet in a rustle of skirts. "I've spent the last several days examining and comparing blood, skin, and other samples from Declan, myself, Joey, and every octopian woman on the *Albatross*." She returned to the worktable and stroked a hand along George's tentacle. "I still want to examine this further, and we won't know for certain what will happen until we try it, but given everything I've observed so far, I don't believe Declan has the capacity to change."

That wasn't as reassuring as Elliot had hoped, but Declan clapped his hands together. "That's settled, then." He looked around the laboratory, then winked at Elliot. "Shall we start?"

Celeste smiled at his impatience. It was typical of Declan— once he decided on a course of action, he was ready to implement it immediately and chafed at unnecessary delay.

"I've a few more preparations to make," she said. "And it would be more comfortable to perform the transfusion at the house. Would Mrs. Carrigan allow that, do you think?"

"Mam'll help," Joey chimed in immediately. "You tell me what you need, and I'll make all the arrangements."

"Excellent," Celeste said. "First, I need to store George's arm so that I can study it further later. I believe there should be a tank large enough in the downstairs laboratory. Would you be so kind as to find it and fill it with seawater?" Joey nodded and clattered down the hatch to the lower laboratory.

Celeste shooed Elliot and Declan from the laboratory, telling them to go back to Nance's and be ready in an hour or so. Declan followed Elliot through the door to the main deck, then caught his arm. He pushed Elliot against the deckhouse, in between the door and window, out of sight of Celeste bustling around inside the lab.

"It'll work, Ellie," he said. He cupped Elliot's face and pressed a soft kiss against his lips. "Promise."

"You don't know that," Elliot protested, but couldn't stop himself from kissing Declan back. If it did work—the hard length of Declan's erection pressing against his thigh revealed how much they both wanted it to work—but Elliot tamped down his hope. "If it doesn't work," he started, but Declan kissed him again, cutting off his words.

"Don't think like that," he said softly against Elliot's lips. "It'll work."

Elliot let Declan's confidence bolster his as they kissed a few more times in the shadow of the deckhouse, then returned to Nance's to wait.

CHAPTER 34

*T*he transfusion worked. Or at least, it hadn't killed either of them so far, and tonight was the supermoon, so they'd know soon enough what effect it had on Declan.

As Celeste predicted, Elliot was weak as a kitten after the transfusion, and it was better that they did it in the comfort of Nance's house so Declan could keep an eye on him. As for Declan himself, after the pinch of the needle going into his arm, which he would never get used to and hoped never to have to suffer again after this, the transfusion was exhilarating.

He felt a rush of euphoric invincibility as Celeste slowly injected him with the mix of Elliot's and George's blood, and if he hadn't watched Elliot's face get paler and paler as Celeste drew more blood from him, Declan would have had him right after the crowd of concerned faces left their room.

He settled for kissing Elliot on the forehead, which led to more kisses along his jaw and neck, his hands smoothing over Elliot's cool skin. Then Elliot turned over and curled into him, and Declan held him while he slept.

He slept for two days, shuffled between the bedroom and Nance's library like an invalid for another four, then perked up as the first quarter-moon passed. They passed the time quietly, Elliot reading through Nance's collection of novels by Wilkie Collins and Declan listening to them argue about the thematic importance of Walter Hartright's first encounter with Anne Catherick in *The Woman in White*.

Thomas popped in to visit daily and play chess with Elliot while Declan burned off his excess energy learning to swim with Celeste. She modified a bathing costume to allow extra room for her tentacles and was a surprisingly patient and helpful teacher.

As she'd also predicted, Declan did not suddenly acquire the ability to shift with George's blood, but if he was going to spend the rest of his life in close proximity to Elliot and his aquatic shifter relations, he should fucking know how to swim himself.

Finally, after a fortnight of waiting, Declan and Elliot were alone in the hot spring. The full moon shone bigger and brighter than Declan had ever seen it—as close to the Earth as it would get this year—and Elliot's face gleamed in its silvery light. He seemed fully recovered, thank God. No more purple shadows under his eyes, and he'd regained a bit of the muscle he'd lost during his convalescence. He was lounging in one of the upper pools, arms spread wide, drops of water clinging to his bare chest, tentacles drifting under the water's surface, a tip peeking up every now and then.

As much as he enjoyed looking at Elliot, Declan couldn't wait any longer. He let his clothes fall where they would and slipped into the pool next to Elliot. The June evening air was warm, but the water was even warmer, and Declan groaned as it soaked into his sore muscles.

"You all right there?" Elliot teased him, splashing water into his face. "I haven't even touched you yet."

Declan splashed him back, which erupted into a wrestling match that only exacerbated Declan's soreness. Swimming was turning out to work his back and arm muscles as much as hauling lines as a deckhand. He'd get used to it the way he'd gotten used to sailing, even if he wasn't as young as he used to be.

After a few minutes of fighting against Elliot's unfair advantage of extra limbs, Declan surrendered. "Uncle," he wheezed, his arms stretched wide by Elliot's hands manacling his wrists. Elliot was sitting practically on his chest and had twined his tentacles around Declan's legs, immobilizing him. "Give your older brother a break, damn it."

Elliot's hands relaxed around Declan's wrists, and he slid them along the insides of Declan's arms, fingers trailing lightly until they reached Declan's chest. He rested them there, flattening his palms and bracing himself upright. He didn't do anything else, and Declan squirmed a little beneath him, to feel the drag of his nipples under Elliot's palms, the velvet-soft wetness of Elliot's web against his belly.

The tide was ebbing but not yet at its lowest point, and Declan could see Elliot's pulse beating in his throat. The thread connecting them was stronger now, with Elliot's blood flowing in Declan's own veins, and Declan stroked his own hands up and down Elliot's arms, wondering what he was waiting for.

"Feeling a little shy, Ellie?" He laced his fingers behind Elliot's neck and exerted just enough pressure that Elliot complied and bent forward enough for their lips to meet.

Declan tasted salt and a hint of sulfur as the tip of his tongue teased the seam of Elliot's lips. They parted, but Declan kept the kiss soft, barely touching Elliot's tongue with his own, until Elliot pushed his tongue inside Declan's mouth and deepened the kiss.

Declan swept his hands into Elliot's hair, cradling the back of his skull, his thumbs caressing Elliot's temples. Elliot broke the kiss and tucked his face into Declan's neck. "It feels a little like this is the first time," Elliot whispered. "I don't know why."

Declan chuckled and nosed under Elliot's ear, kissing that spot that always made Elliot shiver. "At least this time, I know what to expect." Elliot's body stiffened, and Declan tightened his arms around him to forestall Elliot moving away from him in some kind of rush of guilt or shame. "I'm teasing, you half-wit." He closed his teeth on Elliot's earlobe and tugged a bit. "Remember our first time? The very first?"

Elliot sucked in a shaky breath through his nose and nodded, Declan's teeth still gently biting his earlobe. "I'd been trying for months to get you to touch me. You wouldn't, though, no matter how much I hinted."

"You were sixteen," Declan protested. "And my little step-brother. You'd been crawling into my bed for comfort after your nightmares for years. How the hell was I supposed to know your feelings had changed like that?"

"I was seventeen before you would let yourself put a hand on me, and I'd been practically begging you for almost a year," Elliot retorted. "It wasn't until I found that illustration in your sea chest that I figured out what I could do that you might not be able to resist."

Declan pulled back a bit and looked at him. "What illustration?"

Elliot's slow smile was wicked. "The one you brought back from Japan. The one with the two men sucking each other off. I didn't quite know how to get us into that position, but I thought I could try my part first and see how far I could get."

Declan's hips jerked at the memory of waking up with Elliot's mouth around his cock on Elliot's seventeenth birthday. His soft lips, the wispy brush of peach fuzz against his thighs, and the delicate questing of Elliot's tongue around his balls was the most arousing thing he'd ever woken up to, and had made the months and months of wet dreams that came before that worth it.

"I can't believe you went through my things," he protested, but it was weak, and they both knew it. Elliot grinned unrepentantly at him, then wormed a hand between them and wrapped it around Declan's cock.

"You're right," he said, the serious tone in his voice belied by the teasing glint in his eyes and the practiced motions of his hand stroking Declan's cock. "I never should have violated your privacy like that. Especially in order to get you to violate my innocence."

Declan gasped and thrust into Elliot's hand. Elliot's long fingers tightened around the base of his cock. "Not so innocent anymore," Declan murmured.

"No," Elliot agreed, though there was a hint of sadness in his voice.

"None of that, now," Declan said. He moved his hands to Elliot's waist and stroked firmly where his skin changed to the wet velvet of his slippery web. He caressed as much as he could reach of Elliot's muscular tentacles, watching Elliot's eyes darken and his cheeks flush, as Declan's hands circled closer and closer to the cock nestled between the two front tentacles. "Come on, Ellie," he whispered. "Fuck me like you mean it. Or do I need to put you on your back and show you how it's done?"

That permission was apparently what Elliot was waiting for, because he grabbed Declan's wrists and stretched his arms wide again. Declan grunted as Elliot squeezed hard enough to grind against bone, then arched up as Elliot bent to catch a nipple between his teeth. Elliot sucked the stiffened peak into his mouth, then bit down until Declan gave a low shout.

He slid down Declan's body, the rubbery suckers under his web dragging over Declan's skin. It was like a hundred tiny mouths sucking every inch of Declan's cock, and he let his head fall back against the stone edge of the pool, staring up at the stars in the sky above him, blurring and twinkling as his vision unfocused.

Elliot rubbed the soft slickness of his web around Declan's balls and wrapped a pair of tentacles around his legs, spreading him open. The tip of one tentacle traced around his hole and slowly, gently, pushed inside. Declan heard himself groan from a distance, suspended between Elliot's hands holding his wrists and his tentacles spreading his legs wide and his hole open.

The blunt head of Elliot's cock nudged against his hole, and Declan bore down to feel the intrusion even more, then relaxed. Elliot's groan was even louder than Declan's as his cock pushed inside.

It kept pushing, and Declan took everything Elliot gave him, until he was so full there was no room for anything else. Elliot loosened his grip on Declan's wrists and bracketed his elbows on either side of Declan's head. Declan's hands tingled as the blood flowed back into his fingers, and he stroked both hands firmly down Elliot's back.

Elliot arched against him, his cock expanding inside. At Declan's soft grunt, he bent forward and pressed his forehead to Declan's. "Are you all right?" His voice was low and breathless, and Declan knew he was still holding back.

"I'm fine," he said. He clenched against Elliot's cock. "I'm perfect."

And he was. He welcomed the low burn of being stretched around Elliot's cock and the soreness he knew his ass would be feeling later. And whether it was George's blood regenerating his from the inside or Elliot's blood amplifying their bond, or even just because it had been so long since they'd done this, this time, this moment of Elliot inside his body, within his arms, was better than all the other times they'd been together.

Every inch of Declan's skin sparked like tiny fires were set underneath. Wave upon wave of pleasure rippled over him as Elliot's cock expanded inside him and dragged against that spot. The tendons at the top of his inner thighs strained as Elliot's tentacles pressed Declan's thighs open even more. Declan hitched his hips up and up with Elliot's thrusts, seeking more friction against his own cock.

The pleasure kept washing over him, hot tingles flowing from the base of his spine up his chest and along his arms. Heat flushed his chest and face and he stopped straining for his release and just let it flow through him. The press of Elliot's web against his cock and the feel of Elliot moving inside him overwhelmed everything. Elliot was everywhere and everything, surrounding Declan, holding him safe from within. Declan turned his face up to Elliot, who was staring down at him with such intensity that his heart cracked a little. Then his vision whited out, and he lost everything but the rush of pleasure rushing through him, washing his mind clean and leaving him quivering and calm.

CHAPTER 35

The next morning, Declan was at the end of the long pier idly watching small ripples rolling in toward the shore when Joey tried sneaking up behind him. "Morning, Jo-Jo," he said without turning around.

"Shit," Joey huffed in disappointment. "How'd you know it was me?" He held a ceramic mug filled with coffee out to Declan.

Declan took it with a nod of thanks. "A good captain can sense everything around him," he said, hiding a smile behind the mug and taking a long sip of the fragrant brew.

Joey rolled his eyes at him disrespectfully, but Declan was in too good a mood to reprimand him. Elliot had fucked him once more in the hot spring, then Declan had fucked him before he shifted back, and they'd gone to bed in the wee hours. After sucking each other off, just like in that illustration Elliot had found when he was a boy.

Declan hadn't experienced any ill effects from their night of passion. In fact, he felt better than he had in years. All the other aches and pains he'd acquired thanks to a lifetime at sea were gone. Even after so little sleep, he was relaxed and happy, with a coil of energy just waiting to be tapped. He figured he had enough to swim the length of Nance's inlet—now that he had the ability—and was debating whether to do that when Joey nudged his elbow.

"Everything okay, Captain?"

Declan knew what he was asking. He clapped a hand on the lad's shoulder. "Everything's fine, Jo-Jo. Better than fine." He wrapped his arm around his shoulders and squeezed briefly, then let go. "How about you, lad?"

Joey's face broke into an expression of wonder and happiness Declan had never seen before. "So good, Captain." He ducked his head and blushed a little, then peeked back up at Declan like he couldn't resist talking about his new love. "She's so pretty and so smart. And she's funny, too. We was talking last night in between —" he blushed a bright red, and Declan stifled a laugh. "And she said—" he stopped, his mouth open for an instant, then his eyes widened, and he shut his mouth as if he'd just realized what he was about to say out loud. "Never mind," he said, still blushing furiously. "It ain't proper, what she said, and she'd not appreciate me repeating it."

Declan already knew Celeste's ladylike exterior hid a certain irreverent sense of humor, and he grinned at Joey, then winked. Joey grinned back, and Declan gave in to the impulse to hug the lad again.

Joey laid his head against Declan's shoulder. "And you love her, lad?" he asked, speaking into Joey's soft blond hair. "You told her so?"

Joey nodded against his shoulder. "She said she loves me, too," he said, his voice muffled against the wool of Declan's coat. He sounded amazed and wondering and happy all at once. He lifted his head and glanced over his shoulder back at the house. "Mam says I can have her ring, to give to Celeste. I guess she approves."

Declan's throat tightened, and he squeezed Joey against him, hard, before letting him go. Nance's ring, a pair of entwined snakes in rose gold with garnet and pearl eyes, was the only thing she'd gotten from Joey's father, other than Joey. Declan knew she regarded it as the most precious thing she owned. If she was willing to see it on the finger of a woman Joey loved, she'd come a long way since Joey had run away from home.

"Yeah, lad," Declan said, turning his head away to brush the wetness from his eyes, then looking back at Joey with a soft smile. "She approves."

"And you, Captain? Do you approve?"

A splash of water and a high shriek, followed by a deep bellow, distracted Declan from answering. Two dark shapes undulated beneath the water, causing a wake of rippling waves past the pier. A dark head popped up a dozen feet from the end of the pier, followed by another, larger head. Celeste had apparently beat Elliot swimming to some point in the inlet, and she laughed at him, taunting him with something Declan couldn't hear. Elliot splashed a handful of water at her, and then they were off again, chasing each other around the inlet and giggling like fools when they surfaced.

"Of course I approve, Joey." He grinned at Joey's bashful smile, then unbuttoned his vest. "Come on, lad. Let's show these octopians they're not the only ones who can swim."

ACKNOWLEDGMENTS

Well, things got a little weird(er) here, didn't they? I had an inkling at the end of DEVILFISH that it wouldn't be forever smooth sailing for Declan and Elliot, but even I'm a little surprised at the rocky seas they had to navigate.

As usual, the best part about writing historical and paranormal romance is the research I get to do. I dove back into my collection of books about Port Townsend and the saga of the Port Townsend Southern Railroad that almost was. I modeled Celeste's science vessel, *Albatross*, after a real ship of the same name.

Assigned to the U.S. Fish Commission, the real *Albatross* was reportedly the first research ship built specifically for marine research. She did actually operate in the Pacific Northwest waters around the time of the events in this book, conducting fishery and hydrographic investigations along the Washington and Alaskan coasts. I'm betting there were few, if any, women aboard, though, and no octopians. I've dipped into some of the scientific papers produced out of her research, but found no evidence of any hybrid octopus creatures she discovered. George is pretty used to staying out of sight of mere humans, though I expect he'll be back in future books.

I would not have gotten through this book (much less kept writing at all during the global pandemic) if it hadn't been for my community of writing friends and you, dear readers.

Thanks to Carrie, Ami, and Wendy for rescheduling our annual trip to Port Townsend, Washington, which finally happened at a critical point when I really thought I'd lost all my writing mojo.

The folks I write with in the mornings in Becca Syme's Zoom Writing Office have been an absolute godsend and I would pay triple what I do (or more!) for the privilege of virtually writing with them.

My beta readers, Carol, Susan K., and Kate, were extremely helpful in getting this book over the finish line and I couldn't have asked for more helpful feedback.

And finally, thank you, dear readers, for embarking on this wet, wild, and weird journey with me. If you enjoyed SEA CHANGE, give us a review on Goodreads or your usual retailer, eh?

ABOUT THE AUTHOR

Anna Kensing writes steamy paranormal historical romances that flirt with taboo. Her characters are often weird, mostly queer, and always get their happily-ever-after. Eventually. She's obsessed with octopuses and the tv show *Supernatural*, listens to classical flute duets and heavy metal music while writing, and loves her scotch and Irish whiskies. When she's not thinking about writing, she's usually thinking about her next tattoo.

Sign up for her newsletter at https://annakensing.com and get previews of upcoming books, behind-the-scenes glimpses of what goes into her stories, and general news and gossip.

instagram.com/annakensing

goodreads.com/annakensing

twitter.com/annakensing1

facebook.com/annakensingauthor

bookbub.com/authors/anna-kensing